CARDS OF DEATH BOOK 6

# THE SIXTH GHOST

## TAMARA GERAEDS

ISBN-13: 979-8-6768-0569-2
Cover design by Deranged Doctor Design
Editing by Ambition Editing LLC

# FREE SOUL JUMPER ORIGIN STORY!

Looking for a series of stories with just as much action, twists, monsters and magic as *Cards of Death*? Look no further! *Soul Jumper* is the thing for you!

Subscribe to my newsletter now – through www.tamarageraeds.com – and you will receive a *Soul Jumper* origin story FOR FREE!

# PREVIOUSLY, IN CARDS OF DEATH

Another soul saved, but the fight isn't over yet. A couple of days have passed, but it feels more like weeks. Here's a quick recap of the latest events.

Me and my friends have been doing everything we can to prevent the Devil from escaping from Hell to rule over Earth, using the Cards of Death and our powers to save souls. We've only lost one soul so far. I'm grateful for the help we got, not only from Quinn, one of my friends who turned out to be an angel, but also from Mom's best friend and fairy godmother Mona and from Mrs. Delaney, the old lady everyone in Blackford knows because of her daily trips to the baker's and her kindness to others. She has the power to separate molecules, which can be very helpful sometimes.

Still, bad luck has followed us around. We had to kill our "friends" Simon and Paul, who were working for Lucifer.

On our way to Purgatory recently, Vicky and I got into trouble. Some ancient white ents saved us, and their leader gave Vicky a bottle with some sort of liquid. He tried to tell us what it was for, but he died before he could.

The Beach of Mu led us to Purgatory, where we

found the wolf demons that disappeared because of my spell. They ended up in the wrong place, which disturbed the balance of the universe. Trevor, their leader, was also there. He kidnapped my mom and gave her a love potion. I made that potion, which makes it extra strong.

When Trevor showed up with my mother in Purgatory, we tried to free her from him. But everything went sideways, and she fell into the pit to Hell. The Beach of Mu dove after her and so did Trevor. He must really love her.

With pain in my heart, I had to leave Mom in Trevor's care. And then things got worse. We lost Jeep on our way back home. The portal out of Purgatory led us to the silver mine in Blackford. Jeep got stuck in the portal and was taken to an unknown world.

Later, we got a visit from one of Satan's messengers. He told us he's got Mom and Jeep, but we don't believe him. Or we don't want to. I'm not sure which it is yet.

In our search for the fifth soul, a fairy, we also lost D'Maeo. I was convinced that he was doing much better since he got the parts of his soul back that were stolen by the black void that killed him. But it turned out part of the dark creature had clung to him. It took him over and blocked our way out of Heaven, where we delivered the fairy. Now, I can only hope we will be able to reach home safely, and without hurting D'Maeo.

Vicky still has two curses to deal with, and we found out one of them was put on her by Gisella's aunt, Kasinda. Or rather, it was put on my father. It affected the one he loved, my mother, and jumped over to me when Dad died, which means Vicky now suffers from it. Kasinda wants the Book of a Thousand Deaths to bring her daughter back from the dead. Of course, we would never give it to her, even if we knew where it was, but at least now we have a chance to lift one curse soon. The second curse on Vicky has something to do with someone touching her grave. Every time that happens, she is pulled into a memory but also closer to the Shadow World. I'm afraid I'll lose her if she gets pulled much further.

Taylar has been weakening because of his unfinished business, so we needed to take action. We stored the memory of his brother's death in a magical watch to take it to the police as proof. We're planning on visiting Shelton Banks' house in hopes of finding more evidence that he sent the pixie that killed Taylar's brother.

# CHAPTER 1

*Is this bravery?* I ask myself, staring at the black smoke that has half morphed into D'Maeo. *Or is it just common sense that all I can think of is 'I can't let this thing get into Heaven'?*

"What do we do?" Vicky whispers. "We can't attack D'Maeo."

*Of course we can, but I don't want to.*

I remember the words of the ferryman of the Underworld, Charon. He said all my friends are a part of my battle against the Devil. We can't afford to lose anyone. But we fought this black void before, and it almost beat us. That was still with the help of D'Maeo and Jeep. If running away from it was our best option then, where does that leave us now?

"Dante?" Vicky sounds a bit desperate as she pulls at my shirt.

When I blink to clear my head and my view, I see

the smoke growing rapidly. D'Maeo's face is contorted as it stretches higher and higher. The smoke gets thicker and looms over us.

"Our best option is to capture it," I say. "Lock it somewhere until we figure out how to separate it from D'Maeo and kill it."

"With a spell?" Charlie asks, without looking up from the gel wall he's building.

I conjure a ball of lightning in each hand when the smoke hisses. "Yes, but not just any spell. We need to enhance it." I glance sideways at Gisella. "With dark magic."

"What?" She ducks as the void swoops down, the mouth of the monstrous face opening wide.

The rest of us dive sideways. Balls of grease and lightning hit the dark form, but all the smoke does is part.

"I'm sorry," I tell Gisella, "but I can't think of another way to beat this thing. We tried it before, remember? We barely escaped. It's too powerful."

"What do you think it wants?" Vicky asks as the mist spirals up, forming something that resembles a tornado.

I aim some more lightning at it but get no more than a slight shiver as a response. "I'm not sure. We'd have to find out what it is first."

Taylar points at my waist. "Maybe John's notebook can give us some answers."

With a loud hiss, the smoke dives down again, half of D'Maeo's nose and mouth still visible but in the wrong places. It hits my shoulder, and I grab at it as heat stings my skin. It leaves a hole in my shirt.

Vicky shoots me a concerned look, which I dismiss with a wave of my hand. "I'll be okay." I tilt my head to observe the shape in the sky above us. "It's as if the black void is holding back. It was a lot stronger before, wasn't it?"

Maël pauses her time bending mumbling. "That could be D'Maeo's doing. He is fighting it from the inside."

"Can you freeze it?" I ask her.

Her hand wraps tighter around her staff. "No, I can only slow it down. It is still too strong."

"Okay, slow it down as much as you can." I whip out Dad's notebook and open it to a random page.

*Show me how to trap this entity,* I think as hard as I can. To my relief, the pages start flipping instantly. Three-quarters of the book have already filled up. I can't wait to find out what will appear on the remaining blank pages. Secretly, I'm hoping for a spell to lock the Devil in Hell, but I don't think we'll get that lucky.

The pages come to a rest. Before reading the text on the page, I look up to make sure the smoke isn't about to attack again. It's moving left and right, as if it's waiting for something. *No wait, it's something else. It's struggling. Maël is right, it's fighting to stay in control.* While it wriggles and stretches, more of the mouth becomes visible. It opens wide and lets out a scream.

I ball my fists. "That was him. D'Maeo."

I bend over the notebook, gritting my teeth. *Come on, give me something useful.*

My eyes scan the lines, then the letters one by one. I blink. "I know what it is."

Taylar moves a bit closer. "What what is?"

"That black void." I look up at it and then back at the notebook.

Taylar nudges me. "Well, what is it?"

"It's a chaos residue. Listen to this: *A chaos residue comes to life in a place of complete disorder, pain and confusion. Once it escapes its place of origin, it goes in search of locations where it can wreak havoc. Whenever it succeeds, it grows in size and strength. After its hundredth kill, it will change into a chaos demon, which means it can take on solid shape. Once it does, it will be twice as hard to kill."*

"Oh great," Charlie sighs. "So, if we don't kill it now, we never will?"

Vicky frowns. "I don't get it. If this thing is out to create chaos, why did it go after D'Maeo? I mean, it killed him, but obviously that wasn't enough."

I feel my own eyebrows moving up too. "Maybe D'Maeo is the only one who can beat it?"

Vicky shakes her head. "No, that doesn't make sense. If he was, how come the dark void took over? It shouldn't have been able to do that then, should it?"

Maël stops her mumbling again for a second. "Remember what I told you about molecules and balance, Dante?"

I tilt my head. "Eh… sure." *Molecules and balance?* It

hits me. "Of course! When we disturbed the balance of the universe, the molecules inside each one of us could be pulled in any direction." My shoulders sag. "D'Maeo was already struggling with this thing. The imbalance inside him must have given it the opportunity to take over."

A smile creeps upon my lips. "So what we need… is someone who can pull the molecules back to where they belong."

Vicky's face lights up. "Mrs. Delaney!"

"Exactly."

"But how will we get the void to her?"

"And without endangering her life in the process, you know," Charlie adds.

"Give me a sec." I bend over the notebook again. My eyes fly over the rest of the page. "Okay, here's what I think. D'Maeo was the one who brought this thing here to us. If we return to Darkwood Manor now, while they're busy fighting each other, the black void, a.k.a. chaos residue, shouldn't be too hard to lure. All we have to do is create the perfect circumstances for chaos once we get there. D'Maeo will give it the last push in the right direction."

"And then what?" Gisella asks skeptically. "Why would we be able to defeat it then?"

"Because one of us is fighting it from the inside. Once we're back on Earth, Mona can get Mrs. Delaney, who will try to separate D'Maeo's molecules from the chaos residue's. Meanwhile, I'll cast a spell to trap it, in case we can't kill it."

"Sounds like a plan to me." Taylar raises his arm as the dark smoke attacks again. It slams down hard on his shield, forcing him onto his knees. I follow it with my eyes as it moves up and prepares to charge again. I picture it freezing over and getting stuck halfway down, completely surrounded by ice.

"Nice job!" Vicky calls out when the images in my head become reality.

"Thanks." I smile, but I'm not completely reassured. "D'Maeo!" I call out. "I hope you can hear me. We've got a plan. Keep the black void busy while we return to Darkwood Manor. Then follow us."

I'm hoping for another scream in reply, but the smoke is still frozen, unable to move.

Before I beckon the others, I shout out one more message. "We'll get you back, I promise."

Then I take Vicky's hand and start running down the path that leads out of Heaven and back to Earth.

# CHAPTER 2

We've been running for less than a minute when Charlie hollers, "Wait!"

The others bump into me when I come to a sudden halt. Preparing to freeze the chaos residue again, I turn. But what I see is not what I was expecting.

I lower my arms. The clouds are gone. Instead, I'm looking at dozens of pine trees.

There's movement on my right. It's Charlie, back in his disguise of an Asian man. He wipes a dark lock from his face as the wind catches it.

"We can stop running," he says with a wide grin. "We're back home, you know."

He points at something to my left. When I whirl around, my heart leaps. Seeing Darkwood Manor again hits me harder than I would've thought possible. *We're back. We're finally back.* I close my eyes and inhale deeply. I never appreciated the smells of Earth this much before. I never realized it's not just what we see and hear that makes this home. It's every little thing. The smell of the trees and the air, the feeling of the sun on your face. It's all different here, familiar. Or at least, most of it. I'm sure there's lots of magical stuff here on Earth I've never encountered. But still, this is where I belong, this is home, and it feels great to be back.

I turn to grab Vicky's hand and see that everyone is back in disguise again. We make our way to the back of the mansion. At the backdoor, I hesitate. The feeling of elation crumbles when I remember we're three people short. Mom won't greet me with a hug and a concerned look, Mona won't be able to hug and kiss D'Maeo and there's no Jeep to make sarcastic comments about it.

Valery/Vicky takes the lead and pulls me along. "Come on, babe. We'll have D'Maeo back soon, and after that, we're getting the others back too." Her blonde curls bob up and down with every step she takes. I sort of like it, but I still prefer her own straight black hair with the blonde tips.

As soon as we enter the kitchen, sparks appear near the stove.

"You're back!" Mona shrieks, even before she's fully visible. She pulls me and Valery into a big hug but let's go just as suddenly. "Your disguises are wearing off! That's faster than I thought. What happened?"

"What do you mean?" I ask, looking around. "We still look like Valery, Ted, Chung, Grace, Mabel and Dean." I point at everyone as I mention their names. Then my gaze falls upon my feet, and I see what she means. "Ah… My shoes are changing back. Soon the rest will follow, right?"

"We took the fairy to Heaven," Valery explains. "I think that broke the spell temporarily."

Mona nods. "Yes, when you arrive in Heaven, your true form shows."

Valery takes the Cards of Death from her endless pocket, and when she holds them up, they crumble to dust.

Mona's smile lights up the kitchen. "You succeeded! I knew you would!"

I clear my throat and shuffle my feet. "Thanks, Mona."

Finally, she looks up. Her gaze locks onto every face, and slowly her smile falters. "Wait… where's D'Maeo?"

I put my arm around her shoulders and lead her to her chair. "Sit down for a sec."

"Why? What's wrong?"

"There's not much time, so I'll give you the short version." I take a deep breath and look her in the eyes. "D'Maeo has been taken over by the dark void." I grab her hand when it flies to her mouth in horror. "But he's fighting it, Mona, and we've got a plan. A plan for which we need Mrs. Delaney."

She blinks away a tear. "To separate him from the

darkness?"

"Exactly. Can you go get her for us?"

She gives me a confused look. "Now?"

"Yes, we're not sure, but the black void—"

"Which is actually a chaos residue," Valery interrupts, half her face now back to normal, which looks creepy.

I avert my gaze. "Right. It might come to us even if we don't lure it. It blocked our way out of Heaven. D'Maeo kept it busy so we could escape. Now it's time we return the favor."

Mona stands up and wipes the tears from her cheeks with one swift, determined move. "I'm ready. Tell me what to do."

Suddenly, all of the fear, sorrow and despair I've been bottling up inside shoot up to my throat. The words I want to say get stuck before they reach my lips. I look at her, amazed at her strength and resilience. Her best friend fell into Hell and now the love of her life has been taken over by something evil. All she does is shed one tear before turning straight back into battle mode.

Without thinking, I throw my arms around her and pull her close. There are no sparks this time, which probably means she's more concerned than she's leading on.

"We're strong," I tell her. "And so is he. We'll defeat this chaos thing." I kiss her cheek and let go. "We'll prepare a spell from my father's notebook to trap it while you fetch Mrs. Delaney. Once she's here, we'll lure the demon into the protective circle in the back garden. Mrs. Delaney will use her power to tear D'Maeo away from it. I'll trap it, and then we'll have time to figure out a way to kill it."

Mona nods at everything I say. "Okay, that could work."

"It *will* work," I assure her.

She keeps nodding. "Yes. Yes, it will."

"Go," I urge her. "And be careful."

"You too," she says with a sad smile. Then she disappears in a cloud full of dull sparks.

Vicky, now looking like her normal gorgeous self again, pinches my arm. "Well done."

I'm not sure I agree, but this was probably the best I could do in such a short time frame. Hopefully Mona won't need comforting anymore once we're done.

Straightening my shirt, I turn to face the others, who shed the last of their disguises as they stand up again. "Is everyone ready?"

There's a collective yes from their familiar faces, and I swallow to prevent myself from choking up.

"Are you sure?" I press. "This thing is strong, so if anyone is not up to this, tell me now." I give Taylar and Vicky a questioning look. "No unfinished business or fits getting in the way?"

Taylar inspects his slender arms and legs and pats his tummy, that has shrunk at least twenty-five inches. "I'm fine for now."

Vicky cracks her neck and some stray blonde hairs

spiral down and vanish. "Me too. And if I feel a fit coming up, I'll get out of your way."

"Awesome. Let's do this then."

I stride out of the kitchen and into the protective circle we created in the back garden. Vicky pulls most of what I need for the spell from her pocket, and Charlie fetches the rest of it—plus three chocolate bars—from the kitchen.

Soon everything is ready. There's no sign of the chaos residue yet, so we prepare to lure it.

"What we need to do is focus on our worries," I explain, looking at my friends one by one. "But we can't let them take over. We have to release some of the chaos in our heads, but not let it carry us away."

Charlie fidgets with the buttons on his Hawaiian shirt. "I'm not sure I can do that."

I frown, surprised to hear him say that. He's always so light-hearted I thought he never really worried about anything at all.

He clears his throat and finally looks up. "Is there another way to lure this thing?"

"Maybe, but this will work best."

He shakes his head. "Not if I flip out."

"Why would you do that?"

The corners of his mouth twitch. "Well, Dante... normally I push all negative thoughts away, you know... I ignore common sense, even when it's obvious that things... won't turn out alright." He lets out a sigh. "Under normal circumstances, focusing on my concerns wouldn't be a problem, but lately...

we've had some big things to worry about, you know. The comforting phrase 'it's not as if the fate of the world depends on it' doesn't work so well here, does it?"

I reach out to pat his shoulder, but he pulls away. "You make things sound so easy, but some of us are hanging on by a thread, mate. We're not all as brave as you, you know."

My mouth falls open. At first, I want to object, to yell at him that I'm not brave at all, but that won't help any of us. So instead, I nod and say, "I'm sorry I gave the impression that this is all easy. It's not, not for any of us. We're all struggling, and sometimes we need to let off steam or hide under the covers. You say that I'm brave, but I'm not. I just pretend to be brave and confident." I stretch my arm again, and this time, he lets me grab his shoulder and squeeze it. "What you just did is so much braver than anything I've ever done."

He snorts. "Sure it is."

"No, I mean it, Charlie. It takes guts to step up and tell people you've reached your limits. And I'm glad you did, because if I lose one more friend…" My last words are swallowed by a sob. I push the tears back quickly and turn away from him. "So… we need a different strategy."

"I've got an idea," Vicky says. She steps up to Charlie with a smile.

There's a short silence as they look into each other's eyes. Then Charlie visibly relaxes. The tension leaves his shoulders, and his breathing steadies.

"How do you feel now?" Vicky asks. "Do you think you can do it?"

Charlie stares past her for a couple of seconds. "Yes," he says. "Yes, I think I can."

With a triumphant look on her face, Vicky turns back to me. "I can help all of you this way."

I grin. "That's a great idea, babe!" I quickly survey the others' expressions. "Right?"

When they all nod, I clap my hands. "Alright, then I guess we're ready. As soon as Mona arrives with Mrs. Delaney, we can get started."

At that precise moment, the two women step out of the kitchen.

Mrs. Delaney shuffles out onto the grass with a concerned look on her face. She opens her arms wide when her eyes find mine. "Oh, my dear boy, how awful!"

She hugs me so tightly that I can hardly breathe.

"They're not lost yet," I manage to squeeze out. "They will all be fine."

Mrs. Delaney lets go of me so suddenly that I sway on my feet.

"That's the spirit!" she says cheerily. She balls her fists and raises them up to her face. "There's still plenty of us left to put up one hell of a fight."

"Hear, hear!" Mona exclaims from behind her, although it doesn't sound as confident as Mrs. Delaney's words.

I shoot her a comforting smile before turning my

attention back to Mrs. Delaney. "Thank you for coming. Has Mona filled you in on the plan?"

"She has." She rubs her hands together and wiggles her fingers. "I'm ready."

I beckon Mona to join us in the protective circle. "As long as we stay inside, the void won't be able to harm us. Or D'Maeo. Try to keep the entity inside the circle too until Mrs. Delaney has separated them. And stay where you are with D'Maeo until I've finished the spell to trap it."

Mona is nodding feverishly again, saying "okay" after almost every word I utter.

"Hey," I say, catching her eye. "Don't worry. We've got this."

"I know." She takes my hand and leans closer. The worried frown drops from her face. "I heard your speech about bravery. It was beautiful. And very true." Her eyes bore into mine. "You know what I see when I look at you and your friends?"

I shrug. "Determination?"

She tilts her head. "That too. But what I see most is love. You're all so different, but you care about each other, all of you." She presses my hand against her chest. "I can feel it here, the connection. This is what makes you strong. Stronger than any enemy you will ever encounter."

"That's what Dad wrote in his notebook too."

"He was right. Love is what keeps you all together. And you are the light that guides them. You are very special, Dante. I have faith in you."

My lips curl up in surprise. "Thank you, Mona. That means a lot to me."

She kisses me on the forehead and throws some sparks at me. "For extra luck. Now, let's get rid of this cursed thing."

CHAPTER 3

While I tap into my memories and fears, I try not to look at the others. But it's hard to focus when you're worried one of your friends is going to crack. My gaze keeps floating back to Vicky, who's keeping a close eye on all of us. She nods when she catches my eye and mouths something that looks like "concentrate". With a smile, I close my eyes and dive into my own head.

Careful not to unlock too much negativity, I think clear thoughts. *Mom fell into Hell. Is she okay? Will I ever see her again? What if Trevor decides they're both better off dead?*

I breathe in sharply. *Don't think that. It hurts too much. Try something else. The more things to worry about, the better.*

I almost snort. *That won't be a problem. Enough to choose from. All I need to do is keep my thoughts from spinning out of control.*

*Vicky's episodes. Jeep getting pulled away from us inside the portal from Purgatory. Taylar's unfinished business. Maël's guilt about her past.* Images of the people in her tribe bending over in pain fill my vision. *It was horrible to watch them all die, and I didn't even know them. The pain must have been unbearable for Maël. What about Dad? What happened to him? How did he die?* I squeeze my eyes shut tighter. *If only I could see him again. Talk to him about all of this crazy magical stuff.*

My thoughts come to a sudden halt when I'm pushed over with force. I land on the grass hard, and for a moment, I don't understand what's happened. It's not until Mona calls out that I return to the present.

"D'Maeo? Sweetheart?"

I scramble back to my feet and watch the chaos residue soar through the sky above us. It dives at every one of us in turn, knocking us over or picking us up and dropping us from several feet. Charlie rushes over when Gisella plunges down, but she lands on her feet easily. Maël disappears into the ground and returns unharmed and on her feet, her staff raised and ready for action. Taylar uses his shield to absorb the blow, and Vicky makes herself invisible long enough for the black void to miss her. Mona's sparks form a sort of shield that protects her as well as Mrs. Delaney. The old lady remains calm. While she moves her arms and fingers, her gaze never leaves the entity. She's ready.

Soon, the residue gets restless. It has noticed that none of us are getting hurt, and judging by the way it wriggles and howls, this is making it pretty angry. Hovering above me, it starts to change shape. Slowly, it forms a large head with a beard, wrinkles and a fearful frown.

Mona slaps her hand against her mouth. "Oh no."

"Don't fall for it," I warn her. "It's trying to trick us. It wants chaos, remember?"

With an angry glint in her eyes, Mona lowers her hands and throws some sparks into the sky. When they hit the black smoke, it shivers. A mouth forms in D'Maeo's face, and it opens to show a row of tainted, sharp teeth.

"You leave my man alone!" Mona yells, hitting it with a stream of yellow sparks. At the same time, I throw two lightning bolts at it. A ball of gel lands on the smoky nose, and the face shatters.

"Keep going!" I urge Mona and Charlie as the residue prepares to dive at us again.

But then, it suddenly freezes mid-air. It starts to shudder, hissing violently. The particles are pulled apart, and behind it, D'Maeo's face becomes visible. Not the contorted one, but his real face. He's gritting his teeth, and his forehead is scrunched up in effort. His mouth opens, but no sound comes out.

"Hold on, honey!" Mona calls out.

I glance over my shoulder to where Mrs. Delaney is standing. She's moving her hands so fast that they're nothing more than a blur while the rest of her body is like a statue. Even her face doesn't move.

The hissing of the chaos residue gets louder and changes into a high-pitched howling. A human scream gradually mixes with it until, with a crash like breaking glass, D'Maeo and the entity are pulled apart. The old ghost lands in a heap on the grass in front of Mona. A string of smoke still clings to his legs, and when I step closer, I see that his body isn't complete. The black void is trying to pull him back.

Mrs. Delaney grunts. It's taking a lot of energy to separate the molecules. I run to her side to support her while Taylar jumps in front of us and holds up his shield. Mrs. Delaney doesn't even blink, but her jaw sets, and her back straightens when I touch her.

Bit by bit, D'Maeo's legs return, and the chunks missing from his face fill up.

With a nod of my head, I beckon Charlie, who takes my place holding Mrs. Delaney up. Gisella joins them with her blade hands raised while Maël keeps an eye on everything from the other side of the circle.

Hastily, I squat down next to the things I set up for the spell. Most of them have toppled over, but it takes only a couple of seconds to put everything back in place. Vicky takes care of the four candles inside the circle.

"Almost… there," Mrs. Delaney pants.

I grab Dad's notebook, which flips itself to the right page. When I look up, the last sliver of black smoke is pulled away from D'Maeo. Mona holds him close to her, sobbing quietly.

"Now, Dante!" Mrs. Delaney calls out, and immediately I light a match and drop it in the mixture of herbs in the bowl at my feet. In two steps, I reach the first candle.

*"Powers of Air, hear my plea.*
*Trap this evil entity."*

I hurry over to the next candle, glancing at the chaos residue from the corner of my eye. It's wriggling frantically. *I hope Mrs. Delaney can keep the molecules in place until I'm done.*

It takes several seconds for the wick to light, and my hands tremble slightly. Finally, a tiny flame comes to life.

*"Powers of Fire, hear my plea.*
*Make sure this evil doesn't flee."*

The flame rises with a hiss, and I move on.

When I reach the next candle, I realize the flames are not the only things hissing. The black void is putting up one hell of a fight.

"Come on, come one," I mumble, waiting for the flame to jump from my match to the candle.

*"Powers of Water, hear my plea.*
*Let this evil seize to see."*

When I reach the last candle, Mrs. Delaney

collapses.

"Hold on!" I call out to her. "Only one more candle to go."

Mona leaves D'Maeo's side and rushes over to the old lady. Sparks jump from her body to that of Mrs. Delaney.

She gestures feverishly at me when I don't move. "Go on! Finish it!"

I light the last candle and read the words from the notebook.

*"Powers of Earth, hear my plea.*
*Lock this evil in a place with no key."*

The smoke's hissing changes into something resembling the screaming of a steam locomotive. Unable to cover my ears with my hands, I grit my teeth and pull in my head. The others flinch but stay where they are, with their eyes locked on our enemy.

Above me, the residue is swirling and twisting. An invisible force presses it from all sides until it's molded into a solid square.

Vicky hands me a bottle of holy water, which I slam down hard into the bowl of herbs to make sure it shatters. Shards of glass fly everywhere and scrape my hands, but I ignore the sting.

*"Powers of High, hear my plea.*
*Create a prison to hold this enemy."*

The contents of the bowl are lifted. They start to turn, faster and faster, until they've formed a small tornado. Out of it rises a square glass box, covered in brown and green spots.

Lighting the fifth candle, in the middle of the protective circle, I shout out the last lines of the spell.

*"Powers of All, hear my cry.*
*Bring this smoke down from the sky.*
*Lock it in this solid jail,*
*where it can no longer kill."*

With a last violent hiss, the compressed residue drops down into the glass box. I wait for the see-through lid to slam shut and lock it in. *Shouldn't that happen immediately?*

I take a tentative step closer and reach up to close it myself. Suddenly, the box starts to shake feverishly. I try to grab it, but it jumps out of reach. Maël holds out her staff and starts mumbling, in an attempt to slow down time.

"Say the words again!" Vicky calls out.

*"Powers of All, hear my cry!"*

I pick up the notebook I dropped and search for the next words.

*Bring this smoke down from the sky.*
*Lock it in this solid jail,*

*where it can no longer kill."*

Finally, the lid starts to close, but it moves as if in slow motion.

"Please close, please close," I whisper urgently.

Just a couple more inches until the chaos residue is trapped. I look at D'Maeo, who has worked himself up into a sitting position. Our eyes meet, and I give him a short nod, telling him he'll be fine.

But when I move my gaze back to the box, my body freezes. A smoky arm shoots straight at D'Maeo and wraps around him at lightning speed.

"No!" I yell, throwing myself forward to grab the old ghost.

But it's already too late. The smoke has swallowed D'Maeo, and I land on my face in the warm grass.

Mona lets out a horrifying cry, and Mrs. Delaney lifts her arms to use her power again.

Vicky hurries over to the box and grabs it. Immediately, the lid slams shut, but not before dragging the smoke arm and the ghost inside first.

With a desperate look on her face, Vicky pulls at the lid. It doesn't budge. When I join her, she pushes the box into my hands. "You can open it."

Slowly, I nod. My head pounds, and my skin is cold. "I can open it, but I won't."

Her mouth drops open. "What?"

I glance over my shoulder at Mona and the others. "I'm sorry, I can't let it out again. This thing is hard to kill, and as you can see…" I wave vaguely at the spot where Mrs. Delaney is lying with her head in Charlie's lap, "it's also very difficult to catch. We can't take the risk of releasing it. If it turns into a chaos demon, we'll never be able to defeat it."

Vicky yanks the box out of my hands. "So, what… you're just going to leave D'Maeo in there with that thing?"

I swallow at the sight of the fury on her face. "Yes, until we figure out a way to get them both out safely."

Mona pushes herself to her feet and wipes her eyes. "Although I hate to say this, I have to admit that Dante is right. The black void is strong, and it can get much stronger if we set it free. It can kill all of us and, with that, the whole world."

Mrs. Delaney clears her throat and all heads turn to her. "It's true. I felt its power." She takes a couple of deep breaths. "It tried to pull me in too, and it almost succeeded."

When Vicky's expression doesn't change, Mona walks up to her and puts an arm around her shoulders. "If this thing kills all of you, there's no one to stop the Devil. We can't let that happen."

Vicky blinks away a tear. "You just lost the one you love, and you're comforting *me*?"

Mona gives her a sad smile. "We're all sad about this."

With a loud sob, Vicky grabs her and pulls her close, the box wedged between them. "I never told D'Maeo how much I care about him. How much I appreciate what he does for us. That he's such a good

Shield leader and a good man." Tears stream down her face. "And I never told Jeep anything like that either. I lost two of my closest friends, two of my *only* friends, and they don't even know how much that hurts me."

Mona strokes her back and hushes her. "It'll be okay, Vicky. You'll get a chance to tell them both."

"Of course you will," I say, putting my arms around them both. "Because we won't give up, ever."

I kiss them both on the temple and let go. "How about some pizza and a good night's sleep? I think we can all use that."

Vicky shakes herself, and her puffed up face returns to normal. "Sorry about that."

"No need to apologize," I say. "You can't be tough all the time."

She throws back her blonde-tipped hair with a small grin. "Sure I can."

Then she looks down at the box. Her chest moves as she lets out a silent sigh.

"Can you keep this safe, Mona?" she asks, holding the box out to the fairy godmother.

"Of course."

I beckon everyone to follow me inside. In silence, we wait for the pizza to arrive, each of us lost in thoughts and memories.

*No more negative thoughts,* I remind myself. Which is great in theory, but a whole lot harder in reality.

CHAPTER 4

I wake up revived and happy. Vicky is still sleeping, and I watch her for a couple of minutes. It's nice to relax and enjoy a good view for once. No rushing, no fighting, no one throwing ominous predictions or threats at me. Just me and my beautiful girl, lying in bed with the early sunshine on our faces.

Vicky stirs and lets out a soft moan. I reach out to touch her cheek, already looking forward to the moment she opens her deep blue eyes and smiles at me.

"Good m—" The words get stuck in my throat when she vanishes into thin air.

I shoot up and touch the empty spot. "Vick?"

With a loud curse, I jump out of bed and put on my clothes from the day before.

There's a soft knock on my door. "Dante? Is everything okay?"

I shake my head and pull open the door. "No, Mona, it's not." I gesture at the bed. "She vanished again."

With a concerned look, Mona taps her chin. "We should really do something about that."

Images of Vicky's breakdown yesterday fill my vision. "I agree. Vicky has been through enough. Fighting two curses at the same time *and* battling demons in between? No wonder she couldn't take it anymore. We need to help her. This has been going on for way too long already."

"Didn't you make a sketch of the woman who cursed your dad?"

"I did, and Gisella found her. It's her aunt."

Mona nods thoughtfully. "Okay, so I suggest you go see her today. Even if the next Cards of Death arrive, you do this first. I'm afraid there won't be much of your Shield left if you don't."

"I agree, but what if—"

She places a hand on my arm. "No, Dante. No more buts. Keeping the Devil in Hell is your first priority, but please remember that you probably need all of your friends to do that. You can afford to lose one soul, not to lose one of your friends."

With a smile, I shake my head. "How did you become so wise, Mona? It's like you always know exactly what to say."

Her cheeks turn red, and she shrugs. "Hundreds of years of experience, Dante. And still I don't know everything."

I kiss her on her warm cheek. "You know enough."

"Do you want me to wait for Vicky with you, or should I go make some breakfast?"

"Breakfast would be great. I'll be fine here."

"Okay, honey." She turns and blows me a kiss full of sparks from the doorway.

As soon as she's gone, I sit back on the bed and stare at Vicky's spot. "I don't know if you can hear me, babe, but I want you to know that we're going to get rid of the curses today. Or at least one of them. I'm sorry I made it so hard for you by postponing this for so long. It's just… everything that's going on… sometimes I still can't believe it's all real. All that evil and us being chosen…" I close my eyes and shake my head. "It's as if the world has suddenly gone crazy, or as if I got trapped in a nightmare. Or… no, not a nightmare, a dream. With you in it, it could never be a nightmare." I wipe a tear from my eye. "If you can hear me, please follow my voice back. I can't do this without you. And even if I could, I don't want to."

"I don't want to live without you either."

I inhale so suddenly that I get stuck in a coughing fit.

"Not that I'm alive," Vicky adds with a twinkle in her eyes.

"Oh, thank goodness!" I exclaim, throwing myself forward and pulling her close to me. "Are you alright?"

"I'm fine. Although I was in the Shadow World

33

again for a couple of seconds."

I rub my cheek against hers. "Don't worry, we're going to fix all of this first."

She pulls back her head to look at me. "We are? What about the cards?"

"They will have to wait."

She tilts her head in thought. "Are you sure that's wise?"

I plant a small kiss on her nose. "Very sure. A clever old lady told me."

"I heard that!" Mona calls out from downstairs.

"Oh, I'm sorry, I meant a beautiful, clever young woman," I correct myself, winking at Vicky.

During breakfast, I discuss the plan with the others. Or rather, we come up with a plan, because honestly, I have no idea what to do when we meet Gisella's aunt.

"Kasinda is a powerful Black Annis witch," Gisella tells us. "She has protected herself against spells and incantations, which means it will be very hard to fight her if it comes to that."

I sigh. "Which basically means she's just as hard to defeat as the chaos residue. Maybe even harder."

"You know what we need, right?" Charlie asks after a long discussion on how to make Kasinda break the curse.

I rest my head in my hands. "No, please tell me."

"We need something to bargain with."

"There's only one thing she wants, Charlie," I

answer with a sigh. "The Book of a Thousand Deaths, to raise her daughter from the dead. We can't give her that."

"Well, maybe there's something else she wants too without realizing it, you know."

"Like what?"

He stares at the ceiling for a couple of seconds. "Some kind of… weapon?"

Taylar's mouth falls open. "You want to give a weapon to one of the most powerful witches alive?"

"Well, no, of course not," Charlie mumbles with a guilty expression on his face. "But if that's what it takes to make her break the curse on Vicky…"

Vicky shakes her head feverishly. "No way. Who knows what she's going to do with it."

Charlie clears his throat. "I thought we could put a trap in it. Something to strip her powers or kill her."

Gisella slaps him on the shoulder. "That's a great idea! We put a spell on the object instead of on her. That way she won't notice!"

Taylar wrinkles his forehead. "You seem awfully eager to kill your own aunt."

Gisella nods. "I am. You see, family or not, she's dangerous. She doesn't give a shit about me or anyone else, and she cursed one of my friends. The sweet aunt I knew is long gone. In her place there's a woman who wants nothing but to destroy. Why wouldn't I want to kill her?"

"In this case 'family' is nothing but a word," Charlie adds. "Judging by what Gisella told me about

Kasinda, I'd say she has lost all ability to care about others, except for her daughter. She no longer has the right to call herself family. Family is what *we* are."

Gisella gives him a quick kiss on the lips. "Nicely put, Lee."

Taylar shrugs. "A bit cheesy, but I get your point."

I scratch my head. "Did you try talking to her yet, Gisella?"

The werecat-witch throws me a slightly guilty look. "No, not yet."

I push back my chair. "We should try that first. She might have changed."

She snorts. "Sure, for the worse."

"You don't know that."

She smirks at me. "I saw her. Trust me, talking won't do us much good."

I munch on my lip for a second. "I do trust you, but I still want to try. There's good in everyone. I have to keep believing that."

Taylar tilts his head. "Even in Lucifer?"

I can't hold back the sigh that rises. "Come on, you know what I mean. There's good in every human being. And seriously, I'd feel bad if we didn't give Kasinda a chance to do the right thing. I can't really blame her for going a bit crazy. Maybe we can help her deal with her daughter's death."

Gisella raises her hands. "But that will take time, which we don't have much of to start with. We also have Taylar's unfinished business to take care of and three people to search for."

"I know, and I hate it! I hate this pressure of solving everything at the same time. I hate the danger constantly looming over us, ready to strike at any moment. This whole situation scares the hell out of me. But we shouldn't let our fear lead us anymore. That's what we've been doing so far and look where it got us." I gesture irritably at the empty seats around the table.

Silence answers me, and I drop back into my seat, suddenly very tired.

Maël is the first to move. She leans forward and looks at us one by one. "I agree with Dante. Fear is a bad advisor, yet we listened to it. I cannot say that this has led to our losses, but it has played its part. I also agree that we should approach Gisella's aunt with kindness, not hostility. Not with fear, but with caution."

I rub my face and try to find back my optimism. When I look up, Gisella is wearing a reluctant expression.

In a split second, I make a decision. "No one will force you to come with us, although I would prefer it if you did. I understand your anger against your aunt, and I agree that there's a slim chance she will cooperate. Still, killing her without even talking to her will make us just as bad as they are." I hold up my hands when Taylar and Gisella moan at the same time. "I know that sounds lame, but there's a reason you hear this a lot in movies." I look them in the eyes one by one, hoping they will understand. "It's true."

"You're damn right it's true," Vicky responds, slamming her fist onto the table and making everyone jump. "We are the good ones, here to protect everyone on Earth. If we start killing without cause, what does that make us?"

Taylar studies his fingers while Gisella just stares at me. After several uncomfortable, silent seconds, she finally sighs. "Okay, you're right. It would make us horrible people."

Maël leans over the table to take the werecat's hand. "Do not let anger lead you either. Focus on the good in people."

Gisella smiles at her. "I will." She turns her head back to me. "And I am definitely not staying behind. As I told you before, I am with you till the end."

"The end of Satan," Charlie adds, holding up his hand.

Gisella gives him a high five. "Exactly."

"Great," I say, relieved that we came to an agreement without losing anyone else.

I pull out Dad's notebook. "Then I guess it's time for another spell."

While the ghosts vanish to find out as much as they can about Gisella's aunt, I try to write a spell. Charlie, Gisella and Mona jot down what to say to Kasinda.

To my relief, I find a spell called *How to curse an object*. I didn't expect to see anything like that in Dad's book, since it is a book filled with good spells. Cursing an object sounds pretty evil to me, which is why I can't concentrate on rewriting it. My gut keeps telling me it's wrong.

I shake my head vigorously to lose the doubts and squeeze my eyes shut several times. *Come on, focus. We'll only use this if she refuses to lift the curse. There's no reason for her to punish Vicky, so if she doesn't want to help, we have no other choice but to force the curse to be broken.*

I bend over the page again, and finally the words start flowing. Within minutes, I've adjusted the spell.

Mona puts a steaming mug in front of me. "Did you think of an object to use? Something that she will accept?"

"Since there's only one thing she really wants from us…" I tap the notebook with my finger.

Mona frowns. "You're giving her your father's book?"

"Of course not," I answer with a chuckle. "I'm giving her an old book that will look like the Book of a Thousand Deaths."

Gisella looks up from her writing. "Do you even know what it looks like?"

I smile. "Does she?"

She shakes her head slowly. "Probably not."

I tap the lines I've written in my own Book of Spells. "I've put it in here, just in case, so hopefully it will look exactly like the real thing."

As soon as they're finished, Gisella and Charlie go outside for a walk. I don't blame them. I wish I could do the same with Vicky, now that we finally have a small break. But she's still in… well, I don't know, in wherever they go to speak to other ghosts.

Mona takes off to a fairy godmother meeting, leaving me alone at the kitchen table for the first time in what feels like forever.

I try to remember what I used to do when I was alone. *Read a book? Not something I can concentrate on right now. Watch some TV?* I shake my head as I realize I haven't even moved mine here yet. It doesn't matter anyway. I can't imagine anything on TV able to keep my attention for more than a couple of minutes. *I could play darts, if I brought my board with me. Let off some steam. Then again, throwing my Morningstar around would probably work better.*

Eventually, I settle for drawing, with another cup of tea and some cookies on the side. I haven't gotten around to completing my monster collection for a while, and I really want my Demon Guide–the name popped into my head when I flipped through my previous drawings–to be complete.

Soon, I forget everything around me. All I see are lines and shapes. All I hear is the soft scraping of the pencil on the paper. It's been ages since I felt so calm. Until…

I tilt my head and look up sharply. Nothing moves. Still, I'm sure I heard something. A voice calling my name.

"Dante?"

A shiver runs up my spine. I know that voice. It's one I can never forget, one I've been longing to hear for years.

I stand up so quickly that my chair tumbles over and my notebook slips onto the floor. I ignore both, look left and right, behind me, above me. There's nothing, no one.

"Dante?"

"Yes! I'm here!" I call out. My voice trembles. My mind is screaming. *Please let this be real.*

"Son?"

Tears run down my cheeks. I have to hold on to the edge of the table because my legs are suddenly like jelly.

"Dad, is that you?"

# CHAPTER 5

I must be hallucinating. Or someone is playing a trick on me. Because the face, the person, that becomes visible at the other end of the table can't be Dad. He looks so different, but also the same. His strong jawline has weakened, but his dark untamed eyebrows haven't changed. His gray moustache, beard and sideburns, sprinkled with black spots, are still there. But his face and body are smaller. There's hardly any fat in his cheeks or on his arms, and his legs look like twigs. His face is disturbingly pale.

"Dante. Finally." He smiles, and my heart stops for a second.

"It is you, isn't it?" My voice is hoarse.

His brown eyes are wet as he looks at me. "I've been trying to reach you since I…" His voice falters. "Since I died."

I'm torn between slamming my fists against his

chest and throwing myself in his arms. I've missed him so much, and at the same time, I can't forget what I saw. Him burning that Keeper of Life to get the Book of a Thousand Deaths, his face devoid of emotion.

Images of us camping in the woods together are pushed away by a burning man. I want to cry and laugh at the same time. Eventually, I stay where I am, put on a poker face and ask, "Why?"

"To warn you."

"It's a bit late for that, isn't it?" The words come out bitter. I guess the bad overshadows the good after all.

Dad shakes his head. Except for his transparent state, he doesn't look much different than the last time I saw him all those years ago. Years of struggling with Mom's fits and wondering what happened to him. And then…

"It's not too late," he interrupts my thoughts. "There are still four souls left to save. But there's something you should know. Something they've been trying hard to hide from you."

Anger boils to the surface as his words sink in. *Is he really talking about the Devil? He's been gone for years, and this is the first thing he says to me?*

I grit my teeth in an attempt to control the bubbling rage under my skin. Too late. With a frustrated cry, I propel myself at him.

Dad doesn't even move. With a hurt expression on his face, he waits for me to knock him over. The next second, I'm falling through him. I hit my head against the frame of the back door and grunt.

Dad holds out his hand. "I understand your anger, and I'm sorry."

His smile is getting on my nerves. I swat away his hand, and his face goes a shade darker. "I really missed you, Dante. You and Susan."

I push myself up and rub my head. "Sure you did."

I can barely stop myself from burying my face in his shirt. I can't believe my heart still longs for his arms around me. I'm not even sure if he's a good guy. My anger is now partly aimed at myself, and it makes my head hurt more than it already did.

"I'm so sorry. I had to leave you." Dad shakes his head. There's pain in his eyes, sadness, even loneliness. "I had to protect you and Susan, not just for your sakes, but for that of the whole world."

Slowly I breathe out. "I know."

A glint of hope burns in his eyes. "You do?" His lips curl up a bit. "Of course you do. You found my notebook, didn't you? Just like I knew you would." He reaches out to me, and I let him. His hand touches my arm and the hairs on my skin stand up.

"You could've told me, Dad." At the last word, my voice breaks. I sob and lower my head.

Cold arms wrap around me. I don't move, even though I want to pull free. My desire to have Dad close to me again is finally stronger.

After what feels like several minutes, I rest my head on his shoulder and fold my arms around his back.

We enjoy each other and the silence between us for what seems like forever but is too short at the same time.

"I wanted to tell you," he finally says softly. "I wanted to tell you everything. But you were so young, so optimistic and full of life. I couldn't bring myself to tell you. The knowledge you now have would've taken your childhood away in the blink of an eye. And look at you now, you're still so young but so strong at the same time, so grown-up. There are no words for me to express how proud I am." He kisses my forehead forcefully. "My son."

Tears burn in my eyes again, but I'm done crying, so I turn away from him and walk to the kitchen counter. "I know you don't need to eat or drink, but... would you like some hot chocolate?"

"Sure." He walks over to my seat at the table and sits down. "This used to be my chair."

I put some milk in a pan and grab two mugs. "So what happened? The Shield told me you turned evil."

He looks up from my drawings and sighs. "I did. I tried very hard to fight it, but my adversary was too strong. He slowly poisoned my mind."

I stir the milk but keep my eyes on Dad. It's still so hard to believe he's really here. "And the Shield couldn't see it?"

"No, he was invisible to them."

"Couldn't you use a spell on it then?"

"It was a very powerful being, Dante. It still is.

And it's not alone."

It's as if someone presses ice cubes against my arms and neck. "What do you mean? Is it still alive?"

Dad stares past me. "I'm not sure *alive* is the right word." He scrutinizes me for a moment. "I don't want to scare you, son, but this creature will cross your path too someday. Soon, I think."

I turn back to the stove and add the chocolate to the milk. "You can tell me. I can handle it."

He chuckles softly. "You're right. It's hard to see you as a sixteen-year-old instead of an eleven-year-old boy, but I can tell how much you've changed."

I shrug. "Fighting demons and other creeps does that to you."

"I suppose it does."

When I pour the chocolate into the mugs and hand one to him, he finally nods. "Okay, I suppose it might give you an advantage knowing what you're up against. Besides the Devil, I mean."

*Oh great, more enemies to fight.*

The distant look in Dad's eyes tells me he's thinking back to the moment he started changing.

"When I first saw him, I thought he was some sort of angel here to take me to Heaven," Dad says. "Then he stepped into the light, and I saw his evil grin and the bow and arrows on his back. I immediately knew I was dealing with something else, and I knew it had to be something strong if it could step into this house without trouble. I reached for my blade and held up a flame to keep him at a distance." He shakes his head as if he still can't believe what happened next. "It was no use. With one flick of his wrist, I was on de floor, grunting in pain. Power and anger surged through me, but I couldn't use it. It was all trapped inside me, building up until I was screaming in agony. I was sure I wouldn't survive. Until he kneeled down next to me and held my gaze. 'You want power above all. Anger and greed will lead you into war. Your heart will blacken until you feel nothing but hate and desire.'"

In a reflex, I grab Dad's hand. He looks up, startled, as if he really got lost in his past for a second.

"It's not your fault," I say. "You tried to fight it, didn't you?"

He nods. "I did. And when he left, I tried to tell the Shield. But I couldn't. Something inside me stopped me. And after a couple of weeks, I didn't want to anymore. I was angry at everyone and everything. I couldn't think straight anymore."

"So what was it?" We both look up as Vicky's head appears, with an almost invisible body under it. She doesn't greet me but keeps her eyes on Dad. "What kind of creature did that to you?"

I squeeze Dad's hand when he doesn't answer. "This is your chance to tell us all the truth. You couldn't do it then, but you can do it now."

He swallows, his eyes never leaving Vicky's face.

She crosses her arms. "Well?"

Finally, he blinks. "It was the White Horseman."

I gasp. "You're kidding."

"No." He shakes his head, still looking at Vicky.

"He poisoned my heart and mind, and I couldn't tell you about it. I couldn't tell anyone." He lowers his head and buries his face in his hands. Tears flood through his fingers. "I'm so sorry. I should've fought harder. I never wanted to hurt anyone."

"But you did." Taylar's voice is cold as he appears next to Dad. "You did horrible things. You burned people!"

"I know!"

I can't stand the sound of his broken voice. I don't want to see him cry. So I stand up and wrap my arm around him.

"Stop attacking him," I tell the ghosts. "He fought with everything he had." I look down at my father. "Didn't you?"

"Of course!" he exclaims. "But those poisonous feelings inside me were too strong. Deep inside, I knew, even at the end, that I was being used, influenced. I was like a puppet, and I couldn't cut the strings, no matter how hard I tried to. I think this is why the other Horseman killed me in the end. They knew I would keep fighting, so they couldn't use me for their ultimate plan to overthrow the good in this world."

"Other Horseman?" I say, a chill creeping from my toes to my neck. "You've met the other three too?"

I feel him tensing under my grip. "You know about them?"

"Yes," I say. "We trapped the Red Horseman in

the Shadow World and made a deal with the Pale Horseman."

"A deal?" The panic in Dad's voice is palpable.

I wave his concerns away. "Don't worry, it was a good deal."

Vicky straightens her shoulders and walks up to us. Maël has also appeared and is watching us from her regular seat at the table, with just as much interest as concern.

Vicky lowers herself onto her chair and waits until Dad looks at her again.

"What happened with this other Horseman?" she asks.

Dad wipes his face before answering. "I never saw the White Horseman again, but one day I got a visit from his brother, the Black Rider. Weakened as I was already, I didn't stand a chance against him. He took away my ability to eat, and that was that."

Taylar frowns. "He starved you to death?"

"Yes."

"And then what? How did you end up here? Were you a ghost all this time?"

"I'm not sure where I went," Dad confesses. "All I know is that I didn't go to Hell or Heaven. I went somewhere dark and cold. I've been trapped there all this time, trying to get to Dante. I've heard their conversations, their plans, and I knew I needed to warn you all."

Vicky nods. She knows he's telling the truth. She can read it in his eyes.

"How did you finally escape?" Taylar asks.

"The Horsemen have been too busy preparing their big plans to keep a close eye on me lately. It's a great risk coming here, but I had to take it."

"And if they catch you?" I ask.

He shrugs. "They banish me to Hell? Who knows."

Flashes of vile creatures torturing him fill my head. "What? No!"

A sad smile plays on his lips. "It's worth the sacrifice, Dante. For you, for Susan…" He gestures at the others and then at the ceiling. "For everyone."

Maël slams her staff onto the floor, stands up and bows slowly. "I apologize for doubting you, master. And for doing nothing to help you."

Taylar bows as well. "I'm sorry too."

Then Vicky follows their example. "And me. Please forgive us."

With tears in his eyes, Dad rises to his feet and beckons them to come close. He puts his hand on their shoulders, one by one. "My dear friends, there is no need to bow to me. I couldn't have asked for a more loyal Shield than you. I am grateful for the time we had together. There's no Shield braver than you."

Maël straightens up and does something I've never seen her do before. She puts her arms around Dad's neck and pulls him into a hug.

Everyone in the room watches in silence.

When they finally let go, Maël smiles. "It is good to see you again, master."

"You too, Maël." He moves on to Taylar and hugs him too. "And you."

Then he stands still in front of Vicky and looks down at our entwined hands. "And my dear Vicky. I always knew you had a special role to fulfill. And not just in our battle." He pulls us both close to him. "I'm happy you two found each other in these rough times."

Then his forehead wrinkles as he gestures at the empty chairs. "Now tell me, where are D'Maeo and Jeep? And where is your mother?"

CHAPTER 6

Dad stares in the distance for quite some time after I've told him everything that has happened. Or rather, the short version of events, or I'd be sitting here for days.

"Don't be sad," I tell him eventually. "We've overcome so much already, so why wouldn't we be able to get them all back? Besides," I get up to make coffee, "D'Maeo and Jeep are strong and experienced, and Mom has Trevor to protect her."

Finally, Dad smiles. "True." He joins me at the kitchen counter and places a hand on my back. "I'm so proud of you. I wish I could stay here. It would be great to fight by your side. You're stronger than I ever could've imagined."

I snort. "I'm still a rookie. Without the Shield and Mona and Charlie and Gisella, I would've died ages ago."

"And without you, *we* would have died," Charlie's voice says from behind us.

As soon as we turn around, my best friend narrows his eyes. "Mr. Banner?"

Dad steps forward with a big smile. "Charlie? Is that you? You're so big!"

I look away when he wraps his arms around my best friend. Another reunion like this and my emotions will spin out of control. Dad is here with us, but he can't stay. It's just a matter of time before one of the Horsemen comes to collect him, and I'm not sure we're up for that fight. Especially not if two riders come at the same time.

"Dad," I say, flinching a little at the thought that this will probably be the last time I call him.

He turns with a smile. "Yes?"

"I'm sorry to interrupt, but I don't think we have much time to chat. If there's something you want to warn us about, you should do it now."

His face clouds over. "You're right. If the Horsemen find me gone, they'll come to look for me here first. Time to tell you what I overheard."

I lean closer, even though he sits down beside me.

"So far, you've lost only one soul, is that correct?"

We all nod in unison, and I blink away the image of Kale, the boxer, being dragged away.

"Good," Dad says. "The more souls you save, the better our chances of winning. But there's something you should know."

With my eyes, I try to force him to continue.

Instead, he sips his coffee with a content expression on his face. "Oh, how I've missed simple things like this."

"What should we know?" I urge him.

He puts down his mug. "Right. After they lost the first two souls, I heard the Horsemen discussing tactics. You see, after their first attempts to take the souls of every circle, they can start over. It's not as if the soul they have will expire or something. But it could take decades, even centuries to collect nine souls that way. Even Satan doesn't have that kind of patience. Not anymore, that is. That's why they have a back-up plan."

Vicky and I exchange a quick panicked look across the table.

Dad mimics our expression. "There is a way to open the circles of Hell without having all of the souls. If they manage to make the chosen souls commit the sins of each circle, Lucifer can use that somehow to break through the circles."

"What?" we say in unison.

Dad nods gravely. "Unfortunately, I don't know how."

I throw my hands up in desperation. "So we've been saving these souls for nothing?"

"No, not for nothing," Dad corrects me quickly. "Getting the souls is the fastest way to open the circles. But if they fail, they won't give up. They'll just go for plan B."

I hide my face in my hands and shake my head.

"And here I thought we were doing well."

"You are!" Dad gets up and grabs my face with both hands when I look at him. "You are doing better than I've ever done, you all are. You're the golden team, the ones that make it to the end. And I hope I will be there to witness it."

I throw my arms around his neck and blink away new tears. I wish I could hold on to him forever, keep him here with me, and reunite him with Mom. But some things aren't meant to be, and I should focus on the things we *can* realize. Having Dad here, even for a little while, is more than I could ever have hoped for.

I let go of him and wipe my eyes. "Thanks so much for coming, Dad."

He lets out a sigh that could knock a child over. "I don't want to leave you ever again, but I have no choice. Now that I've warned you, I should go back. You're in enough danger as it is. You don't need two Horsemen banging on your door." He places his hand gently against my cheek. "Be careful, I want to see you again, preferably alive." With a wink, he turns away from me. "If I can, I'll visit again and hopefully contribute to the fight."

He doesn't say anything about Mom, which tells me he's not worried. He knows I'll get her back no matter what.

"You be careful too," I say. "If you need help, send a message."

I know it sounds much easier than it is, but I want him to know I'm there for him too.

"We might be able to free you now, master," Maël says when Dad approaches her. "We have a spell to take us to Heaven. You will be safe there."

Dad hugs her without a word. When he finally lets go, there are tears in his eyes again. "You have no idea what your words mean to me. And although it sounds tempting to finally find peace, I can't do it. I believe there's a reason why I haven't moved on. Fate is not done with me yet. My role in this is not over, and I hope that means I can make a difference in the end."

*You already did,* I want to say, but the words get stuck in my throat. It's weird. Him being here, warning us, has given me more hope than any saved soul has so far.

For a second, he meets my eyes again. "Give Mom my love," he says, and before I can respond, he vanishes.

Silence descends on the room, as none of us knows what to say. We're all lost in thought anyway, going through every memory we have of Dad and trying to wrap our heads around the news that he brought us.

My emotions are all scrambled, my mind going back and forth between crying and smiling.

Now that Dad is gone, a lot of questions pop into my head. Things I wanted to ask him.

'How often did you watch Mom and me?'

'Did you know I was the chosen one?'

'Were you able to watch us from your prison?'

I'm grateful when sparks light up the kitchen, and Mona appears. "I'm back!"

She frowns when she gets only weary smiles and mumbled greetings in response. "What's going on here?"

I pull back the chair next to me. For a second, I can see Dad sitting in it again, and I smile. "We got some good and some bad news. You'd better sit down for this."

# CHAPTER 7

"So, what did you find out about Kasinda?" I ask the ghosts as soon as Mona is up to speed.

"Not much," Vicky says with a sigh. "Only that she's a powerful witch. She used to be kind, but she changed when she lost her daughter to a possession, just like Gisella said. Since then, she's been trying to gather more power, but no one knows if she succeeded."

I nod. "Okay, so we'll prepare for the worst."

Gisella dives into a bag she brought and holds up an antique-looking book. "We went by my house to pick up this book. It's a cookbook, but it's as old as the Book of a Thousand Deaths, from what I've heard. It'll be easier to make this look like the real thing than a regular book."

She puts it on the table with a grunt. It's as big as the world atlas we had to buy for school and as thick as the fifth Harry Potter book. It must weigh a ton.

"Thanks," I say as the others pass it over to my side of the table. I flip through it and frown. "Are you sure you don't need this anymore?"

Gisella grins. "I'm sure. We never use it, since all the recipes in there are disgusting."

"It might be worth a lot," I say as I slam it shut. Dirt rises from the pages and tickles my nose.

With a shrug, Gisella leans back in her chair. "It can never be worth more than the safety of the whole world."

"Good point," I say with a smile. "Then I guess we're ready to start. I'll put the spell on the book, and then we can go see your aunt."

Mona stands up and claps her hands together with a delighted expression on her face. "I'll prepare some lunch."

I open my spell book to check the ingredients again and memorize the words. As I read the first line, the page flips on its own.

My mouth goes dry. There's a message on the next page. It's written in a handwriting I recognize. Dad's.

*Dante,*

*If you need some extra power, think of what I did when I was fighting Lucifer. Do not listen to other people's advice in this. Instead, listen to your gut.*

*I love you and miss you,*
*Dad*

After the word "gut", there's a letter that turned into a smear of ink, as if he wanted to tell me more but didn't have the time.

*I wonder what drove him to write this in here. Why didn't he just tell me?*

I read it again. *Do not listen to other people's advice.* That must be it. He thinks my friends will keep me from doing what I think is right. And, of course, they can. I value their opinions, and most of them have more experience with magic than me. And with fighting the Devil.

*So, what's so important that I should ignore them? What does that first sentence mean?*

Vicky nudges me. "Are you done memorizing?"

I close the book fast. "Sure."

She scrutinizes me. "Is something wrong?"

"Besides the fact that saving those souls wasn't enough?"

It comes out harsher than I intended, but Vicky doesn't flinch.

"I feel your frustration," she says. "Literally. And it runs through my veins too. But John said we can still win. We're meant to win. And that's what we'll do."

"Hear, hear," I answer half-heartedly.

But I do still feel it. Hope. Dad has left me tons of it. Even within his cryptic message.

The spell to curse and cloak the book works best on a "natural surface" so I go outside and set everything up inside the circle of protection. Vicky joins me, and we both stare at the spot where D'Maeo was pulled into the box just hours ago.

"We'll get him back," I repeat.

Vicky nods. "I know."

"But first we're going to get rid of the curse on you so you won't go nuts on me again."

She scoots closer and brings her lips to my ear. "I thought you liked nuts?"

With a chuckle, I turn my head and kiss her. "That depends on what kind of nuts we're talking about."

"Nuts about you," she whispers against my lips.

"Oh yes, I definitely like that kind of nuts." I suppress a shiver when her cold fingers touch my neck. "You know… it's really hard to concentrate when you do that."

She pulls back, her shoulders sagging in disappointment.

I lean toward her and kiss her cheek. "We'll save it for later."

The corners of her mouth move up. "I can't wait."

Shaking my head to get rid of the electric pulses flowing through my body, I walk around the protective circle to set everything up.

"So, I had another idea," I tell Vicky once the candles and herb circle are in place. "Since Kasinda is strong, I want to put several layers of spells on the book. A bit like the spell Dad used on the Bell of Izme, but instead of using the same spell more than once, I want to use different ones."

Vicky taps her lips in thought, and I look away, pushing images of my lips touching hers aside.

"What kind of spells do you have in mind?" she asks.

"Well, the ones we talked about for starters. One that takes away her powers and one that makes the book look like the Book of a Thousand Deaths. Then another one on top of that to immobilize her. This will be a fairly simple one, because it's just for show. And the last one would be a spell to hide the immobilization spell." I scratch my head. "It sounds harder than it is when I explain it like this."

"No, I get it, and it's a great idea," Vicky says. "Kasinda will discover the top two spells and undo them. She won't expect other spells to lie beneath them. It could work."

I sense a hesitation. "But?"

"But I might have a better idea for the most important spell." She paces up and down between the candles of north and west. "Stripping her of her powers is a risk. I mean, what if that doesn't break the curse?"

I open my mouth to argue, but she continues without pausing.

"Wouldn't it be better to transfer Kasinda's powers to one of us? Then that person would be able to undo the curse, and they would be more powerful." She stops pacing and looks at me. "We could use some extra power."

With a frown, I look back. "I don't know, babe.

You want to transfer her dark powers to one of us? What if that turns them evil?"

She tilts her head and smiles. "It won't. Gisella can take them. She knows how to harness them."

My gaze flicks to the back door. "You think she'd do that? She already hates her own powers and doesn't want to use them. Kasinda's powers are even darker."

Vicky shrugs. "We can ask her."

She's already on her way to the kitchen, and I don't stop her, even though I'm not sure this is a good idea. But she's right about the other plan. *What if taking Kasinda's powers doesn't break the curse? Vicky could be stuck with it for the rest of her afterlife.*

She strolls back out sooner than I expected with a big smile. "She says she'll do it. But you'll have to write an extra spell now before we go to see her aunt. A spell with which you can take away Kasinda's powers if Gisella is unable to control them. Make sure you strip only her powers, not Gisella's."

My eyebrows move up. "She said that? Great. I can do that. I just need to add a few lines to the spell I wrote."

"You want company?"

I lower myself onto the grass and take out my Book of Spells. "Sure, as long as you don't sit too close. You'll only distract me."

She crosses her arms and glares at me. "You're no fun."

I wave my pencil at her. "You wait until all of this

is over. I'll show you fun."

Her lips split into a wide grin. "You'd better start writing then."

I bend over the book. "Already on it."

With every sentence I write, Vicky moves closer. Once she's leaning against my shoulder, she doesn't move anymore though. We're just two people in love, enjoying a sunny morning in the garden. Or so I try to tell myself. Strangely enough, it works. I feel calm and almost happy. The words flow out of me easily.

"Done." I put away my pencil and kiss Vicky on the cheek and lips.

She jumps to her feet and pulls me up. "Holler if you need me. I'll be right here."

She steps out of the circle I created with the herbs, and I rub my hands. The amount of faith she has in me is comforting, yet I don't feel the same way. These are a lot of spells on top of each other, most of which I wrote myself. If I forget one small detail or make one little mistake, this could go sideways fast.

"You'll do fine," Vicky says. "Just take a deep breath and start. You're good at this, remember?"

*I'm good at this. This is what I was born to do. I can do this.*

I flip back to the first spell and light the black candle in the middle of the circle. Black for banishment.

With the black candle, I walk around the circle to light the four white ones, calling upon the powers of the north, east, south and west. Once the flames burn high, I start my first spell.

I sprinkle the remains of the herb mixture I prepared onto the antique book.

*"With this book we shall control*
*the powers that lie within a soul.*
*Kasinda is the soul we choose.*
*Her evil powers she will lose.*

*When Kasinda's touch is detected,*
*her powers will be at once collected.*
*They will travel through the air,*
*invisible to anyone there.*
*No magic will return these powers,*
*not even in their final hours.*

*To Gisella they will go,*
*but the owner will not know.*
*Once Kasinda's powers are gone,*
*she won't be able to hurt anyone."*

I almost drop the black candle and the book when the smoke rising from it changes into a claw with sharp nails. It shoots forward to grab me but changes direction when I pull back my head. For a moment, it seems to search the air. Then it dives into the book in my other hand, which turns dark as the claw slowly disappears into it.

Vicky steps back into the circle when I don't move. "Are you okay?"

I'm still staring at the book. "I'm not sure." I lift the book higher. "Does this look good to you?"

She bends over it and narrows her eyes. "Not really." Her forehead wrinkles into a concerned frown. "Do you think something went wrong?"

After a short pause, I nod toward the back door. "We should ask Gisella."

Vicky takes off without another word and comes back seconds later with the werecat-witch at her side.

Gisella takes one look at the book and shakes her head. "It didn't work. Your spell bounced on Kasinda's magic." She rubs her temple hard. "I was afraid of this."

"You suspected this?" I ask, incredulous. "Why didn't you say anything?"

She takes the book from me. "I didn't want to worry you. You need confidence to cast a good spell. Besides…" She sighs. "I was hoping I wouldn't have to use my powers again. I hate incantations."

"I'm sorry." I grab the book and throw it into the grass beside us. "You know, you don't have to do this. We can find another way. I understand."

Gisella bends down and picks up the book. "Actually, I think it's the only way to break the curse on Vicky besides killing my aunt, which I don't want to do. So I'll do it. I'll put a curse on this book." She looks at the book in her hands as if it's drenched in blood. "No matter how much I hate it, I'll do it."

I'm still searching for the right thing to say when Vicky throws her arms around Gisella's neck. "Thank you."

The girl in the red catsuit stiffens for a second. Then she relaxes and hugs Vicky back. "You're welcome."

"What do you need?" Vicky asks when they let go of each other.

Gisella picks up the black candle and hands it back to me. "We don't need herbs, circles and candles for incantations. That's the only upside of being an evil witch." With a smirk, she steps to the middle of the herb circle. "A little extra power can't hurt though, so I'll use the circle."

A small nod of her head tells us to back up.

"Please be careful," I say, and she shoots me a look of affection.

"No matter what happens, don't interfere," she warns us. "Your spell bounced on Kasinda's protective magic, which means your spell is reversed. If we use the book now, my powers will flow into her instead of the other way around. I'm going to undo this first. It might look frightening, but I promise I'll be fine."

I back up a little more and pull Vicky along. "Okay. Good luck."

Gisella closes her eyes and places the book on one hand. The other hand hovers over it, going slowly from left to right and back. She starts mumbling words I can't understand. They sound like random syllables put together. Then she starts shaking. It's a good thing she warned us, or I would've thought she was having a fit like Vicky's.

Her free hand is moving up and down now. The black, smoky claw becomes visible inch by inch as she pulls it out of the book. The edges of the pages are getting lighter already. But Gisella trembles more violently with every gesture she makes. Her voice gets lower until she sounds like the evil wizard Jafar from Aladdin, ominous, dark and powerful.

I grab Vicky's hand and squeeze it. "Do you think this is how it's supposed to go?"

What I really want to ask is, 'Does this mean she can't control her powers? Is she turning evil right in front of us?'

Of course, Vicky senses my fear. And she's a good mind-reader, even without her empath power.

"I think it's going well," she says. "She's in control. I can feel it."

I can't say I feel the same way when Gisella throws her head back and coughs up slivers of red smoke. Her voice changes pitch again, growing higher and higher. The volume of her words increases until I slam my hands against my ears against the noise.

Too late I realize my mistake.

I drop my arms when Charlie comes flying past me, cursing at us for not jumping to Gisella's rescue.

# CHAPTER 8

"No, leave her!" I call out, reaching for Charlie's arm but missing him by two steps.

Vicky doesn't hesitate. She vanishes and apparates in front of Charlie. His momentum knocks them both over. Vicky goes up in smoke again and comes back on top of Charlie.

"Stay still," she orders him, pinning his arms behind his back.

When he keeps struggling, I kneel down next to him. "Take it easy, she's fine. She told us it could get rough. We promised to leave her to it."

A tear makes its way from Charlie's eye to his chin. "You call this rough? Something is killing her!"

I place my hand on his shoulder and put every ounce of faith I have into my words. "It's not. Gisella is strong. She said she could do it, and I believe her."

Charlie struggles again, but Vicky is too strong.

We all watch as the book opens, and the black claw frees itself. It hovers in front of Gisella, its fingers outstretched, ready to dig into her face. Gisella keeps mumbling, her voice calm now. The claw starts to rotate, faster and faster. Slivers of smoke rise up from the book, pulled out by the small vortex. Then, the book slams shut. Gisella drops it, and in one quick movement, she slams her hands together, squashing the claw. Puffs of black escape her fingers, but they turn white instantly and are taken away by the wind.

Gisella breathes in and out a couple of times, bends down to pick up the book, and turns to us. With a content smile, she hands the book back to me. "And now you hide my magic with yours."

Vicky lets go of Charlie, who sits up wide-eyed. He's like a statue, frozen in place. His mouth is slightly open.

Gisella puts her arm around him. "Come on, let's go inside."

His head slowly turns toward her. "That was scary."

"I know." She kisses him on the temple. "I didn't want you to see that."

"You need to tell me next time you plan on doing something dangerous like that. Then I can cuff you to the bed or something, you know."

She grins. "That's exactly why I can't tell you." She straightens up and holds out her hand. "Are you coming? I could use something to replenish my energy, and you're the snack expert."

I pick up the book when they walk back into the kitchen, Charlie still arguing that she should've told him.

Vicky points at the antique book. "That looks a lot better."

Nodding, I flip through the pages. "Yes, it looks normal again. I'd better cast the three spells."

First, I cast the cloaking spell to hide Gisella's magic. It goes well, and I move on to the next step. Since memorizing is still not one of my strong suits, I reread the spell I wrote to make the book look like the Book of a Thousand Deaths.

"I can hold it up for you if you want," Vicky says, eyeing me with amusement.

I open my mouth to say I'll be fine, but who am I kidding? It will take precious minutes to remember all three spells, and this is not something I want to risk screwing up. This might be our only chance to get rid of this stupid curse.

Vicky reads my emotions and pulls the Book of Spells from my hands. "Just tell me when."

"Thanks. We can leave the circle like this, but I need dried fern leaf, poppy seeds, dill weed and a few drops of dew. The same things we used for the cloaking spell, remember? They need to be crushed and heated."

"Here you go."

We both turn at the sound of Mona's voice. She's holding out a bowl from which green smoke curls up.

With a frown, I take it from her. "How did you—?"

Her smile is dazzling with a touch of pride. "I'm your fairy godmother, honey. It's my job to keep an eye on you." She winks. "I looked over your shoulder while you were reading the spell."

"Thanks," I say. "This will save us some time."

"You're welcome." She turns, and I watch her walk back inside, not a hair on her head moving and her steps light, almost lifting her completely from the ground.

"She's something special," I say.

Vicky scrunches up her nose. "She sure is, but what she said made me wonder…"

"Wonder about what?"

"How many times she's looked over your shoulder while we were… intimate."

"Vicky!" I scold her. "She would never do that!"

She smirks. "Not on purpose, but accidents happen, right?"

I shake my head feverishly. "I don't want to think about that." With force, I push the rising images from my mind. "Okay, hold up the book, please."

After a deep breath, I sprinkle some of the mixture from the bowl onto the antique book.

*"Shadows, shadows, come to me.*
*Surround me so only I can see."*

With the bowl on top of the book, I start walking

inside the circle, dropping the mixture onto the line of herbs as I go.

*"Wanted by evil, dark as night,*
*I cloak this book in magic's light.*

*Hide its true form from evil breaths.*
*Disguise it as the Book of a Thousand Deaths."*

When I reach the spot where Vicky is standing, I take the last of the mixture and rub it onto the front and back of the book.

Vicky hands me a lit incense stick and holds up my Book of Spells, so I can read the last lines.

*"Evil magic will not see,*
*this book's true identity."*

With the incense held under the book, I wait for the smoke to do its job. More and more of it wraps around the cover until it is no longer visible. It is lifted from my hands. I can hear the pages flipping. The smoke turns red, gold, blue and then brown. With a jolt, the book rises. It's still changing. Pages are added while it spins. The dark cover becomes more solid, and intricate figures are etched into it. Crossed bones, skulls, a pentagram with the tip pointing down to Hell instead of up to Heaven, an inverted cross and, in the middle, inside a deep-set circle, a strange symbol that looks familiar somehow.

While I rack my brain to remember where I've seen it before, the smoke moves along the edges of the pages, nibbling away until they look worn. Then the smoke whirls up one more time before dissipating. Vicky takes the incense stick from me, and I catch the book that drops down without warning. "Wow! It's heavy!"

Vicky steps up to me and studies the thick cover. "What's that symbol?" She points at the one in the middle. "I think I've seen it somewhere before."

"Me too," I say, staring at it again. "But I can't remember where."

I follow every line with my eyes, hoping to jog my memory. There's a cross with a double horizontal line on the top, resting on the center of an infinity sign.

Vicky shakes her head. "Maybe Gisella knows what it is."

I pick up the empty bowl and follow her inside.

"That was fast," Mona says, putting down her mug.

"Oh, we're not done yet," I say, "but we wanted to show you this."

I put the heavy book on the table.

"So that's what it looks like," Taylar says breathlessly.

"It's beautiful," Charlie remarks. "Look at the details. Are those symbols carved into the cover or something?"

"More like burned, with magic," Gisella says in a disapproving tone. "It might be beautiful, but don't forget how dangerous it is."

"It's not the real book," I remind her. "So we have nothing to fear."

"True, but still…" she shivers, "it gives me the creeps."

I tap the carving in the middle. "I wanted to ask you guys if you know what this symbol means. I think I've seen it somewhere before."

"You might have seen it on the Pentaweb," Gisella says, staring at it as if she's afraid it'll jump her. "Vicky showed you the magical internet, right?"

"She did. I know this symbol is called a Leviathan Cross. It's a satanic symbol, but I'm not sure what it stands for exactly."

"I do," Maël says, reaching up to push back an escaped curl. "The double cross symbolizes protection and balance in the eternal universe portrayed by the infinity sign below. Lucifer believes that the balance of the universe was disturbed when he was banished to Hell. The Leviathan Cross is a symbol for all magic used with the intention of restoring that balance. In other words: for Lucifer to rule the Earth."

Gisella backs up a bit more. "The spells in this book are of an evil you can't imagine."

I nod and slide the book back to me. "Well, we knew that already. That's why we're taking a fake book to your aunt instead of the real thing." I shoot her a reassuring smile. "And if this cookbook awakens such strong feelings in you, it must also work on Kasinda."

She shakes her head slowly. "Not necessarily. You're forgetting she's much stronger than me."

I point my finger at her. "She *will* fall for this. Just wait and see."

"I hope you're right."

"I am." Without another word, I walk back into the garden.

Vicky follows close behind. "I still have a feeling I've seen that Leviathan Cross somewhere before. And it wasn't on the Pentaweb."

"Me too." I kiss her on the cheek. "It'll come back to us. Don't worry about it." I gesture at my Book of Spells, which is still in her hand. "Show me the next one."

*"Immobilizing the enemy,"* she reads out loud when the book flips to the right page. "Looks like an easy one."

"It is. It'll only be there for show," I say with a wink.

"All we need is a hex bag. Since we want it to look genuine, Gisella should make it."

I turn to call out to the werecat-witch and am surprised to find her standing behind me.

"Already here," she declares cheerily. She pats her stomach. "And full of energy again."

"How did you creep up on us like that?"

She hops from one foot to the other. "I'm half cat, remember?"

I scrunch up my nose. "I actually don't know what

that means. The only cat feature I've seen so far are your blades, and they're not even that catlike. I'd expect you to have five of them on each hand instead of one big blade."

She throws out her arms, and the blades replace her hands. "We start out like that, but around our tenth birthday, the tiny blade nails, as I call them, melt into one. Which is actually better." She slams them together with a loud clang. "Much more solid, you see."

I smile. "I suppose you have a point. But besides sneaking up on your enemies and piercing them with your blades, what can you do as a werecat?"

Gisella taps her lips in thought. "Well, I can communicate with cats. But that hasn't been very useful so far. Although, I have retrieved something that was stolen from me once that way. Other than that… I can walk on narrow ledges, I'm not afraid of heights, I have nine lives—"

"You what?" Vicky calls out.

I chuckle. "You're kidding, right?"

"Nope." She shakes her head with a wide grin. "If I die, I just come back."

"So, for now, you're immortal!" Vicky's voice is high with excitement.

Gisella tilts her head. "Basically. But I'd still rather not die." She winks. "Furthermore, I could easily win every single gymnastics golden medal in the world… as long as no other werecats are competing." To demonstrate, she does a backflip and several other

77

moves I don't know the names of. It all looks so easy. Her whole body bends as easily as rubber, and it's as if she doesn't weigh anything. She barely touches the ground.

We both cheer and applaud when she gives us a small bow.

"How come I've never seen you do any of that in a fight?" I ask incredulously. "I'd say that's a pretty handy skill. Why don't you ever use it?"

She laughs out loud. "I do use it, all the time. You just can't see it. You only see the beginning or end of a move. Watch."

She walks to the other side of the protective circle and takes a deep breath. "Now, don't move."

Her blades appear again as she throws down her arms. Then she pushes off, takes a couple of ultrafast steps and… disappears.

I can hear movement in the air, but I don't see Gisella anymore until she comes to a halt in front of me, her bright red locks blown out behind her and her blades inches from my neck.

Vicky bursts into laughter. The sound is contagious, but I swallow the chuckle rising in my throat, afraid to move.

"You should see your face," Vicky hiccups. "It's hilarious."

With a content grin, Gisella pulls back. "Glad I could lighten the mood a bit."

"You knew she could do this?" I ask Vicky while I rub my neck, even though the blades didn't actually touch my skin.

Her blonde-tipped locks cascade around her beautiful face when she shakes her head. "No, but I saw this coming from a mile away."

I feel a blush creeping from my neck to my cheeks. "I'm still amazed at the amount of powers in the world. My life feels more like a movie than the real thing at the moment."

Vicky leans over to me and brings her mouth to my ear. "Is it a good movie?"

Her breath tickles my skin and I shiver. "It's a brilliant movie, but as a life, it's a bit hard. If I had a choice, I'd keep the protagonists and throw everything else away."

Her lips are still close to my ear, moving down the side of my face slowly as she asks, "Who's your favorite character?"

Although the answer is clear, I can't stop the joke rolling from my tongue. "Dante is pretty awesome."

She recoils, as expected, and glares at me. "Really?"

My grin stretches so wide it makes my jaws ache. I reach out and pull her close. She resists, but I manage to wrap both arms around her. "Of course not. You know who my favorite is, real and fictitious. I'm looking at her."

As soon as the corners of her mouth move up, I plant a kiss on them.

It's not until I'm out of breath that I realize we're not alone. I let go of Vicky and turn to face Gisella.

"Sorry about t…" My voice trails off when I find nobody there. "She left."

Vicky giggles. The sound fills me with even more hunger for her.

"I think we chased her away," she says with a mischievous glint in her eyes.

I give her another kiss, a short one this time, and sigh heavily. "As much as I would love to continue on this path, I can't." I bend over to pick up the "Book of a Thousand Deaths", which I dropped when Gisella almost decapitated me. I chuckle at the thought and shake my head. Gisella would never do that. I know that now.

Vicky gives me a questioning look, which I wave away. "I was picturing my reaction to Gisella's 'attack'." I make quotation marks with my fingers at the last word.

"Priceless, right?" Vicky grins.

I grab her by the waist and throw her on the ground. She goes down with a startled cry, and I pin her down with both arms. "You were saying?"

She sticks out her tongue.

Gisella's voice makes us both look up. "Are you guys done playing?" She holds out a bowl and a piece of cloth. "I've got most of what we need for the hex bag. Basil, rue, nettle, lavender, hemp and something that once belonged to Kasinda." We scramble upright as she throws the herbs onto the cloth and fishes a tiny doll in a red cat suit with long red hair from her pocket. "Kasinda made this for me years ago. It was the last thing she ever gave me, before..." She swallows.

"Before her daughter died?" I finish her sentence.

"Are you sure you want to use it?" Vicky asks. "You probably won't get it back. At least, not in one piece."

Gisella nods. "It's the best I've got."

Vicky gestures at the herbs spread out over the piece of cloth. "You said you have *almost* everything you need. What's missing?"

"Do you have any wormwood?"

Vicky digs into her endless pocket and shows her a small bottle. "Only wormwood oil, will that do?"

Gisella places the tiny doll on top of the herbs in her other hand. "It's fine. Just pour it over everything gently."

"Anything else?" Vicky asks as she drops the bottle back into her pocket.

"Some goofer dust would be nice. It'll make the spell stronger."

Vicky tilts her head. "I don't think I have any, since it's only used for black magic. But let me see."

She slides her hand back into her pocket and shakes her head. "Nope, sorry."

"It's fine," the werecat says with a shrug. "This spell is just for show anyway. Can you tie the bag for me? There's a leather strap in my left pocket."

Vicky retrieves the strap and follows Gisella's instructions. When she holds the tied bag up, the werecat nods contently. "That looks great. Now all you have to do is cast the spell and make it invisible."

I take the hex bag from Vicky and place it on the grass. "How do we get Kasinda to take it?"

She frowns and stares at the bag. Her eyes move up to the book in my hand. "What if you flatten it a bit and tape it to the back of the book?"

"Great idea!"

After a thumbs up, Gisella walks back to the house. "Holler if you need me again!" she calls over her shoulder.

"We will!"

I watch her walk away and contemplate the changes I've seen in her lately. She kept her distance at first, didn't want to open up to me, to us. Or so it seemed. But now that I think about it, that was probably because of my attitude towards her. The first time I saw her, she scared the hell out of me by making my leg disappear. Her blades are impressive, but to be honest, they only contribute to her "tough girl" look. The catsuit, the bright red hair, the blades, everything about her screams "I want to fight". Which wasn't so bad until I found out what she is: a werecat and descendant of Black Annis, the most feared witch that ever lived, a deadly combination.

"Isn't it great to have someone like her on our side?" Vicky's voice pulls me from my thoughts.

"She can be trusted," she adds.

I kiss her on the cheek. "I know that now."

She holds up my Book of Spells. "Time to wrap this up. Only two more spells to go."

# CHAPTER 9

When we're done, I examine the antique cookbook carefully from all sides.

"Nice job," Vicky compliments me. She runs her hand along the back cover. "I can't feel the hex bag at all."

"Then I guess we're ready."

Her face suddenly clouds over. "What if this doesn't work, Dante? What if we can't get rid of this curse?"

I put down the book and grab her shoulders. "Look into my eyes."

Her gaze darts over my shoulder.

"Come on, look," I press. "Tell me what you see, what you feel."

She blinks and focuses on my eyes. I let my mind wander to what's coming and picture our success in my head. Handing the book to Kasinda, transferring her powers to Gisella, lifting the curse… My mind won't stop there. Next I see D'Maeo, Jeep and Mom standing in the kitchen, hugging every one of us. I even get a glimpse of Lucifer going down. I put every bit of hope in it that I can muster.

Then laughter from the kitchen drifts our way, and the images vanish. Vicky comes into focus again. Her eyes are wet.

"Thank you," she whispers. "I needed that."

I move my hands to her head and press her gently against my chest. "You're very welcome."

We clean up the protective circle, pick up everything we used and walk into Darkwood Manor.

"How's everything here?" I ask the others.

"We didn't find anything," Charlie answers.

"Find anything about what?" I ask, putting the heavy book down on the kitchen table.

"About how to free D'Maeo, you know."

"Or how to find Jeep," Taylar adds.

"And get Susan back," Mona finishes.

"Right," I say, a bit dumbfounded.

"What?" Charlie says when I walk around the table and lower myself into my chair. "You didn't expect us to just sit here and do nothing, did you?"

"Of course not," I answer.

Charlie leans forward and narrows his eyes. "You did think that."

Taylar crosses his arms. "We care about our friends as much as you do, Dante. Why would you think we'd sit back and do nothing?"

Angry faces stare at me, and I shake my head. "I did think you were only chatting and having tea. And I wouldn't blame you if you did. We all need a break at some point. Think about it, a couple of days ago no one would've been mad at me for thinking something like this. But now, everyone is so stressed out and on edge that emotions are flying everywhere." I look at Vicky, still standing at the other side of the table where D'Maeo should be sitting. "Am I right?"

Vicky holds up her hand to silence the others when they start talking all at once. "Dante is not accusing anyone of not caring or giving up. He makes a good point. We're all tired, physically and mentally. Most of our self-control has been slipping away in the last day or so. And as much as I want to lift this curse and free our friends, I think it would be best if we took a break. This constant fighting and worrying is taking its toll. If we continue like this, we're going to make mistakes." She closes her eyes briefly. "Mistakes that could cost us more than we're willing to give up."

All around the table, mouths are closing. All protests die as Vicky meets one gaze after another. Each one of us knows there's no arguing with what she says. Not only do we feel it in our own hearts and bodies, we know Vicky can sense it. And if she says we need a break, we should take one.

I clear my throat. "I'm not willing to risk any more lives. The new Cards of Death haven't arrived yet, and Kasinda isn't going anywhere. If there was ever a time to rest, it is now. A clear head can give us new ideas, and we need those." To put more weight on my words, I stand up and look at my best friend and the werecat first. "Charlie and Gisella, you took some time earlier to take a walk together. That was a good start. You're welcome to stay here and relax, but maybe you both want to go see your families. Mona?" I smile at the fairy godmother. "I know it's your job to take care of us, but no job should demand all of your time year-round. If there's anyone you want to visit, please do. Or gather more stuff you want to move in here. Fix your car... whatever you feel like doing. Go do something you enjoy." She nods gratefully, and I turn my attention to the three ghosts. "I'm not sure if there's anything you guys like to do when you're 'off-duty'? In any case, I order you to go and have fun." I grin to make sure they don't take that order too seriously.

Maël gives me a faint smile in return, and Taylar salutes. "Aye aye, sir!"

"How about another poker game? I enjoyed that," Charlie says. Then he turns to Gisella with a guilty expression on his face. "Unless you want to go home? I can come with you."

The werecat-witch shakes her head. "No, they're on vacation. And although I enjoyed making out with you earlier, a game of poker sounds like fun too."

Charlie's cheeks turn red, and I chuckle. "A game sounds nice, but I don't want anyone to feel obligated to join in. Do whatever you need to relax."

Mona says goodbye, and Charlie and Gisella hunt

for snacks in the cupboards.

Taylar disappears upstairs when I tell him the poker set should be somewhere in my bedroom, which leaves Maël making coffee and Vicky joining me at my end of the table.

"Do you want to play poker or something else?" I whisper in her ear.

She chuckles and kisses my neck. "How about both?"

I conjure a shocked expression. "At the same time?"

She wiggles her eyebrows. "Sure, if that's what you want."

"Are you kidding? I don't want anyone else admiring what's under all that black you're wearing." I pull her close for a kiss.

"Are you in or out?" Charlie shouts inches from my ear.

We both jump.

Charlie places his hands on his waist in mock-irritation. "Make a choice. It's either poker or making out. But if it's the latter, please do it somewhere else. I just got put on the bench and watching all this smooching isn't good for my self-restraint."

Reluctantly, I let go of Vicky. She blows me a kiss before moving to D'Maeo's seat.

"Much better," Charlie says.

"You'd better split up too," I suggest, with a nod toward Gisella.

He rolls his eyes. "Fine. I'll take Mona's chair."

Soon, we're completely absorbed by the game. It's clear that we all needed this. For once, we manage to put our worries aside and truly have fun. Even Maël joins in for the first time. She knows the rules now, and her poker face is the best I've ever seen. This time, Vicky doesn't cheat. We devour an unhealthy amount of pizza and, after that, cookies, crisps and nuts. We also dig into a bottle of champagne that Taylar finds at the back of one of the cupboards.

"Thanks, Dad," I say, holding up the almost empty bottle while Charlie takes half my chips. "Cheers. To our upcoming victory."

# CHAPTER 10

I wake up with a leather tongue, insatiable thirst and a numb arm. My back protests as I sit up and look around. Everyone around the table is in deep sleep, hunched over the table in positions similar to the one I woke up in. Carefully, I move my fingers while I rub my back with my good arm. There's an imprint of my ear on my arm, and I study it with fascination. Then I lean back in my chair and let my gaze move over my sleeping friends again. They look peaceful, some of them more than I've ever seen them.

A pang of guilt hits my heart. *They're all here because of me. They're my Shield, my friends. If they hadn't known me, they wouldn't be in this mess now.*

I clench my fists and take a couple of breaths. I should sneak outside and train. Getting better at controlling my powers will increase our chances of winning.

I imagine everything I might be able to do, but when I picture myself facing Satan, I know it still won't be enough. There's a reason I'm not in this alone. But even with all of our powers combined, of the complete Shield, Charlie and Gisella, I'm not sure we can win. We need another power, something that will tip the odds in our favor.

My heart jumps into my throat, and I gasp. *That's it! Another power.*

My head pounds with excitement while I take out my Book of Spells and flip to the page where Dad wrote his little note. I absorb every word of his message, every letter, and my mouth turns up into a wide grin. *So that's what he meant.*

I don't notice my head moving up and down furiously until my neck starts to hurt. *Yes, this is what I need to do.*

Quietly, I get up and move my chair back. I've never been more grateful for the absence of a squeak from the back door.

I make my way to the protective circle and sit down in the middle. This time, I take out Dad's notebook. "Okay, book, show me how to add another ghost to my Shield."

The first sunbeam of the day pierces the clouds above my head and falls onto the side of my book. *A sign?* I place my index finger on the first illuminated page and open it.

At first, nothing happens. All I get is a blank page. But I know I need to be patient. Some things take a little time.

The ray of light moves up and hits the top of the page. It works like a printer; letters appear where the beam hits the paper. *So, it was more than just a sign. I'm doing the right thing.*

When the last word is etched onto the page, the sunbeam touches my face, as if to say "Go ahead!".

But I can't. Not yet. Dad's words flash before my eyes. *Do not listen to other people's advice in this. Instead, listen to your gut.* My friends might try to talk me out of this. Tell me there's no time to train another ghost, to tell him or her everything they need to know. They might even think we can't trust them. But I know deep inside that this is what we need. This is the thing that will change everything.

After a quick look at the back door, I sneak around the mansion. I search my pockets for the car keys and curse under my breath. *Why didn't I think of taking them with me when I left the kitchen?*

I tiptoe back and peer into the kitchen. My keys are on the kitchen counter, next to the coffee maker. There's no way I'll be able to grab them without anyone noticing, since the others are starting to wake up. *I could use my powers to manipulate the wind or something, but that's too risky. Maybe I should just walk.*

While I'm contemplating my best option, something moves in the corner of my eye. I turn my gaze back to the kitchen counter and slam my hand over my mouth to smother my cry of surprise. The keys are floating!

I take a step back when they hover in my direction. Gisella lets out a deep sigh and rubs her eyes. Immediately, I step out of sight. The keys fly through the back door and come to a halt in front of me.

"Take them," a voice whispers.

I frown. "Mona?"

"Yes. Go on, take them. Go, before they all wake up."

"But… why… how?" I stutter quietly.

"I checked in on you and read the spell over your shoulder. The others might not agree with your choice, but I do. Another ghost in your Shield can also help you get back D'Maeo, Susan and Jeep. Now go. I'll make some noise in the kitchen to cover up the sound of the engine."

"You're an angel," I say, holding up my hand.

"Not quite, but pretty close." With a wink, she places the keys in my palm.

I wrap my fingers around them and hesitate. *Shouldn't I take Vicky with me?*

"This is something you need to do on your own, Dante," Mona says. "Oh, and before I forget…"

Sparks fall down from the sky, and the fairy godmother becomes visible. "Take this."

She shows me a glass globe the size of a golf ball and holds it up into the sunlight. "You see those sparks wriggling inside? I filled them all with so-called *tracing vibes* and told them, or programmed them if you like, to obey you." She presses it next to the keys in my hand. "Use it to request a ghost with a certain power. The book will tell you how."

"Dante?" Charlie's voice calls out from inside.

I pull Mona into a quick hug. "Thank you."

"Any time. Take these bottles too. They contain more ingredients for the spell."

With my arms stuffed with glass bottles, I hurry to Phoenix. I gently drop everything in the passenger seat, walk to the driver's side, start the car and pull away fast. Several glances in the rearview mirror tell me no one is following. I'm as relieved about that as I am scared. *Is it actually wise to go somewhere on my own? What if demons surround me?*

The radio plays a soothing song, and I slowly relax. *This was Dad's idea, and Mona supports it. She'll keep an eye on me, and if I get into trouble, I can always summon the Shield.*

I hit the brake hard. *Summon the Shield... Why didn't I think of that before? Summoning them to me might also bring Jeep and D'Maeo back.* Although that does sound too easy to be true, I have to try it. *As soon as I finish this,* I decide. Adding another ghost to the Shield is my top priority now. I have a feeling this is the right time for it, and that time might not come again.

I pull over on Mrs. Delaney's street, where I have a—probably false—sense of safety. I scan the instructions for the spell again. *Must be cast in a place of motion to ensure maximum conduction between the realm of the dead and that of the living.*

*A place of motion. What does that mean? Water? A river? No, I won't be able to draw the circle and all the symbols I need in a river. So, what else moves?*

I tap the side of the notebook. *A train moves, but that's a bit too crowded for a spell.*

The answer lies on the tip of my tongue.

"A train station!"

I drive to the Silver Family Market and collect every ingredient on the list and some extras, just in case. Then, I make for the train station. My shoulders sag when I see half of the station is fenced up because of renovation work. Then, I realize no sound is coming from the site. I pull my phone from my pocket and smile. *It's Sunday! See, I knew this was the moment to do this.*

I jump out of the car, collect all my things in a large bag from the trunk, and make my way into the train station.

People are walking in and out, trains are pulling up and announcements rise above the noise. No one pays attention to me. Still, I look around four times before slipping through the space between two fences. I disappear behind the plastic curtains and walk further into the construction site. After turning two corners, I find stairs leading down to a dimly lit corridor. It smells damp and earthy here, and a draft awakens the goosebumps on my arms. The only sound that breaks the silence is the occasional train that moves above me. *A place of motion. The perfect spot for my plan. This should work.*

One by one, I take out the ingredients and compare them one more time with the instructions.

This is the most intricate spell I've cast so far, and as I pull Mona's glass ball from my pocket, another line appears in the book. *Draw a pentagram inside the circle.*

"Easy enough," I say to myself. "If only the rest of it was so simple."

*What if I summon something evil?* I shudder at the thought.

*But no, Dad used this same spell, and his father did it before him. It worked out fine, it'll work out fine again.*

I study the cracks between the tiles in the wall. *What kind of power should I ask for?*

After several minutes of blankness in my head, I sigh. *Why did Mona give me that ball? Why can't I just let the universe, or whatever, decide which ghost to send to me? What if I make the wrong choice?*

I walk over to the wall and kick it a couple of times in frustration. "Stupid insecurity. I'm done with it!"

And I am. *No more doubting myself. I'll just pick a power that will complement what we already have, and that will be fine. And if the power I come up with doesn't exist, I'm sure the spell will give me something similar.*

I pace up and down for a while, trying to come up with the thing we need the most. *Telekinesis? A Pyrokinetic like my father? But he might be able to join the fight, so another power might be more useful. Someone who can't be killed? No, that's no use if you don't have a power to fight with. Maybe I can summon someone with incredible strength. That could be helpful.*

I scratch my head while I walk up and down the corridor. *Isn't there something that has several of these characteristics?*

Abruptly I come to a halt. I feel my grin stretching, and it feels great. *That's it!*

Grateful for the epiphany, I look down at Dad's notebook, which I put on the ground next to the ingredients.

The first part is easy. It's almost similar to the protection spell I cast on Darkwood Manor.

I put down four candles, yellow for protection, after checking the compass app on my phone for the wind directions. Around the candles, I draw a circle made from the herbs listed at *step one* of the spell.

I read the first part a couple of times before starting. The jar with the remaining mix of herbs is in my hand. I shake it nine times.

> *"Salt and herbs, nine times nine,*
> *guard well this circle of mine."*

I place the jar on the ground in the middle of the four candles and create a line of salt following the outline of the herb circle. There's no need for salt under doors or windows here, since I'm only protecting this summoning circle. I pick up the sage stick, light it with a match and walk around the circle until the air is thick with smoke. Then, I put it down next to the jar and walk over to the candle placed on the east.

*"Powers of Air, hear my cry!*
*Grant me your protection, from all in earth and sky!"*

The candle of the south is next. The wick hisses when I light it.

*"Powers of Fire, hear my cry!*
*Grant me your protection, from all in earth and sky!"*

I pause for a second when a soft tapping echoes through the corridor. *Is someone coming?*

With all my heart, I hope not. How would I explain all of this to someone without magic? They'll think I'm crazy.

But no one rounds the corner, and the tapping stops. *It was probably a pipe or something.*

*Still, I should hurry. I don't want to be interrupted in the middle of this spell.*

I move on to the third candle.

*"Powers of Water, hear my cry!*
*Grant me your protection, from all in earth and sky!"*

The sound of an approaching thunderstorm rolls in. This time, I'm relieved to hear something. It means the spell is working. I only hope no one will come to investigate.

The last candle is the one on the north side.

*"Powers of Earth, hear my cry!*
*Grant me your protection, from all in earth and sky!"*

The four flames burn bright and reach for the ceiling. I follow the smoke that rises from them with my eyes and call out to the forces of magic.

*"Powers of High, listen to my plea.*
*May I always be protected by thee!"*

The jolt of power inside me is stronger than any I've experienced before. It nearly knocks me down, but I manage to stay upright. The flames move in a strange pattern, almost twirling. When the surge of electricity inside me reaches my ears, I take a deep breath to finish the first part of the spell.

*"Air protects us!*
*Fire protects us!*
*Water protects us!*
*Earth protects us!*
*Whatever may appear,*
*no evil will enter here!"*

There's a soft whoosh, and all four candles are blown out. I pick up a handful of salt, stand in the middle of the circle and turn slowly while I drop the salt and recite the last words.

*"Pure salt protect this place,*

*keep out all with evil pace.*
*Make this circle a place to hide,*
*keep us safe from harm inside."*

Shivers run down my back when I think of what the last line means. *Us. Another ghost for my Shield. What kind of person will it be? Male, female, young, old?* The thought of someone new to protect me makes me nervous and excited at the same time.

I rub my hands together. *Part one is done. Only two more to go.*

# CHAPTER 11

The next step is drawing a pentagram inside the circle. And… I curse and hold the book closer to my face. *Was this here before?* I'm positive it wasn't, because part three of the spell has moved to the next page. Under *part two,* there's now a collection of intricate symbols that should be painted over the pentagram I was about to draw. Painted in my blood too. *Great. Not only am I going to need more blood than I feel comfortable with, this is also going to take a lot longer than I anticipated.*

I consider casting a spell to prevent people walking in on me, since I'm going to be here for a while, but I simply don't have the time to do that. *If I want to finish this today, I'd better get on it. Good thing I have some drawing skills.*

The pentagram is easy, I've done it several times before, and it's made of only a couple of simple lines. I'm glad I left the candles in place, even though I need another color for this part. Now I know where to draw which symbol, since the placement is also important, according to the explanation.

Every symbol is different. There are some with sharp lines, there are curved ones, some consist only of tiny dots, and others need to be formed without lifting your hand. I don't recognize any of them, which means I have to keep the book close to make sure I copy them exactly. Who knows what could happen if I make a tiny mistake?

I squint to make out the lines of each symbol, since most of them also overlap. Thankfully, the book has listed all of the symbols separately too. The order in which I draw them doesn't seem to matter, and I'm grateful to find that when I accidentally step on them, they stay intact.

Although time breathes down my neck, I don't rush. If I do this right, I'll come out stronger, we all will.

When I finally draw the last line, I'm a bit dizzy from all the blood I had to use, and my body is stiff from sitting in the same, bent-over position for too long. I stretch my back and legs and go through my pockets, looking for a quick snack. Unfortunately, I find nothing of use.

When I turn my attention back to Dad's notebook, the symbols have all disappeared, and the spell is on one page again. At the end of *part one,* there's a new sentence.

*If you're low on energy after this part, stand in the middle of the pentagram, turn left three times and repeat the following*

101

*words threefold.*

I shake my head incredulously. *This book is amazing. It knows exactly what I need and when I need it. Or is this also part of the spell? It could be designed to keep the spell caster safe.*

With the book in my hand, I step to the middle of the circle, which is also the middle of the pentagram.

*"Circle of power, three times three,
refill the power that was taken from me."*

Turning makes me even dizzier, but as soon as I finish my last turn, my muscles all lock. I can't move, and for a second, I'm convinced I was tricked. Then, a blue flickering trail of light crawls from the points of the pentagram to my feet. A buzz goes through me like a thousand volts. My teeth chatter, and my fingers stretch by themselves. It's like being electrocuted, but somehow… in a nice way. All the little pains I didn't even notice anymore, stiff limbs, bruises, small cuts, they all vanish. Suddenly, I have so much energy that I could run a marathon. Even my eyesight and hearing seem to have improved. Control over my body is returned to me, and I flex my arms, that seem bigger.

"Thanks!" I say to the book.

I half expect an answer to appear on the page, but all the letters stay where they are.

I hop up and down to get the blood flow in my legs going again, and once the tingling of the blue light has left me, I read the next part of the spell.

*Use thyme, acacia leaves and althaea roots to form a strong connection between the worlds of the dead and the living. Add basil leaves as a symbol for extending your family. Take some black candle tobacco to help you reach someone you don't know the whereabouts of. Crush all of the above and mix it with agrimony oil to keep evil entities from clinging to your ghost. The blood root will tie the ghost to you, but you need it later. Orange candles will help you attract the ghost you want.*

I take a look at all the herbs spread around me. *It's a good thing Mona handed me those bottles too. Too bad I have no idea what blood root looks like.*

My phone buzzes, as if to remind me there's a thing called Google. I pull it from my pocket and grit my teeth when Charlie's number flashes across the screen. I swipe him away, muttering an apology, and open Google. Thankfully, the blood root pictures are clear. To make sure I don't mix the wrong herbs, I google all of them.

I swap the yellow candles for the orange ones I bought and repeat the words of the spell a couple of times in my head.

Before I continue, I check for Mona's glass globe. It's still in my pocket.

After a deep breath, I turn to the candles one by one.

*"Powers of north, south, east and west,*
*please fulfill my one request.*
*For my fight to save the world,*

103

*I need another boy or girl."*

I repeat the lines four times, lighting an orange candle after each verse and placing three dots of herb mixture on each one. The flames flicker when I return to the middle of the circle and draw a miniature herb circle there, around my feet.

*"Powers that be, hear my call.*
*Send me a ghost that can help us all.*
*Complete my Shield with a sixth addition,*
*to increase the chances of our mission."*

I rub some of the mixture under my shoes, on my neck and onto my eyelids and spread the remains onto my hands. I take out the glass ball and hold it between my smudged palms.

Now is the time to focus on the power I want, the gift this ghost must have. Doubts rise in my mind again. *What we could really use is more than one ghost, but since I haven't got all day, I'll have to choose one power.* I'm still convinced that a shapeshifter will be very helpful, so I repeat that word over and over in my head while I think of all the things it could turn into. I guess it could even mimic a demon or Satan himself. *How convenient would that be? We'll have a ghost with almost limitless powers.*

I grin at the thought and lift the glass ball above my head.

*"Powers of all, hear my plea.*
*See the wish that lives in me.*
*Send me the ghost that I desire,*
*make it rise from the flaming fire."*

I raise the ball higher and crush it between my fingers. The glass shatters easily but doesn't cut my hands. Warmth floods down from it, covering me from head to toe. The sparks are so brilliant that I narrow my eyes. I don't close them, because I don't want to miss what comes next. My heartbeat speeds up in anticipation. Mona's sparks touch the outer circle, and all the herbs go up in golden smoke that surrounds me. Through it, I can see the flames of the candles rising high. The crackling gets louder, and the light brighter. I have no other choice now than to squeeze my eyes shut.

A loud bang reverberates through the corridor. The tiles in the wall rattle, and a strong, hot breeze hits me. I sway but stay upright. Carefully, I open one eye. The candle flames have settled. The sparks are gone. In front of me lies a girl, dressed in a short, leopard skin dress that hugs her curves.

"Ahem," I say in a half-cough.

"Wow." The girl wipes her bleached locks from her face and scrunches up her forehead. "What the heck happened? Where am I?"

I'm wondering if I should help her up when her gaze locks onto mine, and her eyes grow wide.

"Wow!" she says again. Then she scrambles to her

knees and lowers her head until it touches the ground. "Master. It's an honor to meet you."

When I stand there speechless, hardly able to believe it worked, she continues to talk to herself. "I can't believe someone chose me for a Shield."

"Ehm… miss?" It sounds silly, since she can't be more than a year older than I am, but I don't know what else to call her. "You can get up now."

She does, and when she's done smoothening her dress, I hold out my hand. "My name is Dante Banner. I'm sorry to have summoned you here, but we have an important task to fulfill."

"Oh, my gosh," she gasps, and she takes my hand and kisses it.

I pull it back and shuffle uncomfortably. "You don't have to do that. We're not in the middle ages anymore."

She giggles. "Oh, I know." She waves her hands around uncontrollably and laughs. "It's just such an honor." She shakes her head as if she still can't believe it.

I shoot her a reassuring smile. "Well, I asked for a shapeshifter, and here you are." I scratch my head, unsure of how to continue this conversation. In the end, I bend down and start picking up everything I used for the spell.

"Let me help," the girl says, squatting so fast that she loses her balance.

I frown at her attempts to get back up. "Are you okay, miss… I still don't know your name."

She pauses her struggles and smiles brightly. "It's Kessley, but you can call me Kess. Everyone does." Her forehead wrinkles again. "Or did."

"Okay, Kess." I smile back, although I'm starting to think that something went wrong and that I got a handful instead of more help. "Did something happen on your way here?"

She leans closer. "I might have peed myself from shock."

I stare at her, unsure what to think of that answer.

She bends over, laughing hysterically.

"I'm sorry," she pants when the corners of my mouth don't even twitch. "I'm really sorry, I can't help it." She wipes her eyes and straightens up. "I died drunk."

I must have heard that wrong. "You what?"

"Yeah, it's a sad story. I was drunk, tripped, got knocked out and froze to death."

I gape at her. "You're kidding."

"Wish I was!" she says with a sad smile. "But on the bright side... your spell seems to have made it better." She points at her head. "I can think straight again."

With my eyes on the ground, I try to hide my frown. "Are you sure?"

She slaps my shoulder. "Yes, I'm a bit wonky on my best days. Hey! I can touch you. Brilliant!" She rubs my back and squeezes my shoulder. "I can feel again!"

Quickly, I step away from her. "Please don't do

that."

She pulls back her arm and presses her hands against her chest. "I'm sorry." Her eyes dart to the ground. "Please forgive me, master. This is all a bit strange for me."

"Strange for *you*?" I hold back a snort. *Maybe I should find a way to send her back. Maybe this was a mistake after all.*

Kessley shapeshifts into a hairy monster with a wide mouth, gets down on all fours and starts gobbling up all of the salt and herbs. In the blink of an eye, everything is gone. There's no trace of the spell left.

With a shake of her ugly head, Kessley turns back into herself. She licks her lips and burps. "Excuse me."

*Okay, maybe I should give her a chance.*

I put the rest of the stuff in my backpack and smile at her. "Are you ready to go to your new home? I'll tell you as much as I can about why I summoned you on the way there."

She nods and follows me to the stairs. When we reach the plastic curtains, I come to a halt.

Kessley waits patiently for instructions as I turn to her. *At least she seems to take her duties seriously.*

"Can you make yourself invisible?" I ask her.

Hope flickers in her eyes. "I don't know. Should I be able to do that?"

"Yes. We don't want to freak out the non-magicals."

"Of course." She flexes her arms and hops around excitedly. "So how do I go invisible?"

"Eh... no idea. I think you just concentrate on it?" I shrug. "I know from the rest of the Shield that they need a lot of energy to hide themselves. Concentration too, I think. They can't fight and stay invisible at the same time."

Kessley's eyes grow wide. "Wow."

"What?"

She grins. "Sorry, I still can't believe I'm part of a Shield. I mean, I have a purpose now. I can make up for all the stupid shit I did in my life."

"Yes, you can," I say patiently. "Starting by learning how to become invisible. It's only for the ride home. Once you meet the others, they can give you tips and fill you in on everything you need to know about being a ghost."

"Brilliant. Give me a sec."

She scrunches up her nose and breathes in and out deeply. "Here I go."

It shouldn't be funny but looking at her pulling a face as if she's having a hard time on the toilet without any effect makes me laugh.

"What is it?" she asks, genuinely surprised. "Did I make my head disappear?"

"Actually..." I try to wipe my smile from my mouth, but my lips keep moving up. "Nothing changed. Try again, but maybe not so hard. You're a ghost. This should come naturally to you."

She places her hands on her hips. "Are you pulling

my leg?"

"No." I wave my hands defensively. "I promise I'm not. I'm sorry I laughed."

She grins. "Don't worry about it, it happens to the best of us."

She shakes the tension from her shoulders and tries again, a lot calmer this time. But still, nothing happens. "Great, I suck at being a ghost."

"Come on, don't be so hard on yourself. I summoned you from Heaven ten minutes ago. You're not used to being a ghost. We'll just have to come up with another solution." I look around, searching for ideas. The plastic curtains give me one. "Okay, stay here for a minute while I search for some clothes to cover you up."

I'm about to walk through the gap when Kessley speaks up. "You mean something like this?"

My hand flies to my forehead when I turn back to her. "Of course! Why didn't I think of that?"

She twirls around, dressed in a long gray coat, a cap and shawl covering most of her face.

I tap my finger against my lips. "Still, I can see your hands and chin, and even your hair is see-through."

The clothes disappear and she tilts her head in thought. "Maybe I can disguise myself as a human? A living human, I mean."

"You can do that?"

Her shoulders move up. "I don't know. Let me try."

She closes her eyes, wraps her arms around herself and performs a graceful ballerina turn. When she comes to a halt again, she's a thirty-something woman with dark hair and solid skin, dressed in jeans and a pink top. "How's this?"

The only answer I give her is a wide smile. She looks down at her hands and copies my expression.

"Well done!" I compliment her. "Your powers will be very useful to us. Are you ready to go?" I hold out my arm, and she pushes her hand through it.

"Yes, master."

"Please, call me Dante."

CHAPTER 12

Of course, the ride home is too short to tell her everything, so I start with what's most important. "Do you know what our mission is? Who we're fighting against?"

She shakes her head. She obviously hasn't been following the news of the Underworld.

"You've never heard of me?"

"No, why? Are you famous?" she asks eagerly.

I blush. "Sort of. But not in a good way."

"Well, tell me!"

"Okay." I brake to let some pedestrians pass. "Lucifer is trying to escape from Hell so he can rule the Earth. I'm the one chosen to stop him."

She nudges me in the side so hard it hurts. "And that's not a good thing? Are you kidding me? I'm going to fight the Devil side by side with the chosen one? That's brilliant!" She puts up her hands and shakes her upper body. "We're gonna rock this!"

I chuckle. "Well, I'm glad I finally found someone who's happy about this instead of worried."

"So," she says as I pull up again, "who else is in your Shield, and what are they like?"

I tell her the basics. Who the others are, what they can do. I tell her what happened to D'Maeo and Jeep and that Mom is missing. I also mention Mona and Charlie and Gisella, which brings me to my other friends. "Me and Charlie used to be part of a group of friends who turned out to be a lot different than we thought."

"Different how?" Kessley asks. "You mean evil?"

"Two of them, yes. Paul and Simon were working for the Devil. They tried to get me to join them, and when I refused, they tried to kill me."

"Oh my gosh, that must have been hard on you both!"

I nod. "It was. It still is, actually. When I think back to all the good times we had together, it's hard to wrap my head around it all. We had so much fun, and they seemed like good people." I rake my hand through my hair as I turn onto Oak Street. "We had to kill them both."

I clench my jaw to hold back the tears. Deep inside, I still think Paul and Simon couldn't have been all bad. *They were probably manipulated, brainwashed. If only I'd had a way to reverse that.*

Kessley pats my leg, which feels awkward and normal at the same time. *Could that be because she's now part of my Shield?*

"You had no choice," she says.

I shake my head sadly. "How do you know?"

Her gaze bores into mine when I turn my head. "I can see the pain in your eyes. It tells me you'd do anything to get them back in one piece. But you can't. Some people are evil, no matter how much we want them to be different."

"Are you speaking from experience?" I ask before I can stop myself. Immediately, I raise one hand. "Sorry, you don't have to answer that." I frown. "Unless you have unfinished business. Then I need to know everything."

She throws back her head and laughs so hard I almost drive Phoenix into the forest.

"What's so funny about that?"

"You don't have to worry about unfinished business. My life was a sob story, but there's nothing to finish."

I slow down, giving us both some more time to chat before we reach Darkwood Manor. "Do you want to tell me the short version? We can talk more about it later if you like."

"That's sweet. I dealt with my problems after I died, so I'll be fine." She sighs. "I guess I could tell you the very short version of it."

I drive even slower and wait for her to continue.

Even though she says she's processed what happened to her, her body language tells me otherwise. Her fingers fidget with the hem of her

114

shirt, and she blinks rapidly. I stop the car and turn off the engine. "Take your time."

She gazes into the forest where a squirrel jumps from tree to tree. "I grew up in a normal, happy family. That is, until my grandfather moved in with us. He was a tyrant. A drill sergeant with a hunger for domination. He never touched us in front of my father and threatened to kill him in his sleep if we told him. So, at first, we didn't. But my father wasn't stupid. He knew something was wrong and pressed me until I told him." She breathes against the glass until it fogs up, and draws two stick-figures. "They fought, only with words at first, until my grandfather hit my father. I was surprised when my father remained calm. He just grabbed him by the collar, dragged him to the front door and threw him outside. He promised to kill him if he ever came back."

"And did he?"

"He didn't get the chance. My grandfather kept harassing us, threatening us, but from a distance. Setting up traps in our back garden, leaving bloody packages, calling us in the middle of the night. It drove us all crazy, and the police couldn't do anything about it." She smirks at me. "No evidence."

"What a horrible man."

"Yes, he was. And since we couldn't stop him, my parents decided to move. It was a hard time for us. We all had to leave our friends, and my father was diagnosed with a heart condition."

I shoot her a sympathetic look. "And did it help?

Moving?"

"It did. It took him two years to find us, and then he broke into the wrong house. Our neighbor killed him. Self-defense." She shrugs. "So he got what he deserved. Sort of." Her face turns from mid-thirties back to seventeen-ish. Her hair gets longer, changes color and falls against her cheek to hide her eyes. I don't think she even notices. She's wrapped up in memories. "But it was too late for my father. He had nightmares about him. Kept thinking he saw him in the street, checked the locks every five minutes when we were home. He was afraid to leave our side." She wipes her eyes. Her jeans and top are replaced by the short dress. "He died in his sleep. Cardiac arrest." Tears fall onto her bare legs. "My mother was never the same after that. She blamed herself, kept saying she should've known. That her father probably killed her mother too." I grab her hand and squeeze it. She lets me. "I told her she was too young to realize it, but she didn't believe me. She started drinking, and that helped a bit. At least she felt good when she was tipsy, and I guess she forgot all of her problems when she was drunk. I wanted to experience the same numbness, so I followed her example. I didn't drink as much as she did, since I was the only one left to take care of her. But one day, I went too far. I drank too much and was punished for it." She tilts her head back until it leans against the head rest. "And now I'm here to do some good."

There's a long silence while I process her story.

"I'm really sorry," I say eventually.

"Thank you." She relaxes a little, which gives me the courage to ask another question.

"Do you know what happened to your mother after you died?"

"Yes, I saw her."

"In Heaven?"

She smiles. "No, she's still alive. She met a sweet man who helped her through everything. She's quite happy."

I breathe out slowly. "I'm so glad to hear that."

She pulls back her hand. I forgot I was holding it and blush.

"So that's my story. Pretty sad, but there were good times too. I saw my father, and he's at peace. I'm fine with how it turned out, really. And I'm grateful for the opportunity to mean something to the world." She nods at the keys in the ignition. "Can we go? I can't wait to meet the rest of the Shield."

I clear my throat. "There's one thing I forgot to tell you."

"What is it?"

"They don't know you're coming."

She giggles. "Well, I've always liked surprises."

"I can only hope they feel the same way."

"From what you told me about them, I don't think you've got much to worry about. They want what's best for the mission."

I give her a sideways look while I start the car. *She might be a good addition to the team after all.*

"Shall we go find out?"

She gives me the thumbs up, and I smile. She's already growing on me.

After a couple of turns, I steer onto the road that leads to Darkwood Manor.

"This is a nice place to live," Kessley comments, taking in the trees and wildlife. "Really nice… Wow!" She pushes her body against her seat and pulls her knees up. "Wow, wow, wow! Stop!"

I hit the brake and follow her gaze. "What? What did you see? Was it a demon?"

"That… the…" she stutters. Her hand slowly moves up and she points at the mansion. "You don't see that?"

I squint and lean forward for a better look. "See what?"

"The house! It's… it's alive!"

## CHAPTER 14

With a frown, I look from her to the house and back. "It is?"

I roll down my window and stick my head out.

Kessley grabs my arm. "Be careful!"

I pull my head back in. "I don't see anything out of the ordinary. Can you describe what you see?"

She wraps her arms around her knees. "Well, it's staring at me, and not in a friendly way." She shivers. "And its mouth is open. The vines are reaching for us... It's horrible, can't you see that?"

Her voice rises at the end of the sentence, and I pat her arm in comfort, ignoring the fact that her dress has crawled up to reveal red lace panties. "I'm sure it's only a trick of the light or something, but I'll call Mona, just in case, okay?"

"Great," she says without moving a muscle.

"Mona? Can you come out for a sec?" I ask

119

calmly.

Almost immediately, the fairy godmother appears in a cloud of golden sparks. "You did it!" She walks to the passenger side and pulls it open. Her smile wavers when Kessley goes rigid, and she shoots me a questioning look.

"Tell her what you see, Kess," I say.

The girl repeats what she told me. I still don't see it, but Mona lets out a relieved sigh and throws some sparks onto Kessley to make her feel better. "There. You can stop worrying, honey. The house won't try to eat you. What you're seeing is the way it appears to non-magicals. It's a protection put up by the previous owner, and Dante's father decided to leave it. Keeps out nosy people."

I wave a hand at my new ghost. "But Kessley is magical, so why is she seeing it?"

Mona stares at the ghost girl for a moment. "When did you die?"

Kessley lets go of her knees. "About a year ago."

Mona nods. "That's probably it. In the first year after people die, they are more subjective to impressions than they normally are. Which means you sometimes pick up things you would otherwise never have seen."

"And, of course, I couldn't have picked up something nice," Kessley grumbles. "It had to be scary."

I bite my lip, thinking of all the demons we've fought. *If this frightens her so much, what will happen when we're facing true evil? Will she react the same way?*

"Don't worry about this too much," Mona continues with a smile. "It's not easy being pulled from Heaven to serve the chosen one." She winks at me. "Even when he's as cute as Dante."

Warmth creeps up my neck. "Mona!"

Kessley giggles. "Well, she does have a point."

That doesn't make it any better. Now I'm sure my cheeks are the color of ripe tomatoes.

"I'm kidding!" Kessley laughs, poking me in the side playfully. "You're cute and all, but you're not my type. Besides, you're with Vicky, and I hate girls that steal other people's boyfriends."

"How do you know I'm with Vicky? I didn't tell you that."

"Oh, come on!" She throws back her head and laughs even louder. "It was written all over your face when you spoke about her. You were practically drooling."

"I wasn't."

Mona chuckles. "It's nothing to be ashamed of, Dante. You two are crazy about each other."

"Okay, I think it's time to go inside and introduce Kessley to the others, don't you think?" I get out of the car before the two of them turn up the heat even more.

To my relief, Mona and Kessley follow me without comment. There's movement behind the window of the study, but when I look closer, there's no one there. *Were they spying on us?*

*Not that I would blame them. After all, I took off quietly and without explanation, and when I got back, I stayed in my car with an unknown girl.*

"Guys?" I call out as soon as I open the front door. "I want to introduce you to someone."

They're all sitting at the kitchen table, just like I left them.

I clear my throat and look at them one by one. "I'm sorry I took off without telling you or talking to you about my intentions. I don't have a good excuse for it either. I acted on instinct." *And I listened to my father*, but I leave that part out. I'm the master now, so I need to take responsibility for my actions. "The truth is, I wanted you to have a bit more carefree time." I cough and follow a scratch in the table with my finger. "Okay, and I was afraid of a discussion that would take too much time. We needed more power, so I went and got some."

When I look up, I expect to see angry faces. Disappointment too.

When Vicky opens her mouth, I brace myself. "It's fine. Mona told us you needed to do this on your own."

Maël pulls her cape closer around her. "Whether to expand a Shield or not is a master's decision and his alone."

I scratch my head. "Well, normally, sure, but in our case…"

"It's fine," Vicky repeats. "We're not offended."

"We're grateful for the help actually," Taylar adds,

leaning forward to peer past me into the hallway. "So, where is our new Shield member? It did work, didn't it?"

I breathe out slowly and straighten up. "I…"

"Well?" Charlie asks.

Still surprised about their indifferent response to my sneaking off, I turn to see where Kessley is. She's hovering near the front door with Mona waiting patiently beside her.

I mouth a "thank you" to the fairy godmother and raise my arms. "May I present to you… the sixth member of our Shield… the one… the only… Kessley!"

My cheerful announcement spurs her to step inside. With a wide smile and a twirl, she enters the kitchen.

The others cheer and applaud.

"Welcome!" Taylar says, hopping from his chair and holding out his hand.

"Thank you!" Kessley says, shaking off her nerves and pulling Taylar into a hug.

"We're sort of family now, right?" she says when he doesn't respond.

The white-haired ghost grins and wraps his arms around her. "We sure are."

It's strange to see Kessley changing back into her half-drunk state so suddenly, but I kind of like it. It helps break the tension that has hung over all of us for too long. I can't help but smile when I see the others' faces. They have their doubts about her, like I did, but I'm confident they'll warm up to her soon.

"Kessley is a shapeshifter," I explain.

Taylar's mouth falls open. "No way! That is so cool!"

Kessley blushes. "Thank you."

I rub my hands together. "So, are we all reenergized and ready to go see Gisella's aunt?"

As if on cue, Taylar vanishes and reappears in the same spot.

"Are you okay?" I ask him when he shakes his head vigorously.

He shoots me a guilty look. His face is even paler than usual. "I'm weakening again."

"Weakening?" Kessley asks before I can respond. "Why? What's wrong with you?"

I gesture at the chair next to Maël. "Have a seat."

She does, and when Maël glances at her bare legs, she pulls her dress down as far as it will go. Which isn't very far.

I clear my throat, and all heads turn back to me. "I'll have to give you the short version. Remember our talk about unfinished business?"

Kessley nods.

"Well, Taylar has some of that, and it will be the end of him if we don't do something about it. We stored one of Taylar's memories in a magical pocket watch. Now we're going to copy it to a flash drive and deliver it to the police."

"Why?" Kessley asks excitedly. "What's in the memory?"

I glance sideways at Taylar. *Maybe he should tell her that.*

The young ghost shifts in his seat. "It shows a gravity pixie killing my brother. The man who ordered the kill was never punished."

"Wow," Kessley says.

Taylar smiles at her. "Yes, definitely wow. He needs to pay."

"I agree." Her forehead wrinkles. "But will the police take you seriously if you hand them footage with a magical creature in it?"

Dumbfounded, I stare at her. I can't believe I haven't thought of that.

Gisella laughs. "Don't worry, the watch will turn anything magical into something more acceptable for non-magicals. All you have to do is push one button to activate that function."

I relax again.

Kessley sits up straighter. "Is there anything I can do to help?"

"Not with this," I say, "but we can use all the help we can get for what's next." My gaze moves around the table. "Can you guys fill Kess in on Kasinda and our plan? Be ready when Vicky and I come back."

"Of course," they say in unison.

Vicky is already on her feet, the pocket watch in her hand. "We'll take care of this, Taylar. Don't worry. We'll get him."

Taylar gives her a grateful nod. "I know."

"We'll be back as soon as we can," I say. "If you

have any time left, do some training in the circle. And if there's an emergency, summon me with the spell." I turn to walk out of the kitchen but change my mind. "That's an order," I add, smiling to take the edge off my words.

"Yes, master," they all say in unison, Kessley loudest of all.

With a chuckle, I take Vicky's hand and pull her along as I walk upstairs to my room.

Although I've been sleeping here for a while now, it still doesn't feel like mine.

"You should put something on the walls and bring over more personal stuff," Vicky comments after obviously reading my feelings. "When you have time, I mean."

I snort. "Which will be never."

"Don't be so gloomy," she says, dropping down onto the bed and taking my laptop from the nightstand.

I huddle up next to her. "I'm not. I'm being realistic."

"That's not realistic. It takes a couple of days for us to save each soul. We've got four more souls to save. That means it could all be over in about two weeks."

I kiss her in the neck. "It could be, but I doubt it. Think about what Dad said. They have another way of opening the circles of Hell."

She pulls her head back and looks at me. "And you think it'll take weeks again for them to do that? No way."

I tear my gaze away from her lips. "A plan B is always harder, isn't it? That's why it's a plan B."

She shrugs. "Sure, but I have a good feeling about this. It'll be over soon, no matter what the outcome."

I lift her hair with my hand and trace the outline of the mark in her neck with my finger. She shivers. I bring my mouth close to her ear and whisper, "We're going to beat him."

Before she can answer, I take her earlobe between my teeth and pull softly.

She giggles and pushes me away. "Stop that."
"Why?"

"Because we've got work to do."

With a loud moan, I drop backwards onto the mattress. "I hate it when you're right."

She's still smiling. "No you don't. You love how smart I am."

I grab my head theatrically. "Oh, I hate it when you know exactly what I love." I scoot closer again and run my fingers up her side.

"Stop that!" she chuckles. "We've got important things to do here." She turns to face me and pulls my head closer with one hand. "You can have one kiss. Then we're going to finish this. Think about Taylar, okay?" She presses her lips against mine shortly, but I won't let her pull back. I grab her and ruffle her hair while our tongues intertwine. My other hand slips under her black top. She swats it away, and I let go.

"Oh, come on!" I call out when she places a hand

on my chest to keep me at a distance. "How can I concentrate with you looking so hot? This is so unfair!"

She grins. "I can't help it. I died this way." With a smug look on her face, she turns back to the laptop. "Now keep your hands and mouth to yourself for a couple of minutes so I can finish this."

"Only for a couple of minutes?" I taunt, folding my arms. "I can do that."

Carefully, I bring my head closer to hers. "Do you need help?"

"No, your father taught me a thing or two about computers. I can do it."

"Good."

I lay back with my hands folded behind my head and watch her every move.

Then a thought hits me. "Wait. Why are we handing this evidence over to the Blackford Police Department? Taylar's brother wasn't killed here, was he?"

Vicky turns her head to face me. "You're right. But Taylar lived far from here. We'll need a way to get there quickly."

"Or…"

She throws her hair over her shoulder. "Or what?"

"Maybe Shelton Banks lives closer. Do we have an address?"

Her hands fly over the keys of the laptop. "We're in luck. He lives in Mulling, which falls under the Blackford Police Department's domain. They'll take the case."

I rub my face. "Thank goodness, that'll save us a lot of time." I wave at the pocket watch lying beside her. "Sorry for the interruption. Please continue."

She pulls a cord from the nightstand drawer and connects the pocket watch to the laptop.

I frown. "It has a USB port? That's convenient."

She shakes her head. "No, but you can insert any kind of connecting device into it, and it will follow the cord to the device." She holds up the pocket watch to show me the inside before clicking it shut. The cord seems to melt with the watch, and the laptop lights up.

*I wish I'd found something like this years ago. It would have saved me a lot of frustration about cords that didn't fit or didn't work. The watch itself would've come in handy too. There are lots of things I'd like to forget, such as the first day of primary school, when my belt snapped, and my pants dropped to my ankles in the middle of a game of tag. Or that time I confessed my love to Daisy from next door, and she laughed in my face.*

My heart suddenly stops. I push myself up so quickly my head spins. "That's it!"

Vicky's hand flies to her heart. "Jeez! You scared me!"

"Sorry." I rub her back. "But I've got a brilliant idea."

"Yeah?"

Hope crawls up from my toes and fills my whole body with pleasant warmth. "Yes. I know how to get

Trevor off my mom's back."

CHAPTER 15

While I wait for Vicky to finish the transfer of Taylar's memory, I try to summon D'Maeo and Jeep to me. It doesn't work, just as I expected. The magic that's holding them is too strong.

I put away the laptop and shake off the gloom that looms over me.

"We'll find another way," Vicky assures me. "Just like we always do."

I nod, and we hurry downstairs.

"Listen up, I've got a plan," I say as soon as I step into the kitchen.

All eyes turn to me. Kessley sits up straight and alert. She's obviously ready to jump into action.

I take the pocket watch from Vicky and hold it up. "We can take Trevor's memories of my mom, make him forget he loves her or even knows her."

Gisella frowns. "But how? You have to think

131

about the memory you want to store. You'll never get Trevor to think about all those memories, especially once he knows what you're doing with them."

I grin. "I know! But I can write a spell to make him think of them. And once we've got all his memories of her, he won't know that he lost them."

Charlie slams his hands down on the table. "I like it!"

More hope builds up inside me. "You think it'll work?"

"Sure, if we prepare it well."

I hand the watch back to Vicky. "You keep this safe. We'll use it later when we've dropped Taylar's memory off and reversed the curse on you."

She smiles. "Sounds good to me."

"Great." I stand up and turn to Mona. "Can you disguise us as FBI agents?"

The fairy godmother stands up and waves her hands. "Of course."

In the blink of an eye, Vicky and I are dressed in black suits. Vicky still has her own face, but it's about twenty years older. I imagine mine has undergone the same change, but I don't bother going upstairs to look in the mirror. I don't want to know what I'll look like twenty years from now, if I even make it till then. So instead, I wave while I turn and leave the kitchen. "Thanks! See you all soon!"

"Wait!" Mona catches up with us at the front door. She hands me a business card. "Give them this. It'll connect them to me and prevent them from finding out you're not actually FBI."

With a frown I study the card. "How?"

Mona winks. "I put some of my sparks in it. If they try to call the FBI to ask them about you two, I'll get notified, and they will reach me instead."

I grin and put the card away. "Sounds great."

Outside, I pat Phoenix gently on the hood before opening the door.

As we drive into the center of Blackford, the corners of my mouth start to ache from the constant smile playing with my lips. I whistle a tune I don't even know the name of. My head bobs up and down to the beat.

When I glance at Vicky, I see that she's watching me with a thoughtful expression and a glint of annoyance. Somehow it suits her current official looks.

"What?" I ask her.

"You know we haven't solved anything yet, right?"

I recoil. "When did you become so pessimistic?"

She shrugs.

"I know we haven't solved anything yet," I continue, "but we're getting there. We're taking the first steps toward solutions. Plus, Dad… is… here… to… help!" I hit the steering wheel to emphasize each word, making Phoenix groan. "Sorry, love," I tell her, stroking the wheel.

Vicky swallows half a snort.

"Come on, you must see the bright side too here,"

I say, pulling up in front of the police station.

"I do," Vicky answers. "And I think there's a good chance that most of our plans will work. But I think we shouldn't get too excited. A lot can still go wrong."

"Sure, but it won't." I turn off the engine and bend sideways to kiss her. "And if it does, we'll find a solution again. That's what we do, isn't it?"

Finally, she smiles again. "Yes, it is."

We get out of the car, and I stare at the police station. "Are you ready for this?"

Vicky straightens her back. "Let's do it."

I hold the door open for her, and we walk to the counter.

"Hi," Vicky says cheerily while she flashes a badge that Mona conjured into her pocket. "We're here about a murder that took place years ago. We've got security footage from the crime scene." She hands over the flash drive, and the woman behind the counter puts it in a bag and writes something on it.

"The perpetrator was sent by Shelton Banks," I add. "He had ordered the kill because the boys stole some food and a goldfish. The boys are both dead now, which is why we are handing over the evidence to the proper district. With our prime witness gone, we're providing all of the evidence to this district so you can prosecute Mr. Banks. Unfortunately, we had to drop the case." I give her a sad smile. "New priorities."

The woman nods. "Thank you both. I will pass it

on to our homicide detective. Can I have your name and phone number so we can contact you if we have questions or news?"

I'm surprised she doesn't ask any more questions but give her our fake names and Mona's business card. After a thank you from both sides, we walk back to the car.

"That was easy. Do you think they'll take this seriously?" I ask Vicky when we drive back to Darkwood Manor. "I mean, it's an old case."

"True, but they take every murder very seriously, especially if they get evidence from the FBI. And I've seen this detective a couple of times when your dad was still our master. He's a good man."

I nod. "That's a relief. Then we'll definitely hear from them again."

She taps the window, as if she's counting the trees we pass. "They won't let us know when they pick him up, so I think you should ask Mona to keep an eye on Shelton Banks. That way we'll know when the coast is clear to go check out his house."

I pull up to the mansion. "That's a good idea. I'll do that right now."

Mona agrees immediately and disappears to take a first look.

The rest of us gather our weapons and file into the car, Charlie instead of Jeep beside me and the backseat filled with blended faces. I hate to admit it, but I'm going to need a bigger car when we get

135

D'Maeo and Jeep back.

"Everyone comfortable?" I ask when I start Phoenix.

Discontent mumbling rises from the back seat, and when I look in the rearview mirror, only Kessley is smiling. I wink at her, grateful for her optimism.

"Don't worry, it's not far." I turn on the radio and sing along to "Bohemian Rhapsody" at the top of my lungs.

Soon, everyone joins in. Maël hums along and taps the back of Charlie's seat rhythmically.

I know most of us are thinking of Jeep and D'Maeo, who should be here singing along too, but no one says anything about them. We fear for them inside, but none of us dares to put our worries into words.

The whole way to Kasinda's house in Buke, which is about seven miles north-east of Blackford, we sing and hum. We only stop when I turn left onto a street that the sun can't reach for some reason. In silence, we study the old houses. They haven't been painted for a long time, and all the fences are rotten or half collapsed. Some of the windows are broken, and there's no movement anywhere. Large oak trees stretch their crooked arms out to the roofs threateningly.

"Is this where she lives?" Taylar asks, leaning away from the window.

"Yes, it's a bit further up the road," Gisella answers. "I think all the neighbors fled."

"From her?" Taylar swallows.

Gisella pats his leg. "Yes, but I think they were all non-magicals. They couldn't defend themselves against her. We can."

I slow down as I drive past the houses. "Which house is it?"

Gisella bends forward and points through the windshield. "That one."

I hit the brake. "Then I'd better park here."

She frowns. "Why? We're going to ring the doorbell, aren't we?"

With a sigh, I place my foot back on the gas. "Right."

"Are you afraid?" Gisella asks. She sounds surprised.

"Well… yes, a bit."

She squeezes my shoulder. "We'll be fine. The spells will work."

I nod, and she leans back again, apologizing when Taylar and Vicky scoot over.

The house Gisella indicated is bigger than the other ones on this street. It's also a lot darker, because of the oak trees surrounding it with long branches, as if they're protecting the place.

It looks like a square block of wood. Moisture has peeled off some of the black paint that covers the wooden boards. Leafless branches reach up to the windows from the ground. The porch slumps in the middle, weighed down by years of gloom. Gray clouds hang above it, blocking out the sun. Even inside the car the temperature seems to drop several degrees.

Charlie shivers. "Well, this is going to be fun." He smirks at me when I turn my head.

"Ready?" I ask.

He pulls out a half-melted piece of chocolate and stuffs it in his mouth. "I'm owways weady."

I turn to the back seat. "Remember, we don't want to come off as intimidating, so stay invisible."

"Yes, master," Kessley calls out enthusiastically.

I chuckle. "There's no need to call me master. Dante is fine."

"Yes, Dante."

"Can you make yourself invisible?"

"I can." She demonstrates it with a wide grin on her face. "I practiced with the others, mast- I mean, Dante."

I hold up my thumb. Still chuckling, I open my door and step out. After a glance at the house, the sound dies in my throat though. I clench my jaws and walk to the back of the car. I open the trunk and hoist the heavy book out. Gisella joins me and closes it. "This will work," she says again.

"Yes, it will." My voice is hoarse when I answer, and I clear my throat. "She's already waiting for us."

Gisella turns while my eyes stay fixed on the doorway of her aunt's house. Standing there is a plump middle-aged woman with layer upon layer of clothes. Scarves or coats, I can't tell. She reminds me of the fortunetellers I've seen in movies. Her hair is as bright red as Gisella's, but she's got streaks of black in it. Even from this distance I can see the hostile look in her eyes. Goosebumps rise on my arms as I approach her slowly, the book held closely to my chest. I beckon Vicky, who is still visible to Kasinda.

"I'm sorry to bother you," I say when I'm five paces away from her, "but Gisella said you could help us."

"Why would I help you?" she spits angrily.

"We have what you've been looking for, Aunt Kasinda," Gisella says, stepping up next to us with Charlie in tow. She nudges me softly. "Show her."

I lower the book so she can have a good look at it.

Kasinda's hand flies to her mouth. "You found it?"

I nod and press the book against my chest again. "Yes, and we want to ask you to lift the curse in return for it."

Her red eyebrows shoot up. "The curse?"

I look her in the eyes, anger rising inside me. "The one you put on my father, John Banner."

Her eyebrows drop down to form a solid 'V'. "I see. You think I'll go soft if you give me the book." She reaches out to me with bony fingers and sharp nails. "Who says I won't just take the book and kill you for what your father did to my daughter?"

"Gisella did," I say, trying hard not to step back. My lips are dry, but I don't wet them.

Kasinda drops her hand by her side. "Did she now?"

The werecat steps forward. "I did, because I know you, aunt."

The woman shakes her head. "Not anymore, child. I've changed."

Gisella stops in front of her and places her hand on her aunt's heart. "You're still you deep inside. Somewhere behind all the grief and anger, you're still the person that read me bedtime stories and sang me happy songs when I was sad."

Kasinda snorts and pushes her hand away. "Sure, and what good did those do? Huh?"

"Please listen to what we have to say," Gisella begs her. "And if you still want the book after that, you can have it. As long as you lift the curse on Dante's girlfriend."

They stare at each other for at least a minute. The book is getting heavy in my hands, and a chill creeps up from the ground to my ankles.

Kasinda grins. "Fine. Come in. After all this time, a couple more minutes can't hurt."

# CHAPTER 16

"Thank you." Gisella tries to grab her hand, but her aunt turns quickly and walks inside.

The hallway behind the front door is not very inviting, but Gisella steps inside without hesitation, and I follow close behind, afraid of the door slamming in my face, trapping the werecat inside. Thankfully that doesn't happen, and the others follow us in too.

The hallway is damp, and the flickering lights on both walls do little to chase away the darkness. A soft scratching sound comes from the middle of the floor. I walk around it carefully. Shadows seem to move everywhere, closing in on me if I walk too slow. If the molded, scratched up wallpaper could speak, it would tell stories that would give you nightmares.

"Sit down," Kasinda says, pointing at the chairs and couch in the living room.

I try not to stare too much as I walk in, but it's hard to ignore the brown stains on the carpet and the pieces of wallpaper that have been burned away. Part of the ceiling is black. The shadows are still moving, but they stay away from the middle of the room where we are. When I sit down and place my hand on the armrest of the chair, I can feel something that resembles claw marks.

"So…" Kasinda says. "Let me see that book."

I hold it tightly to my chest again. "Not until you lift the curse."

She snorts. "Oh, come on. Any dimwit would understand that I can't take your word for it. You probably cloaked another book or something."

I look down at the book with an expression that hopefully tells her the thought of taking another book here never occurred to me.

*I could give her the book. But if I do that, she'll know something's up. I would never hand the real Book of a Thousand Deaths to her unless I got something in return.*

"Well," I say after a brief silence. "You've been searching for this book for so long you must know what it looks like." I hold the book up to her as she stands only three paces away beside the coffee table with the staring eyes carved into it.

She doesn't move but takes in every millimeter of the cover. I see her eyes glinting with pleasure. *She's falling for it!*

Suddenly, she dives forward. "Give it to me."

I press the book against my chest and step back.

"No!"

She looms over me, her eyes full of hate, her mouth twisted. Gray veins pop up in her neck. "Give me the book, boy."

I stare back angrily. "Not until you lift the curse. It's not Vicky's fault you lost your daughter, nor is it mine. I never even knew her!" I leave Dad out of it on purpose, since I already know she's not willing to even consider the possibility that it wasn't his fault.

Kasinda brings her face even closer to mine. The smell of rotting flesh escapes her mouth, and I suppress a shiver. The lines in her neck move to her cheeks and maim her face. It's as if they're pulling her whole head out of proportion. Her nose gets wider, her eyes turn up, and it looks as if her skin is melting away. Her fingers grow longer, just like her nails. For a moment, I'm sure I'm looking at a monster instead of a woman. Maybe, in this case, they're one and the same.

My breath is shallow, but I manage to sound confident when I say, "I'm not giving you the book unless you give me something back. We need Vicky for our battle against Satan. If we didn't, I would never give you the book."

She straightens up so suddenly it's as if someone pulled a cord attached to her head. Her face returns to normal, making her features look soft in comparison to the monstrous one from a second ago. "A battle against Lucifer? Really?" She grins. "How very interesting."

I swallow. "Is it?"

She turns and paces up and down between my chair and the one Vicky is sitting in. "Of course! The Devil has always fascinated me. He makes a great example." She stops and stares down at me. "Expect for the part where he got himself locked in Hell." A nasty chuckle rises from her throat. "I certainly won't make that mistake. That's why I kicked my husband out long ago."

I clench my fingers around the book. *What is she going on about?*

"Okay," she says after a quick look at her niece. "Fine. I'll do it. I'll lift the curse, and you give me the book. Sounds like a fair trade to me." Her eyes rest on the book in my hands, greed shimmering through them.

I wet my lips. "What are you going to do with the book?"

"Bring back my Lily of course. And after that, who knows." Her grin widens. "I've got some nice plans for the world. It could use a make-over."

My knees tremble when I rise from the chair. "Forget it." I beckon Vicky. "Come on, we'll find another solution. I'm not handing the world over to some lunatic."

Kasinda's hand is wrapped around my neck before I realize she has moved. I hear the others standing up, but I can't see them. Gray threads shoot before my eyes, stinging viciously. They crawl from Kasinda's hand onto my face, leaving hot marks all over my cheeks and chin. I gurgle as boiling grains move down my throat.

"Please let him go," Vicky begs with panic in her voice. "We'll hold true to the deal we offered."

The pressure on my throat grows. I drop the book. My hands fly up to the squeezing fingers.

"Aunt Kasinda?" Gisella sounds as calm as ever. "Please let him go. He's my friend."

I land in my chair hard, gasping for air. My fingers move over my face, once, twice, searching for the gray that crept beneath my skin. Everything feels hot, but I seem to be in one piece.

When my vision clears, I see Kasinda bending over to pick up the book. I hold my breath as her hand wraps around the cover. *Will she notice? Will she feel what's hidden at the back?*

The witch caresses the book as if it's a long-lost loved one. "Finally," she whispers.

Then she stiffens. Her hands stop moving, and her face is frozen.

"Did it work?" Charlie whispers.

I shush him and shake my head to get rid of the crawling inside me. Then I push myself up.

Slowly, I reach for the book. In Kasinda's eyes, I can see she's fighting our immobilization spell, and I have no doubt she's going to beat it. That's why I have to keep pretending to want the book back.

I pull back my shoulders, my hand still outstretched. "Now listen up, Kasinda," I say loud and clear. "You're under our spell now, and you'll do exactly as we say, or we'll leave you like this forever."

Anger flashes across her face. It won't be long until she pulls herself free.

"We tried asking you nicely. We would've helped you to see your daughter again. Not alive, because it's never a good thing to bring people back from the dead. But I'm sure her ghost can be summoned to give you some time together. And then she would tell you that my father did everything he could to save her."

Kasinda's hand moves. A couple more inches and she'll touch the hex bag attached to the back of the book. I can only hope that will be before she turns me to dust.

Her mouth opens, bit by bit. The shadows around the room lunge at us, apparently waiting for her command to charge, but already eager to grab us.

"You think…" she growls in a low voice, "that a simple… immobilization spell… can hold me?"

Her fingers twitch. Her eyes flicker. Instinctively, I pull back my hand and conjure a lightning bolt.

"You'll… be… sorry," Kasinda pants. "You cocky… little… bastard."

With a jerk, her hand moves down to get a better grip on the book. I glance at it. *Did she touch the hex bag?*

The answer comes in the form of a scream, coming from deep within Kasinda's throat. She gurgles and tips her head back. I take a step away from her. A thin red thread shoots out from her mouth towards Gisella, whose head also snaps back. The thread disappears into her throat while she stares at the ceiling wide-eyed.

Charlie grabs her by the shoulders. "Gis? Are you okay?"

She doesn't move or make a sound.

Charlie shakes her. "Gis? Answer me!"

I step up next to them and pull my best friend back gently. "Don't interfere. Our spell is working."

Black and blue mud crawls out from Kasinda's throat and along the thread to Gisella.

"Are you sure this is safe?" Charlie asks, his voice trembling.

"It'll be fine," I try to assure him, although I'm not so sure myself. "This is what we wanted, remember? Her powers are transferred to Gisella."

Kasinda's body starts to shake. She must be fighting my spell with everything she's got. Her eyes are also still open, and light shoots out from them. They hit the ceiling, and the shadows pull away. They fold in and out like bed sheets and form a solid roof above us, like a tent. The middle slowly moves up and down, as if it's breathing.

More light shoots from Kasinda's eyes, and the giant shadow drops a couple of inches.

Suddenly, I understand what's happening. "She's trying to get the shadows to pull her from her trance! Freeze them, Maël!"

To buy her some time, I smother the shadows with ice. Crystals cling to the edges, but I can't make them spread.

Charlie tries to help by building a wall around Kasinda. Unfortunately, the whole thing tumbles down when the shadow curls its edges and touches it.

The mud is halfway down the thread when it slows down, seemingly hesitating.

The plume agate on the top of Maël's staff lights up, and her mumbling fills the room. The shadow's ascent is slowed down, but it hasn't stopped yet, and it almost touches Kasinda's head.

Then a soft, high voice calls out from behind me. "Mommy?"

The shadow freezes, the tips turning toward the sound.

Kasinda blinks rapidly.

"I'm here, Mommy, don't be scared."

With my mouth open in shock, I watch a little girl approach. She's wearing a light blue dress, and there's a ribbon in her dark hair in the same color. She looks like an angel.

*Is this Lily? Did we accidentally summon her here?*

Suddenly, I feel guilty for trapping Kasinda. She only acts like this because she lost her daughter.

Vicky frowns at the girl as she passes us. "Lily?"

The girl smiles radiantly. "Yes. I came to help. My mommy thinks you are bad people, but I know you're not." She stops in front of Kasinda and looks up at her. "Don't fight them, Mommy. I want you to be good. I want you to be like my mommy again."

Tears fall from Kasinda's eyes. They're still the

only parts of her that move. Slowly, the black and red mud crawls further across the thread again. My heart beats unnaturally fast. *Is this actually going to work? If it is, we have Lily to thank for it.*

The light in Kasinda's eyes dies, and the shadows move back to the ceiling in slow motion.

"Thank you, Lily," I say to the little girl. "We don't want to hurt your mother. We want to help her, and we hope that she can help us too."

Still smiling, Lily turns to me. "I know," she says, and then she winks.

I frown, but she's already turned back to her mother. "I can't wait to hug you, Mommy."

A soft moan escapes Kasinda's lips. When I turn my head, I see the mud has almost reached Gisella. In a couple of seconds, she'll have Kasinda's powers. *Will she be strong enough to control the evil within them? Or will she break under the pressure?* I chew on my lip. *We'll find out soon.*

Kasinda's breathing has steadied, and Gisella seems more relaxed too. Charlie is rubbing her back silently, his head bent. I think he's afraid to look at her. I can imagine. I wouldn't want Vicky to go through this.

"You're doing fine," I tell her. "You're both doing fine."

Kasinda starts gurgling again. This time, it doesn't sound angry. It sounds more like "Lily". Tears still fall from her eyes.

The mud has reached Gisella's mouth. In the blink

of an eye, it shoots down her throat. The thread snaps in half, and the werecat-witch starts trembling forcefully.

"Oh no, oh no," Charlie whimpers as she drops to the ground.

On the other side of the table, Kasinda collapses too. Lily quickly steps out of her reach, and when I blink, she's gone. In her place is a smiling Kessley.

I gape at her. "That was you?"

"Uh huh," she answers with a content grin.

"Great job!"

"Thanks." She points to where Gisella is lying, motionless now. "Will she be alright?"

"Of course," I say confidently. "She's strong."

Gisella gasps loudly and sits up straight. When she coughs violently, I'm afraid she'll spit out all of her guts. But she doesn't. All that comes out is some red and black dust. Little specks that dissolve instantly. She doubles over, grabbing her stomach and then her head. Her fingers claw into her red locks, and she screams. The shadows above us roll her way so fast we can't stop them. They wrap around her arms and lift her to her feet.

For a moment, the whole room is quiet. We all hold our breaths and pray that Gisella is okay.

She has stopped screaming, and her whole body is relaxed now. The shadows let her go and pull back to where they belong. The werecat takes a deep breath and shakes her long hair over her shoulders. "Oh yes, this feels good."

A chill runs from my ankles to my neck at the sound of her low voice. *Please no.*

"Gis?" Charlie whispers. "You need to control the evil, babe. You can do it. Look within your heart."

Very slowly, she turns her head to him. It creaks alarmingly. When her eyes meet his, all the white in them disappears. She opens her mouth and laughs hysterically.

Cold fills every inch of my body as I watch her. *We made a mistake. She can't handle the power. We've turned her into a nightmare.*

## CHAPTER 17

From the corner of my mouth, I whisper to Maël, "Freeze her, please."

Bit by bit, the ghost queen moves her staff until it points at Gisella. The words falling from her mouth are inaudible. The tip of her wand lights up. With a jerk, the werecat turns her head. She raises her arms over her head and brings them down with force. Before her hands reach chest height, all the shadows in the room untie themselves from the walls and furniture and lunge at Maël.

The African queen is knocked off her feet. Her staff falls from her hand, and the light is extinguished.

"Gis," Charlie continues in a panicked voice. "You must stay calm. Control this before you hurt our friends."

Gisella turns back to face him. A manic grin twists her mouth up. "I don't care about friends anymore,

Charles."

She raises her hand, and I scream, throwing myself forward before I can think about it.

But I bump into someone solid before I can push Charlie out of the way. I land hard on the tainted carpet. Ignoring the pain that climbs from my arms to my shoulders, I look up.

If the wind wasn't already knocked out of me, my breath would be cut off now.

Facing Gisella is… another Gisella.

"Stop this now," she says firmly. "This isn't you."

The werecat-witch with the dark eyes lowers her hands without taking her eyes off her double. The shadows retreat, and I hear Maël pushing herself to her feet behind me. She starts mumbling again while the copy keeps Gisella busy.

Slowly, I sit up and take out Dad's notebook. *There's bound to be a spell that can make the good inside someone overcome the bad.*

I open the book at a random page and wait for it to start flipping the pages by itself.

*If only I had thought of this before. We could've used it on Kasinda. It would've been much safer than what we did now.*

The book shows me a page that reads:

*How to suppress the evil inside you*

I scan the ingredients needed and signal to Vicky. She doesn't respond.
"Vick!" I hiss.

I wait for her to meet my eyes… and freeze. There's nothing but anger and hunger in them. Saliva drips from her mouth as she snarls at me.

I back up hastily. "Why?" I ask out loud. "Why now?"

Both Gisellas face me and follow my gaze. The real werecat tilts her head in interest. The other one gasps. Her lips form something that resembles "Oh crap". In a reflex, she grips Gisella's arm. "Our friends need us. Please help me. Do the right thing."

Hesitation flickers in her eyes, but there's no time to wait for her response, since Vicky jumps me with her hands outstretched. There's no escaping her. I'm trapped between the couch and the table. Which means that the only option I have is to hold up my hands to catch her and hope she doesn't bite my fingers off.

I brace myself for impact and drop my chin to protect my neck.

She doesn't hit me. Instead, she comes to a halt mid-motion.

Taylar grabs me under the arms and pulls me out from under her.

I thank him and then nod at Maël. "Thanks. Nice save."

Meanwhile, the two Gisellas haven't moved. They're both staring at Vicky as if they can't believe what's happened. When I look around the room, I finally realize the copy must be Kessley. This is the second time she has proven herself to be a great addition to the Shield. I can only hope she can get through to Gisella.

There's movement to my left. Kasinda is waking up. I had forgotten about her for a moment.

Taylar acts quickly. He takes out his sword and pushes it against her throat. "Don't move."

She holds up her hands in defense. "Don't worry, I won't. I only want to help."

After checking on Vicky, I step up to Kasinda. "Why would you suddenly want to help us? You seemed eager to kill us a minute ago."

She bows her head. "I was, and I'm sorry about that." She holds her hands higher and looks me straight in the eyes. "I promise I don't mean any of you harm. Why would I? You've sucked all the evil out of me."

I can't argue with that. Still, I'm hesitant to trust her too soon.

I open my mouth to ask her to prove her goodwill somehow, but her attention has shifted to her niece.

"Please let me help," she says. "I don't want her to go down the same path as I did. And I know what to do."

Her eyes are full of sorrow, but it could still be an act. For all I know, she's trying to get close to Gisella, waiting for her chance to get her niece on her side. *If they manage to transfer her powers back to her, we'll be screwed. We'll never get a chance like this again.*

*If only we had Vicky to read Kasinda's emotions.*

Before I realize what she's doing, Kasinda is

155

crawling to where Vicky is still suspended in the air, frozen in time by Maël's power.

"Don't!" I yell, but she has already grabbed Vicky's hand.

She brings her face close to Vicky's and takes her other hand too.

Gisella's copy takes a step toward Kasinda and stretches her arm. "If you hurt her, you'll suffer."

Kasinda smiles at her. "I'm not going to hurt her."

Taylar and I exchange a brief look, not sure what to do. *Should we pull her back?*

Meanwhile, Charlie has approached Gisella. He's talking to her softly. She still hasn't moved, which gives me hope.

Kessley's true appearance blinks through, and I whisper to her, "Don't change back yet."

She might be the main reason that Gisella has not killed us all yet. The werecat-witch seems to truly believe that Kessley is her benevolent side. *We should keep it that way until we're certain that Gisella can contain the evil inside her.*

Kasinda's whispered voice pulls me back to our other problem. "What's her name again?"

"Vicky," I say.

"I'm sorry for what I did to her, and to your parents, Dante."

I clench my jaws. *Is she serious?*

"When Lily died, my malevolent side kept whispering about fault and revenge. I tried to block it out, but the grief and anger were so overwhelming. In the end, I couldn't withstand the pull of evil anymore. It felt so good to make someone pay for what happened to my daughter. And once I'd succumbed to that side, there was no turning back." She wipes away a tear. "Which is why I want to stop Gisella from going down that same path. It's horrible. Somewhere deep inside, there was still a part of me that wanted to break free, that wanted to stop all of the hurt. But I couldn't."

"How are you going to stop her?" I ask, holding on to the desire to be mad at her.

"By doing what your father told me to do."

"Which is?" She's starting to get on my nerves. *Why does she keep speaking in riddles?*

Kasinda lowers her voice even more while Kessley distracts Gisella with a speech about listening to the good inside you. "He came by a couple of weeks after I cursed him, to beg me for help. I refused, and he told me the good in me would never die, but it would be out of reach soon. He gave me an egg and told me to eat it if I wanted to overcome the evil within me."

Taylar sticks out his tongue in disgust. "An egg?"

Kasinda nods and takes another look at her niece. "Or you take Gisella's powers away. That works too, as you can see." She gestures at her own body.

"Don't let her fool you," Charlie says. "She just wants her powers back."

Kasinda shakes her head. "Oh, trust me, I don't. I haven't felt this good in years. All anger, resentment and need for revenge has left me. You liberated me."

157

Charlie frowns at her, then shifts his gaze to me. "In that case, maybe we should take Gisella's powers and destroy them somehow. She told me several times that she's always struggling to keep her evil side under control."

I bite my lip. "Sorry, Charlie, we can't do that. Not yet anyway. We need every power we can get to defeat Lucifer. I didn't add another ghost to the Shield for nothing after all."

He sighs. "Yeah, you're right."

"And we need Gisella to undo the curse on Vicky. But we can take her powers away afterwards, if she still wants to get rid of them." I turn back to Kasinda. "So, what kind of egg are we talking about? Do you still have it? Will it still work?"

She's still looking at Gisella, who's caught up in a conversation with her double. She looks less threatening. Her eyes even seem lighter. *Maybe we don't need the egg.*

"It's the egg of a Ryu, a Japanese dragon. They lay fifteen to twenty eggs each month but choose only one to hatch. The others are thrown out of the lair and collected by magical people. Those who eat such an egg will be blessed with the wisdom to make the right choices in life. Since Ryus are benevolent dragons, this also means you receive the wisdom to choose right over wrong, and, therefore, good over evil." Kasinda takes a couple of steps back, watching Gisella like a hawk. "I will go and fetch it."

Kessley seems to do fine, so I walk over to Maël.

"Can you keep Vicky like that a while longer?"

She nods without taking her eyes off Vicky. Her lips never stop moving.

"Good," I say. "It won't be long now." *Hopefully.*

I meet Charlie's eyes. He still looks worried, so I tell him everything will be fine.

"I hope so." He gestures at the second Gisella. "I don't know how long Kessley can keep this up."

Gisella blinks rapidly, then narrows her eyes.

*Oh no... Why did Charlie say that?*

CHAPTER 18

"You!" The werecat holds out her hand, and Kessley recoils. "You are not me! You're a traitor! A trickster!" The white in her eyes disappears again as she draws the shadows to her.

"No, don't!" Charlie shouts, and he pushes Kessley out of the way.

Of course, that doesn't help. The shadows follow their target. They lift Kessley from the ground and wrap her up tight. Her face changes back to her own as she gasps in pain. "Help!"

"Gisella, look at me!" Kasinda's voice rings out, and to my surprise, Gisella's hand stops moving. So do the shadows around Kessley, but they still hold her tight.

While Kasinda carefully approaches her niece, Charlie and I each grab a shadow and try to pull it free.

Kessley screams in agony.

We let go, and I take her face in my hands. "Kess, listen. You're a ghost. You can slip through the shadows. Make yourself invisible."

"I can't," she says. "I can't… breathe."

"Sure you can," Charlie says after a quick look over his shoulder at Kasinda and Gisella. "You're dead. There's no need to breathe, you know."

"But it feels… that way, and I… suck… at turning… invisible," she says.

It looks like Kasinda could use some help, so I gesture at Charlie to keep talking to Kessley. I can only hope she won't be taken away from us this soon.

Gisella has aimed her rage at her aunt.

"You can't stop me," she says in a low voice that doesn't suit her. "I can do things you can't even imagine."

"Oh, I can imagine," Kasinda chortles. "And I don't want to stop you, I want to help you. Don't you remember why you're here?"

Gisella's eyebrows move down. "Don't play with me."

"I'm not playing." Kasinda halts in front of Gisella. "You came to take my powers, and now you've got them. I want you to put them to good use. Combined with your own powers, you can do what I could only dream of."

A grin forms on Gisella's distorted face. "I sure can."

"I brought something to help you." Kasinda holds

out her hand. On it rests the dragon's egg.

I press my lips together to keep in a warning. *If Gisella breaks it, we'll have no way of controlling her. She'll be too powerful to defeat with a spell. I don't even want to think about what she could do.*

"What is it?" she asks curiously.

"It's the egg of a Hornback Dragon, the foulest dragon alive. If you eat it, the strength of your powers will double."

"Really?"

Kasinda holds out a book with her other hand. "If you don't believe me, look it up. I brought you the Dragon's Encyclopedia. The real one, not the incomplete one you can find on the Pentaweb."

Gisella releases the shadows, and Kessley rolls away from them, clutching her chest.

The werecat takes the book from Kasinda and flips the pages until she finds both the Hornback and the Ryu. "This does look like a Hornback egg, but you probably put a spell on this book to make it show me what you want," she scoffs.

Kasinda laughs a sweet laugh without joy. "Come on, how would I do that? I have no powers left, remember? No more spells for me. Which is why I want you on my side."

Gisella licks her lips slowly. "Well, in that case." She grabs the egg, holds it above her mouth and squeezes until it breaks.

I look away when the yolk slides into her mouth and down her throat.

"Ugh," Gisella says, wiping her mouth. "That's gross."

She hands the book back to Kasinda and stretches her arms above her head. "These powers feel great. They fill me with energy."

Her aunt gives her a pitiful smile. "I know. They feel so good in the beginning, don't they?"

Suddenly, Gisella doubles over in pain. "What the…?"

I hold back Charlie, who wants to rush to her side.

Kasinda glances at us. "Don't worry, it's just the magic of the egg kicking in. Her battle with her evil powers has started."

Gisella is practically screaming, and for the first time, I'm glad Kasinda doesn't have any neighbors left. The last thing we need now is a police squad knocking down the door.

Gisella is on the ground, her hands resting on the floor. She's panting hard. Her teeth chatter as she pushes them together over and over.

Charlie pulls himself from my grip and kneels down next to her. "You can do this, Gis. You're strong, you know." He rubs her back, and she lets him. As her breathing steadies and her face relaxes a little, I calm down too. *Finally it's going in the right direction.*

My heartbeat shoots up at the sound of a thump beside me. I take two steps back when I see Vicky laying on the floor between the couch and the table.

"I am sorry, I could not hold her any longer,"

Maël apologizes. She steps forward. "But I can hit her in the head with my staff if you want."

*Of course I don't want that.* I hold up my hand. "Wait. Maybe the fit ended while she was frozen."

Vicky lifts her head and scans the room.

Her eyes are still wild. Her mouth curls into a snarl.

"Okay," I say, "hit her in the head."

But it's too late. Vicky jumps over the table and knocks Maël down. They roll around in a ball of teeth and arms. I try to grab Vicky, but she digs her fingernails so deep into my arm that I pull back.

Maël fights her off as best as she can, but the fit is making Vicky stronger than she usually is, plus more determined to win. She pins the ghost queen to the ground and brings down her head to bite her in the neck. I'm about to scream when Maël disappears. Vicky lands on her belly, hard. Her head hits the floor with a bang. Maël drops out of the sky above her and lands on her back. Without hesitation, she pulls Vicky's head up and slams it down.

I turn away and swallow. Tears form in the corners of my eyes.

"I had no choice," Maël says, picking up her wand and pointing it at Vicky again.

"I know," I say hoarsely.

I kneel down beside my girl and slip my hand into her endless pocket. I pull out some rope and hand it to Taylar. "Tie her up with this. That will at least keep her busy for a while when she wakes up again."

The young ghost nods silently and goes to work.

Meanwhile, I walk over to where the others are standing. Gisella shoots me a guilty look. "I messed up, didn't I?"

"Don't worry about it," I say. "The evil was stronger than we thought, but you're okay now. We all will be if you fix Vicky now."

Blackness clouds over her eyes again, and she cracks her neck. "I'm not sure I want to."

Her voice has lowered once more, but this time, I don't back up. Instead, I place my hands on her cheeks and force her to look at me.

*"Let the goodness in your heart*
*obliterate every evil part.*
*Keep the magic alive inside.*
*And let benevolence be your guide."*

At first, she struggles, but when I finish the spell, she freezes. The black retreats from her eyes, and she lets out a sigh. Her legs give way, and I can barely keep her upright. I pull her closer. "Lean on me."

Her head bumps against my chest, and I can feel her breath slowly turning from ice cold to warm. Charlie is rubbing her back again and whispering sweet things in her ear.

"I'm okay," she says after a while. She lifts her head and smiles at me.

I smile back when I see a shadow rise up from her head. The red of her hair is suddenly a lot brighter. I hadn't even noticed the change.

"How did you come up with that spell so fast?" she asks when I release her.

I scratch my neck. "It was in Dad's notebook."

Behind us there's moaning, and we turn as one.

Vicky blinks and stares at us in surprise.

"Are you back?" I ask cautiously.

She sits up and blows a lock of dark hair from her face. "I think so." She shakes her head. "That was some bad timing, huh?"

I chuckle. "It sure was. But I think we'll be okay now." I glance at Gisella. "Right?"

The werecat-witch nods. "Let me take care of that curse."

Taylar unties Vicky, who walks straight to Kasinda. "First things first."

The woman stands still while Vicky checks her emotions. With a content smile, she turns to me. "She's fine. The evil has left her."

"Before we start," Gisella says, "can you check me too? I want to make sure these powers are not going to hurt you."

The fact that she's asking Vicky to do this tells me enough, but I still feel relieved when Vicky gives her a thumbs up.

"Can we please lift the curse now?" I ask. "I don't want anything else to interfere."

Gisella and Kasinda exchange a few words, after which the werecat fetches a knife from the kitchen. She pierces the tip of her finger and presses it against

166

Vicky's forehead. The red dot she leaves behind wriggles.

*"Shadows, hear these words of mine.*
*Take back all that is malign.*
*Kill the curse that plagues this girl,*
*and burn it with a simple twirl."*

The shadows come to life again. They dive straight for the glowing red dot and disappear into Vicky's head in one long wisp.

Vicky's head moves from side to side. Her eyelids flutter. Her hands tremble. She coughs and retches and out comes the string of shadows, red smoke trailing behind it. The string flies up to the ceiling and starts twisting until it takes on the shape of a tornado. The red smoke is trapped inside it and slowly pulled apart into tiny dots.

Vicky sneezes, and a handful of red specks join the others near the ceiling.

I catch her as her legs give way underneath her.

Together, we watch the smoke being pulled into smaller and smaller pieces until there's nothing left.

I stroke Vicky's hair as she rests her head against my chest.

Gisella bends down and presses her finger onto the same spot on my forehead. When I narrow my eyes, I can see a faint blue light pulsing around her. She radiates pure joy now.

*"Shadows, hear these words of mine.*
*Take back all that is malign.*
*Lift the curse that lingers here.*
*Make all evil disappear."*

I press Vicky firmer to my chest as something turns my organs upside down and inside out. My chest heats up and freezes at the same time. Nausea hits me hard, and I bend past Vicky to throw up. Instead of the contents of my stomach, a long black string comes out of my mouth. It's as thick as the rope I pulled from Vicky's pocket, and it grinds against the inside of my throat.

I cough and spit until I'm dizzy. Still, more string keeps coming out. My body is on fire, yet I shiver as if I'm hypothermic.

"Don't block it," Kasinda says. "Give it room."

"How?" I cough.

She walks up to me and pushes me back against the couch. "Try to relax. I know it's hard, but it'll be over soon."

Vicky strokes my arm. "Look at me, Dante."

I meet her eyes and try to smile, but the string coming from my mouth prevents my lips from curling up.

"Relax," she whispers, and calmness falls over me.

My body stops twitching, and my head bobs sideways. I watch the heap of string on the floor get bigger. It looks a bit like a snake, wriggling and hissing. Then, a bomb goes off inside me. Stars dance around the room. I can finally close my mouth again. My throat is raw, and my head pounds.

"Look." Vicky points at the string on the floor. The sparks in my vision wrap around it and get bigger until there's only light.

"Are you seeing this?" I ask hoarsely.

"Yes," Vicky whispers.

Another explosion, this time outside my body. There's so much light in the room that all the shadows flee. When the huge spark flickers and dies, the floor beside me is empty, save for a brand-new burn mark.

I wipe my mouth and sit up. "Did it work? Is it all gone?"

Gisella presses her hand against my forehead. She closes her eyes. A strong vibration goes through me, but I keep as still as I can.

When she finally pulls back her hand, a wide smile lights up her face. "The curse is gone."

Vicky lets out a deep sigh while I cheer. I pull them both into a hug. If my legs didn't feel like they're filled with lead, I would dance around the room.

"Thank you so much," I say to Gisella, and then I repeat it to Kasinda. "Thank you, thank you, thank you."

"Yes... yes..." Vicky breathes, lost for words for the first time since I met her.

Kessley is sitting up too, a relieved expression on her face.

I nod at her. "I'm proud of you." I gesture at the others. "I'm proud of all of you."

# CHAPTER 19

While Vicky and I gather our strength again, helped by some special tea from Kasinda—"No evil ingredients, I promise!"—Gisella and her aunt hug and talk, and hug and talk some more. They've got a lot of catching up to do.

When we finally feel good enough to get up, Gisella exchanges a sad look with Kasinda.

"You could stay here, you know," Charlie says. "You're not obliged to come with us."

I slap him on the back. "That's what I wanted to say."

I expect Gisella to brighten up, but she shakes her head. "No, I belong with you guys. We're doing this together, remember?"

I flex my arms and stomp my feet to get blood flowing again. "As happy as I am to hear that, and to have you as part of the team, I feel I should remind you that the next set of Cards of Death haven't arrived yet. It's okay if you stay here a bit longer. We can call you when the cards arrive."

"No." She shakes her head more adamantly. "Thanks for the offer, but I'm not in only for that part of the battle." She lowers her gaze and kicks the table with her foot. "You have all grown on me, and I want to help. There's more to this battle than just fighting demons and saving the souls." She gestures at Vicky. "There are curses to lift, there's unfinished business to deal with and we have three people to search for. I'm not abandoning you now. I'm with you all the way."

There's a long silence, in which I try to find the right words to respond to this since "thank you" won't be enough. Eventually, Charlie is the first to react. He throws himself forward and almost squeezes her to bits. "I love you so much! There are no words to express it, you know."

She frees her arms and wraps them around him. "I know."

When they finally let go of each other, I open my arms and wait for Gisella to walk into them.

For the first time, I see a glimpse of shyness, the shadow of a blush on her cheeks.

"You are amazing. A thousand times thank you," I say while I hug her.

"No problem. You are my friends. I don't want to lose you."

"We don't want to lose you either," Vicky says,

patting her on the shoulder.

Gisella grins and shakes her arms. "You won't. I've got a shitload of powers inside me now. Thanks to you guys. I can't wait to use them."

Vicky grins back. "They won't know what hit them."

"That's the spirit!" Kasinda calls out.

She is answered by a handful of frowns and gulps. "I am *really* sorry for all the trouble I caused you. I mean it."

Vicky nods. "I know."

I pull Kasinda toward me and wrap my arms around her. "Come here. You deserve a hug too. It's not your fault that fate dealt you some nasty cards."

She slaps my back. "Thank you, Dante. That means a lot to me. And to set things right: you're a good person and so was your father. I know now that he did everything he could to save Lily."

"He did," Maël confirms.

"I am so sorry," Kasinda repeats.

I release her. "It's fine. I'm glad you're on our side now."

Her eyebrows move up. "Even without my powers?"

"Sure. Every person on our side is a good thing. Even if it's only because they won't help our enemies."

"True." She nods at the empty teapot on the table. "Do you want more tea?"

"As lovely as that sounds, we can't. We need to get

going. Like Gisella said, there are lots of other things on our to-do list. And with our luck, probably not a lot of time to do them in."

Kasinda bends toward me. "Well, maybe your luck has changed now."

"I hope so."

We walk to the front door and say goodbye to Gisella's aunt. The cloud above her house is gone, and the street looks a lot more inviting now.

I breathe in the fresh summer air and perform a sloppy quickstep. The others laugh as Kessley joins me with an excited shriek. "I love dancing!"

She starts singing some song I don't recognize, because it's completely out of tune, and throws up her hands. Then she does a good impression of a twerk. Her dress crawls up even further, and I shield my eyes. "Stop! Enough!"

Giggling like a five-year-old, she pulls down the fabric, and we exchange a high five.

She dances around Phoenix several times before getting in, and we watch her with lazy smiles on our faces.

"I like her," Vicky says.

Taylar nods. "Me too. She lightens up the mood a bit."

I frown at him. "A bit?"

With a grin, he steps through the car door. "Okay, a lot."

Once we've all settled into the car again, we wave at Kasinda one more time.

"So, what's next?" I ask while I steer Phoenix around the first corner.

Before anyone can answer, I hit the brakes hard. My heartbeat quickens, and nausea rises to my throat at the sight of the giant hole in the road.

"Wow!" Kessley shouts. "What is that?"

I back Phoenix up a little. "I'm not sure."

The answer comes in the form of a loud rumbling that shakes the ground so hard that we're all thrown from side to side. The rip in the road before us grows wider and out comes a familiar figure. Tall, hulking form, glowing red eyes, horns on his head.

"Lucifer."

"Oh crap," Kessley says, pushing herself against her seat hard.

I place a hand on her arm. "Don't worry, he's not real. It must be a projection or something. He can't get to Earth, remember?"

"But he can send demons here, right?"

I squeeze her arm. "We've beaten five armies of demons already, Kess. We can handle a few more."

"Dante Banner!" The Devil's voice rattles the car and my teeth. The sound reverberates through my stomach. "Show yourself!"

I reach for the door handle.

"Don't," Vicky says. "It might be a trap."

A ball of lightning comes to life in my hand. "I'm prepared."

I can almost feel her shaking her head in disbelief as I step out of the car.

The slamming of two more car doors tells me my friends are following.

"Okay, I'm here!" I yell at the huge monster rising from the cracked asphalt.

When he doesn't answer, I place my free hand on my waist. "What do you want?"

He narrows his eyes, and flames burst out from under his skin. "You know what I want. And you could have been a part of it. But you declined my offer, so I decided to send you a gift."

A voice inside my head is screaming at me to back up and run. But I can't. Satan is taking desperate measures to either get me on his side or destroy me. Now that the first didn't work, he's going to throw more demons at me. Well, good for him. We're ready.

"I don't want anything from you," I hiss at him. "And if you're so scared of me, staying away might be a better plan than sending me more armies to take out."

Lucifer chuckles. An unnaturally low sound with no joy in it.

"You stupid boy," he says. "I'm not sending you any armies. I've got something much better than that."

I give him my best poker face, but he sees right through it, judging by the way he shakes with laughter.

"Yes, you laugh now," I say through clenched teeth, "but you'll never win. The prophecy says I'm going to beat you, and I will."

A giant hand moves up to support his red chin. "Oh yes, the prophecy. I've heard it." He leans forward, and it takes all of my will to stay where I am. "You do know that all prophecies come from crazy people who mistake the voices in their heads for that of my father, don't you? Relying on things like that is a bit like..." He taps his chin. "Well, like fighting the Devil with a drunk ghost by your side." He smiles sweetly at me. "Wouldn't you say so?"

To my surprise, Kessley doesn't storm past me. The only thing I hear is a loud, indignant huff behind me and some mumbled words I can't make out.

"Your words and threats don't impress me, Lucifer. You can send whatever you want my way, but you will always be trapped in Hell."

He tilts his head, flames burning in his eyes. "You know, Dante, I like you better than your father. You must have inherited your wits from your mother, because your daddy was such a boring opponent. He never spoke back to me. This..." He moves his finger from his chest to me and back. "This is nice. I will miss our little get-togethers when you're dead."

"Whatever," I say with a loud sigh. "Are you going to send someone to fight me or not? Because I've got more to do."

He laughs again. "I am. And I'm sure you'll like them a lot. You met two of their brothers already, and I have to say, your tactics against them surprised me. You're a smart boy. It's such a shame you're on the wrong side."

*Brothers?* The word echoes through my mind. It bounces against my skull harder and harder. *Oh no, please don't let it be true.*

Vicky's voice pierces through the echo of Satan's words. "Dante!" she hisses. "Get back here!"

The Devil leans back, reaches inside the hole in the road and pulls out the last two creatures I wanted to meet. They seem tiny in his hands, but once he releases them and drops out of sight with a laugh that sounds like thunder, they grow to full height.

They are both on horses, one white, one black, like their riders. The rider in black is wearing motorcycle clothes hanging loosely around his bony body. The sight of his face and hands makes the hairs on my arms rise. His skin is stretched way too tight over his bones. His eyes lie deep in the sockets, and his lips are a barely visible line around the few stumpy teeth he shows in a grin. He's like a skeleton brought back to life.

The other one looks a lot healthier but just as intimidating. Instead of slouching, like his brother, he sits up straight and proud. A bow and a quiver full of arrows rests on his back, and a golden crown is placed on his white hair. His pale hand lazily strokes his horse's mane.

"The White and the Black Horseman of conquest and famine," Charlie whispers from behind me.

His voice trembles with fear, and I flex my fingers as the same feeling seeps through me. Then I ball my hands into fists. *No, we won't let them intimidate us. We defeated two of them already. We can do it again.*

## CHAPTER 20

I hear my best friend ripping open a chocolate bar and munching on it as if he's afraid someone will take it from him. The rest of us stay still. I can almost hear the cogs in everyone's brains squeaking.

I turn my head slightly and whisper, "Maël?"

Very slowly, she starts to move. My muscles tense as she whispers the words that will freeze the Horsemen in time. Hopefully.

I thrust my elbow back to nudge Charlie, who's still munching like a madman. "Stop that, enough is enough."

"But I need the energy," he says between bites. "And I'm freaking hungry, man."

The moment he says the word "hungry", the emptiness in my stomach hits me like a ton of bricks. Very light bricks. I stretch out my hand behind me. "Give me one too."

With a dissatisfied grumble, he slams a bar onto

my palm. I gulp it down in two bites, but the hunger is still there. From the corner of my eye, I see Vicky reaching into her endless pocket and pulling out snack after snack. Chocolate bars are yanked from her hands and not just by Charlie. Suddenly, everyone seems to be famished.

While I bite down on a cookie Vicky hands me, I eye the two Horsemen. They haven't moved since they got here, and it's not because of Maël's spell, which can't be working yet. *What are they waiting for?*

It's only after my third cookie that it hits me. Around me, everyone is fighting over the last snack, meanwhile complaining about an insatiable hunger.

"I'm always craving for something greasy," Charlie says, "but this is crazy, you know?"

It's actually Maël's sudden urge to devour a handful of potato chips that wakes me up.

I turn and grab Vicky's wrist just as she's about to dig into her pocket again in search of more food. "The Black Horseman is playing with us. If we don't stop, we'll eat ourselves to death."

Vicky looks at me curiously before shaking her head. "No, Dante. We will die if we *don't* eat. Don't you feel that? The emptiness in your stomach?"

I let go of her arm and nod. "Yes, I feel it."

There's no use trying to stop them. They're all under the spell of the Horseman of famine. And although none of the ghosts can die from either hunger or overeating, I'm sure the Horseman of conquest has a solution for that. I don't know why

I'm the only one "awake", but I can't let the Horsemen know, so I pretend to search for food and grab my stomach every few seconds while my mind goes into overdrive. I picture the two men on their horses and focus on cold. *Maybe I can create a layer of ice around them to block their powers.*

When I reach Kessley and pretend to beg her for something to eat, she squeezes my hand hard, meets my eyes and winks.

At first, I just stare at her, then she pulls herself free with a hysterical yell. "Get away from me! You can't have my food!"

Behind me, the Black Horseman chuckles. The sound sends chills from my neck down to my ankles.

I press my hand against my stomach again, but this time, I stretch my fingers. Kessley gives me a convincing angry look before dropping her gaze to my hand. I pull in my thumb and then another finger, counting down to zero. With a small nod, she acknowledges it. I see her muscles tensing. It would be better to discuss some sort of plan before attacking, but there's no way to do that unnoticed. It's up to the two of us to break the Black Horseman's spell on our friends, and we *will* do it.

While the last two seconds count down, I picture a huge, powerful wave appearing out of thin air next to the two Horsemen, rising above their heads and slamming down on them like a flying bulldozer.

I pull in my last finger, and Kessley and I turn to face the Horsemen as one. To my surprise, the wave I created in my mind is already rising beside them. But they don't move, distracted as they are by our sudden attack. I bring the wave down on them and conjure another one on their other side, blocking their escape. The horses neigh and rear.

I wonder what Kessley is doing, but I need to focus to keep the waves under control.

From inside the wild water, I can see the White Horseman raising his arms. Slowly, the drops move away from him. I grit my teeth with the effort of keeping the water where it is. I can only hope I'll be able to trap the two Horsemen in there until everyone is awake again.

Thankfully it doesn't take long. As I expected, the Horsemen need all of their focus to fight us. I can hear hushed instructions from Vicky behind me. The Horseman's hold on my friends has been broken.

My thoughts move back to Kessley, and immediately I lose focus. Drops of water fly everywhere as the Horsemen break free of their makeshift prison. Then, just as suddenly, the water comes to a halt midair. The horses stop rearing, and the Horsemen take the reins, preparing to attack.

*Freeze!* I think as hard as I can, aiming my thoughts not only at the Horsemen, but also at the water. The edges of the waves change into ice, and the Black Horseman shivers. *More ice, more cold,* I urge.

Both Horsemen shake their heads to lose the drops of cold water hitting them when Maël loses control.

"Keep trying!" I call out to her. When there's no answer, I turn my head to see what's wrong.

Behind me, I find a lot more people than I expected. It's no longer just my friends backing me up. Or... actually it is, but instead of one Kessley, there are about a dozen of her.

*How the heck is this possible?*

The Kessleys all wink at me while my other friends stare at her.

Suddenly, I remember the thoughts I had when performing the spell to add another ghost to my Shield. I was thinking I could use more than one ghost. *So that's why I got Kessley. She's not only a shapeshifter, she can also multiply herself.*

I almost throw back my head in laughter. This is the best surprise ever. Taylar looks pretty pleased too. The odds are turning quickly.

"Your tricks don't work on me, Horsemen," a dozen Kessleys say in unison. "I've been tricked too many times in my life. I've learned to protect myself." Every single Kessley raises a sword, that must have multiplied with her. "Leave and you won't be harmed."

I turn back to face our enemies.

The Horsemen frown at each other and start to laugh. They haven't noticed their horses moving in slow motion yet. They're too focused on us, on their task to kill us.

I see Maël tearing her gaze away from the Kessleys. The tip of her wand starts to glow again.

This time, it's not only her spell and mine that hit the Horsemen. The black rider has lost his power over all of us. A grease ball hits his sunken cheeks, and he tumbles from his horse. When he struggles up, panic falls over his face. His hands fold around his horse's head.

"Void, my baby! What's wrong?"

The White Horseman holds out his arm and points at Maël. "It's that wretched woman. Don't worry, I'll take her out."

Taylar and Gisella rush forward to protect Maël. The voice of the African queen rises until it fills the air around me, and I can't hear anything else anymore. I see the White Horseman's lips moving but can hear no sound.

When someone nudges me in the side, I almost shriek in surprise.

"Shh, it's only me." Vicky leans close to me. Her words tickle my ear. "I've got an idea. Can you cast a simple invisibility spell on one of the horses?"

*Without ingredients? Is she kidding?*

She shoves a bowl filled with herbs in my hand and a candle in the other. "This should be enough. We'll only need it to work for a little while."

I nod and walk backward until several Kessleys hide me from the Horsemen's view.

Charlie takes my place, and Gisella lifts her arms and calls shadows from all around us to her. While Maël keeps slowing the Horsemen and their horses down in time, Charlie's grease sticks to their arms and legs and blocks their view. A giant shadow drops down on them and forms into a wall, strengthened by Charlie's grease. Taylar takes several steps to the side and holds up his shield to protect the Kessley copies.

I see Vicky explaining her plan to one of the copies. She looks up and gestures at me to hurry.

"Okay, the spell," I mumble to myself.

When I dig into my memory, I find only part of it. I thought I was getting better at remembering lines, but I guess my memory doesn't work so well under stress. It doesn't matter anyway, because the spell I used on Mom and me before won't work now, since anyone could see the shadows wrapping around the horse to make it invisible. I'm guessing Vicky wants me to turn the horse invisible without the Horsemen noticing. So I need a different spell anyway. I'll have to make it up.

Cracks are appearing in the wall that Charlie built around the Horsemen.

I squeeze my eyes shut. *Come on, give me some good words.*

"You think you can stop us?" the White Horseman bellows. "We've been around for centuries. We've beaten all kinds of Mages."

*Not the chosen one*, I think, but I don't say it out loud. They are trying to distract us, and it won't work. I won't fall for it.

Another look at the herbs in my hand gives me the inspiration I need. I practice the spell in my head a couple of times before saying it out loud.

With a lightning ball, I light the candle, press my hand into the bowl three times and cast the spell in a whisper.

*"Herbs of power, three times three,*
*listen to my plea to thee.*
*Turn the white horse from the rider*
*Invisible, like a tiny spider.*

*Herbs of power, listen well.*
*Help me with this secret spell.*
*Make no sound or magic spark,*
*let this spell release no mark."*

While I repeat the words twice, I see Vicky staring into one of the Kessleys' eyes until she blinks out of sight. I smile as their plan dawns on me. Vicky helped Kess to turn invisible so she can sneak close to the Horsemen and take on the shape of the white horse. I'm not sure why yet though. I hope their plan works.

The herbs swirl around in my bowl when I say the last word. A breath of wind blows out the candle. Nothing else happens. At least, not that I can see or hear, which is exactly what I was hoping for. Only problem is, that because of it, I have no idea whether it worked or not.

A small explosion interrupts my thoughts. I hold up my hand to protect my face. Slivers of shadow and hardened pieces of grease rain down on me.

When I look up, the walls separating us from the

Horsemen have shattered. Gisella is reeling in the shadows for another attack while Maël's mumbling grows louder again. Charlie is munching on something indefinable. His energy must have run out. Taylar is picking up stones from the side of the road and hurling them at the Horsemen as a distraction.

I hold my breath as I watch the Horsemen fight Maël's power. Although they can still speak normally, their movements are broken up in phases, like an online video loading bit by bit.

"You can't hold us forever," the Black Horseman says, stroking his horse with almost robotic movements.

Then it happens. Without any warning, spark or sliver of smoke the horse under the White Horseman vanishes. The Horseman blinks in surprise, but before he can react, he topples sideways.

Now the horse is clearly visible. It's lying on its side, moving its head wildly from side to side as if in pain.

The Black Horseman's gaze shifts from his brother's horse to us. "What are you doing?"

With the bowl still in my hands, I walk to the front of the group. "We warned you to leave us alone."

The White Horseman doesn't respond. He drops onto his knees and buries his face in his horse's neck, sobbing loudly. "No! Stay with me, Victory. Don't give up."

The authority and confidence in his voice have changed to pure horror and fear.

The Black Horseman rises to full height and steps in front of his horse. He stretches his finger in my direction. "I will kill you for this. And it will be painful." I hold up the bowl and let my finger hover above it. "I wouldn't do that if I were you. Who will heal your horses if we're all dead?"

The Horseman opens his mouth… and closes it again.

One of the Kessleys steps out next to me. "This is your last warning. Leave now or your horses will die."

While the White Horseman is still sobbing against his horse's head, which is actually Kessley's head, his skeletal brother balls his hands into fists. His sunken eyes darken, and I can see the muscles of his jaw move.

"Don't think for too long," I say, lowering my finger into the bowl. "We've got things to do."

The Black Horseman still doesn't answer. I can tell by the look in his eyes that he'd like to make a hobby out of torturing me.

A quick glance at the white horse tells me Kessley is fine, but I don't know how long she can keep this disguise on.

Taylar nudges me from the left. "Just kill it, Dante. They're not leaving."

"No!" The White Horseman stands up and holds up both hands. "We *will* leave. Don't kill him."

"Alright…" Slowly, I lift my finger again. "You leave first. We'll send the horses after you."

"What? I'm not leaving without him!" the Black

Horseman roars.

I shrug. "It's either that or no horses at all. We can't trust you."

He snorts. A weak sound coming from a small nose with barely any skin on it. "And *we* can trust *you*?"

"Of course you can," Kessley says, folding her arms across her chest. "We're the good guys. We keep our word."

Maël's body slouches slightly, and Taylar rushes to her side to hold her up. She won't be able to keep the horses in slow motion for much longer. If she collapses, the real white horse will stand up, and the Horsemen will know we tricked them.

"You know what," I say with a sigh. "This is all taking way too long."

I slam my hand into the bowl.

*"Herbs of power, three times three…"*

The White Horseman grabs his brother's skinny arm and pulls him from his horse as he walks back. "Don't! We're leaving!"

The road opens up behind them, and they jump into the hole.

The Black Horseman's raw voice carries out to us. "We'll get you later!"

I bite my lip. *He's right. If we let the horses go now, their riders will come after us later. We won't be able to trick them again, I'm sure of that. They won't give us the time to do that.*

"What are you thinking?" Vicky says as she approaches.

I nod at the two animals. "We should kill the horses. If we do, the Horsemen will also die. This might be our only chance to beat them."

A Kessley on my left grabs my arm. "We can't do that! The horses aren't evil, are they?"

I stare at the white horse that changes back into Kessley. "Maybe not, but I see no other way."

All the Kessleys melt into one again, and she walks past me. "Go ahead then, but I'm not watching." She crosses her arms with a stubborn expression on her face. Taylar hesitates but stays by Maël's side.

"I don't want to do it either," I say, "but sometimes we have to make tough decisions."

When she doesn't respond, I look at Vicky. Her eyes are sad, but she nods. "Let's get it over with."

As we approach the black horse, the white one becomes visible again too. It's on the ground with a dazed look in its golden eyes. It moves its head an inch to the right, then stops, then moves again.

"I cannot... hold them... any longer," Maël says, and before I can respond, she collapses.

Gisella rushes over to catch her.

When I turn my eyes back on the horses, they have gotten up. With a loud snort, they shake their bodies like wet dogs when they step out of the water.

Vicky and I move in, but we're too late. They jump gracefully into the hole behind them, which closes over their heads faster than I can walk.

I slam my fist into my hand and curse.

Kessley joins us, with a big smile on her face. "You should be happy that you didn't get a chance to kill those beautiful, innocent creatures."

My fingers burn with the force of clenching them. "I am, but I'm not too thrilled that we'll run into the Horsemen again. They are almost impossible to beat, Kess."

"Well," she says, still smiling brightly, "almost impossible is still possible."

Vicky laughs out loud. "She's got a point."

Shaking my head, I walk away from them to check on Maël.

She's sitting on the road, leaning heavily on Taylar and Gisella, while Charlie keeps her talking.

"How is she?" I ask him.

"Resisting the strength of the Horsemen and their horses drained most of her energy, but I think she'll be fine."

I place my hand on hers. Ripples go through it, and I frown. "Is this normal? Don't ghosts usually get more see-through when they're ill?"

Charlie holds up his hands. "I'm no expert. You know more about this stuff than I do."

"No," Maël whispers.

I lean closer to her. "Do you know what it is?"

"I have felt… this… before."

A chill grabs my neck. "When?"

"In… the Shadow… World."

# CHAPTER 21

The cold takes over my entire body as flashes of memories appear before my eyes. Maël, captured by the black tree in the Shadow World. The branches almost ripping her apart. Her head slowly disappearing into the mud below.

"What do you feel?" I ask her.

"Something…" She takes a second to think. "Crawling around… inside me."

Vicky crouches down next to me. "Part of the black tree?"

I look down at Maël's arm. The ripples are turning darker, black dots fill her fading skin. "That's it. The black tree must have left something behind inside you."

"And it woke up when your powers collided with those of the Black Horseman," Vicky finishes my thoughts.

"What?" Charlie asks with a frown. "What does he have to do with it?"

"Each Horseman is connected to a tree in the Shadow World," I explain. "Didn't I tell you?"

His frown deepens.

"That's how we got rid of the Red Horseman," Taylar says from behind Maël. "We tied him to his tree so he couldn't leave the Shadow World."

Finally, Charlie nods. "Oh yes, I remember that."

Maël's natural color is returning, and I gently rub her arm. After a couple of deep breaths–force of habit–she's back to her normal transparent state. Her tiny curls catch the sunlight again, and her eyes shine.

"What happened?" Taylar asks. "Did it leave?"

With an un-queenlike grunt, Maël pushes herself up. "No, I forced it back to where it came from."

Taylar takes her in from head to toe. "Where's that?"

The ghost queen taps her chest. "Somewhere inside. I put it back to sleep." She looks down at my hand, that still rests on her arm. "You can let go now. I am fine."

I pull in my hand. "I'm glad to hear that, but what if it happens again?"

"Do not worry. I got overwhelmed because I needed to resist the Horsemen's powers and control the remnant of the black tree simultaneously, and because it was the first time the remnant woke up. Now I know what to do."

Kessley jumps up and down excitedly. "This is

brilliant! You can fight the Horsemen using their own power!"

I open my mouth to object, but Maël is faster. "Yes, I think I can."

"Wait, you can?"

My mouth must have fallen open, because Kessley points at me, laughing hysterically. "You should see your face!" She does a silly imitation of it and snorts with laughter.

"Yes, thank you, Kess. I don't think this is something to laugh about. This remnant inside Maël can be very dangerous. Not just to her, but to all of us. What if it takes over, like the black void inside D'Maeo or the ghosts trapped inside Jeep's tattoos?"

"I'm sorry," Kessly hiccups. "I can't help it. Sometimes my drunk state takes over." She swallows a couple of times and wipes the tears of laughter from her eyes. "I know it's not funny. Really."

Taylar steps around Maël and whispers in her ear, loud enough for me to hear, "His face was pretty funny actually."

Kessley giggles softly.

Deciding to ignore both of them, I turn back to Maël. "As soon as we're back at Darkwood Manor, we can find a way to get it out of you."

To my surprise, Maël shakes her head. "No, Dante, we should leave it where it is. I can control it, trust me. This happened for a reason. We can use it to defeat the Horsemen."

Thoughts of doom build up in my head, followed

by visions of the Four Horsemen lying dead at our feet. For the trillionth time, I wonder how I am supposed to decide on things like this. I'm only sixteen, and I have barely begun to understand half of all the magic in the world.

"Vicky?" I say after a long silence. "Would you mind?" I gesture at Maël and step aside.

The two of them stare at each other for what feels like forever.

"She's right," Vicky finally says. She sounds as relieved as I feel. "The remnant of the black tree is in there, but it's under control. I sensed a vague desire to obey."

"What about evil? Did you sense any?"

She shakes her head. "Nothing."

Kessley pushes hard against my shoulder. "See? I told you it was party time!"

Back at Darkwood Manor, I walk straight through to the back garden and beckon the others.

I feel like a football coach when I address them. "I'm so proud of all of you. Even without D'Maeo and Jeep, we accomplished two things today that seemed impossible." I let my gaze move from one ghost to the other. "We finally got rid of the curse on Vicky by defeating one of the most powerful witches on Earth. And we chased off two of the Horsemen of the Apocalypse."

Vicky nods with a smile while Taylar is almost glowing with pride. Kessley is hopping excitedly from one foot to the other, and Charlie throws his blond hair over his shoulder as if to say 'I know we're awesome'. Both Gisella and Maël have lost their serious expressions.

"I am pleased with how well we all fought together and particularly proud of Gisella and Kessley," I continue.

While a wide smile forms on Kessley's face, Gisella looks away with a shrug.

"I'm serious," I say. "Absorbing those dark powers wasn't easy, Gisella, let alone controlling them. You are much stronger than you think and look at the way you steered the shadows when we were fighting the Horsemen! That was amazing!"

"Yeah!" Charlie yells, making Gisella jump. He looks at the others. "I'm always telling her how great she is, you know."

I smile as the werecat's cheeks turn red. It's so funny to see how difficult it is for her to take a compliment. Her usual confident demeanor is replaced by an awkward shuffling of her feet and an inability to look me in the eye.

"You deserve a big compliment, Gisella," I say, "and so does Kessley, for blending in so easily and taking control when no one else could. I'm glad I decided to summon you, and I'm glad I was thinking about needing more than one extra ghost too. Your duplication ability is…" I search for the right word.

"Brilliant?" Kess suggests.

I nod. "Exactly." I let out a satisfied sigh. "I'm

starting to believe that we will actually be able to pull this whole thing off, guys. Even with all our misfortunes, we're still standing. Sure, we've lost contact with two members of the Shield, but we *will* get them back. Our progress is slow, but we're getting there. Eventually, we will come out as winners."

"Hear, hear!" Vicky yells, and the others join in. Cheering fills the air, and warmth floods through my body. *I hate the reason why we're all here together, but I like the company. I wouldn't mind if they all stuck around for the next forty years or so.*

When the cheering dies down, I conjure a lightning bolt in my hand. "I expect the next Cards of Death to turn up soon, so I suggest we do some training. Even though it went really well today, it can't hurt for us and Kessley to get used to each other and for Gisella to practice with her new powers."

Kessley slams her fist into the palm of her hand. "Brilliant! I can't wait!" She's hopping up and down feverishly again, and I chuckle.

"Okay, you're with me."

"I've got an idea," Gisella says.

"Shoot."

"Since we normally don't fight one on one, wouldn't it be a good idea to train in groups?"

Maël nods. "I agree. We can fight two against two. This will also train our abilities to combine our powers."

I hold up my thumb. "Great idea."

We walk into the protective circle. "So, how's

this?" I tap my chin in thought. "I fight with Taylar against Vicky and Gisella. Kessley, you fight against Charlie and Maël, since you're more than one person." I wink, and she grins from ear to ear. "Next time, we can switch."

Everyone takes in their positions, and soon, sparks and grease fly everywhere, and the relative silence is broken by huffing, yelling and the clang of iron against iron.

Our fighting is more fierce than usual. I can tell we're all feeling reenergized, not only by our short break, but also by our recent victories.

Sweat pours down my temples. I get knocked down several times, but I don't mind. I could do this for hours.

In the end, we do train for hours. We even forget to eat, so when the sun sets, I call everyone into the kitchen and order pizza. That's when I realize there's been no word from Mona. *I hope she's okay.*

Before I even finish my thought, yellow sparkles appear next to my chair.

"Everything okay?" I ask as Mona comes into view, her hair and clothes as pristine as ever.

"Everything is fine. Shelton Banks is still at home." Her expression changes to one of disgust. "I don't think I like this man very much."

I laugh. "I can't say I'm surprised. He's a first-class ass…" I cut off my sentence when she gives me a stern look. "Jerk," I say quickly.

"That's an understatement," she says.

"Well, I wanted to use another word."

"Which would still be an understatement." She steps back to the kitchen counter and leans against it. "I overheard some of his phone calls, and I've seen the way he treats his staff."

"He has a staff?" Kessley asks, her mouth slightly open in awe.

"Sure," Mona nods. "He's extremely wealthy. He's got a house full of slaves, basically. I'm surprised there hasn't been any kind of revolt yet."

"There probably was, years ago," Maël says. "But if you punish someone hard enough, no one will dare to stand up again."

Mona is still nodding. "True. But anyway, I should get back. I'll tell you more as soon as the police come and pick him up. I hope to see you all soon again! Stay safe!"

"You too," I say, and I blow a kiss at her vanishing form.

Shortly after that, the pizzas arrive, and I'm happy to see that even Maël takes a slice. Diving into her memories really was a good thing. Showing me her past and the reason why she hated food gave her some peace. One by one, the ghosts in my Shield are resolving their problems, with a little help here and there. *Soon, we'll be an unbeatable team. Or so I hope.*

# CHAPTER 22

The house is silent when I wake up, but there's movement beside me. With a yawn, I push myself up until my back rests against the headboard. Vicky is sitting cross-legged at the foot of the bed, all kinds of stuff spread out around her.

I rub my eyes and frown. "What are you doing?"

She looks up with a surprised smile. "Oh hey, you're awake." She crawls over her stuff and kisses me on the lips. "I was pulling some forgotten things from my endless pocket."

I grab her wrist when she backs up. "Can't you do that later? Come and lie down with me for a while."

"Don't you want to see what I've found so far?"

I let go and look at her with my best puppy eye imitation. "I'd rather examine you than your pocket."

She giggles and bends over me again. Her hands rest on both sides of my chest. "You can examine my lips if you want. But only for a minute."

With a soft moan, I pull her closer. "You're such a tease."

I kiss her and let my hands slide under her shirt. Electricity shoots from her waist to my fingertips, and I shiver.

Vicky pulls herself free and places a kiss on the tip of my nose. "Okay, enough for now. I want to finish tidying up my pocket."

"Oh, come on!" I protest. "That was way shorter than a minute!"

She sticks out her tongue.

I settle back against the headboard and watch her silently for a while. She rearranges some of the things that are already on the bed. An old book, half a bag of sweets, some pencil stumps, an eraser that almost crumbles to dust when she touches it, a pair of glasses, a glowing feather and some stuff I don't recognize. Her hand slides into her back pocket, and she stares past my head. After several seconds, she retracts her hand and shows me a small ball.

"What is it?" I ask, leaning forward for a closer look.

She turns it around and around, then bounces it on the ground. "I think it's just a ball."

I catch it when she throws it at me. "Then why were you carrying it with you?"

She shrugs. "You never know when you come across a dog that wants to play. And it's also useful for family visits when there are small children."

"Sure," I say, rubbing some sand off. "If you clean it first."

She holds up her hand, and I throw it back.

"I think I'll keep it," she says, before digging into her pocket again.

"So how does this work exactly?" I wonder out loud. "You said that you need to think of a certain object to be able to pull it from that pocket, right? How do you find these if you don't even know they're there?"

She presses a finger against her lips. After a short, concentrated silence, she pulls something out again.

"I literally think *I want to find something that I lost* or *I wish to find something that I forgot about.* And then I do." She unfolds her fingers and shows me a small bottle, filled with a brown-greenish liquid.

We move closer to it at the same time so fast we almost bump heads.

"It's that liquid the ent gave to you before we left that strange world the Beach of Mu took us to!" I say excitedly. "What was its name again, of the tree that saved us?"

Vicky's eyes grow sad. "Althan. His name was Althan."

I place a hand on her arm. "It was so sad to see him die, but there was nothing we could do, babe."

"I know."

Carefully, I touch the glass of the bottle. "What do you think it does? It must have been important for him to risk his life like that."

She nods slowly, her eyes never leaving the liquid. "He said 'this will help you'."

I remember the moment. The white tree leaning into the portal, Vicky reaching up to take the bottle from him, and him tumbling to his death.

"Help you with what though?" I say. "We don't even know what it is."

Vicky looks up with a hopeful expression on her face. "Hey, maybe your father's book knows!"

"Good thinking!" I lean over to my nightstand, where I keep everything that's normally tucked behind my waistband. It still baffles me that the two notebooks seem to shrink when I put them there. All this magical stuff is even more awesome than in the movies.

Vicky shuffles forward until she's sitting next to me and hands me the bottle.

I place Dad's notebook on my lap and hold the bottle above it.

"I'd like to know what this liquid can be used for," I say, loud and clear.

Vicky nudges me with a grin. "You don't need to say it. The book can read your mind, remember?"

I give her a quick kiss on the lips. "I know, but this might give us the answer we seek sooner."

The pages of the book start to flip by themselves, making my heartrate go up. My hands get sweaty at the thought of discovering something important.

The pages seem to keep moving forever. I bite my lip. *What if the book doesn't know the answer?*

Vicky leans closer and closer until her head blocks my view completely.

With a chuckle, I pull her back. "I can't see anything, babe."

"Sorry." She fidgets with her dark hair. "What's taking so long?"

"It must be a difficult question." I switch the bottle to my right hand and wrap my left arm around Vicky. "Don't worry. We can always search the Pentaweb if the book doesn't know the answer."

Just when I lose faith, the pages finally settle down. I expect to see some sort of revealing spell, but instead, I find a couple of scribbles. I recognize the handwriting immediately.

Vicky frowns at it. "Did your father write something about it?"

I hand the bottle back to her, pull back my arm and pick up the book. "I think so. Let's find out."

*"Although I've never used it myself, I've heard that tree sap can be a powerful ingredient to certain spells. The older the tree, the more powerful the sap will be. I've added a list of uses for several trees here. The most powerful and useful tree sap, however, is that of trees from other worlds. Ents, preferably."*

I exchange a quick look with Vicky. "This is so weird. It's as if Dad knew we'd run into some ents in an unknown world someday."

She shrugs. "Maybe he had a feeling you might need this information. Magic works in mysterious ways." She points at the next line. "Read on."

*"I'm not sure if this is true, but I found a story on the Pentaweb that spoke of an old race of Ents in a world that has no name. These Ents are neither good nor evil. Their goal is to help keep the balance in the universe."*

"This is them," Vicky says excitedly. "I just know it."

I nod. "I think you're right. Listen to this.

*These Ents are as old as the universe itself. They look like dead, white trees, and their language consists of moans and creaks. However, they can also speak many other languages."*

"So, what does their tree sap do?" Vicky interrupts.

I skip a couple of lines. "Here it is.

*The tree sap from these Ents is only useful if it was given to you voluntarily. If you take it by force, it has no power. The Ents don't give it away easily, and if they do, it is to protect or restore the balance of the universe."*

Vicky snatches the book from my hands. "Yes, but what does it *do*?"

"Hang on, I was getting to that." I take the book back and search for the spot where I left off.

*"The sap can be drunk by someone plagued by a curse. The*

*curser will be revealed to the cursed one, even if they are*
*protected by a spell."*

Vicky slides from the bed and jumps up and down.
I've never seen her so happy. "Yes! Finally!"

Vicky takes the book and tosses it to the other end
of the bed before grabbing my hands and pulling me
with her around the room. "This is my chance to get
rid of the other curse! I can finally find out who it is
that touches my grave."

I grab her by the waist and twirl her around. "Soon
you'll be freed of both curses!"

We hug and dance until someone knocks on the
door.

"Come in," I yell, elated.

When the door opens, Taylar peers around the
corner. "Is everything alright?"

His face lights up when he sees our smiles. "Did
you get good news?"

"We did!" I let go of Vicky and look for my pants.
"Let me get dressed. We'll be downstairs in a minute,
then we'll tell you all about it. Can you gather
everyone?"

"I think everyone is already in the kitchen. Kessley
is making breakfast." He snorts. "Or something
resembling it."

With a wink, he vanishes.

I put on my clothes from yesterday while Vicky
hops up and down impatiently. "Hurry up! I want to
tell the others."

"Hang on, I'm not going anywhere without my notebooks, my Morningstar and my athame, you know that."

When everything is in place, I grab her by the waist and give her a long kiss. For a couple of seconds, she seems to forget her haste.

I look her in the eyes when I let go. "I love this happy, carefree you. I hope to see a lot more of her."

She ruffles my hair. "You will, once we've kicked my curser's ass."

"I can't wait." With a wide smile, I follow her down the stairs.

# CHAPTER 23

Kessley's breakfast is actually not bad. It's whole wheat toast topped with sliced banana. Simple, but satisfying. Even Maël takes a slice once we've told them the good news.

"Works great when you have a hangover," Kess claims.

I swallow a bite of my toast. "That doesn't work anymore once you're dead though, right?"

She grins. "Probably not, but it can't hurt to try."

"So, when are you going to drink that tree sap, Vicky?" Taylar asks.

"Yes, what are you waiting for?" Charlie pipes up.

Vicky stares at the bottle of tree sap placed before her on the table. "Well, I was thinking…" She scratches her head. "Maybe we should save it for a more important curse. We don't know what's waiting for us in the future, what surprises Lucifer has planned for us."

My heart grows at her words. *She's willing to risk getting stuck in the Shadow World forever in order to save one of us.*

Judging by his deep frown, Taylar isn't too happy with Vicky's suggestion. "How many times do you think you have left to get pulled toward the Shadow World and come back?"

Vicky leans back in her chair. "I have no idea. But I think at least one more time."

Maël taps her staff on the floor, and all heads turn to her. "Vicky makes a good point. We have a powerful tool in our possession. One we might be able to use later. But perhaps not." She twirls the stick around in her hand. "We know we can use it now. Freeing Vicky of her second curse will also free us of some unexpected disappearances. It will make Vicky a stronger and more reliable fighter. But it might get us into trouble later."

There's a short silence as we ponder her words. When no one else speaks up, I lay down my thoughts. "I think there's a reason why we received this bottle now and not later. We were able to find out that Kasinda put the curse on my parents, which was transferred to me and Vicky, but we have no idea who put the other curse on Vicky. This is our chance to find out and hopefully get rid of it."

Charlie and Gisella don't look convinced, and although I'm in charge, I want this to be a joint decision.

So I lean forward with my hands folded on the table. "The last thing we want to do now is risk losing another member of the Shield." I hold up my hand when Charlie opens his mouth in protest. "Or another friend. We cannot afford to lose anyone else, even though we've got Kessley now." The longer I talk, the more I get convinced that this is the right thing to do. "I say we use the tools we were handed to solve the problems we have now instead of holding on to them—with the risk of losing them—for a moment that might never come. We need to get our team in the best shape possible, not only to beat Lucifer, but to get our friends and my mom back."

Charlie opens his mouth again, and this time, I let him speak.

I'm surprised by what he says. "I totally agree."

I rub my forehead. "You do?"

"Well, I wasn't sure, you know, but when you put it like that, I can see the logic behind it."

Gisella nods. "Me too."

My gaze moves back to Vicky. "What about you?"

She shrugs. "You're the master."

I shake my head. "That's not the answer I want to hear. I know you don't feel comfortable putting yourself before others, but we need you as much as anyone else."

Finally, she looks up. "Okay then, if no one has a problem with it."

Reassurances fly over the table, mixed with smiles and the shaking of heads.

I point at the bottle. "You'd better do it now, before something comes up."

She picks up the bottle and uncorks it.

"Wait," Charlie says, and her hand freezes midair.

My best friend gestures at the half-eaten toast with banana in front of Maël, Vicky and me. "Can I have that? I'm famished."

We all laugh, the tension broken for a second. Three plates are shoved in Charlie's direction. The silence that follows is only broken by the crunching of bread between his teeth.

Vicky lifts the bottle to her lips, and after an encouraging nod from me, she empties it into her throat in one go.

"Hmm." She tilts her head and licks her lips. "It doesn't taste bad."

With a surprised "oomph", she's pressed against the back of her chair. Her eyes roll back, and she grits her teeth. Her hands grasp the edge of the table so hard it creaks in protest.

I jump to my feet, but Maël holds up her hand. "Leave her, this is part of the process."

Vicky's head start to move from left to right in erratic, shivery moves. It looks like she's having a fit. My muscles tense at the thought. Then I remember we lifted the curse. We finally got rid of the fits.

"I see him," Vicky says, her head still shaking like crazy. "He looks like an average man, an office manager or something. He's wearing a dark blue suit with a white shirt underneath and a blue, striped tie.

His face is round. He has dark hair streaked with gray, brown eyes and heavy eyebrows. Most of his hair is combed to one side. There's a disgruntled look on his face, as if someone has just brought him some bad news."

"Do you recognize him?" I ask, barely able to look at her with her eyes rolled to the back of her head.

She stops shaking. "No, I've never seen him before." She relaxes a little. Her hands lie calmly in her lap. "Why would a businessman curse me?"

"No idea," I answer. "What about a name? Can you hear it or see it?"

She lifts her hands and presses her fingers against her temples. "Not yet, but maybe… yes, he's on the move. He's stepping into a black car that looks expensive. He drives down a driveway to a set of iron gates that have initials in them." She tilts her head slightly. "S.B."

I rack my brain for a name that matches those initials. Nothing comes up, and the others keep quiet too.

"He gets out of the car and walks over to a post box. There's a name on it."

I shift in my seat. "What is it? Can you read it?"

"It's… Banks. Shelton Banks." She lowers her hands, blinks and opens her eyes.

"It's Shelton Banks," she repeats.

I stare at her beautiful face that has confusion written all over it. "The man that killed your grandmother?"

"We don't know that for sure. All we know is that he got very angry when my grandmother found a certain book in his library and that she was killed soon after."

"So, he killed her," I conclude again.

She smirks at me. "Probably."

"What else do we know about this Banks guy?" Charlie asks.

Vicky turns the bottle over and over in her hands. "Mrs. Delaney knew him. She said he always gave her the creeps."

"Didn't he also order the kill on Taylar's brother?" Kessley interrupts.

I frown and see my puzzled look reflected on the others' faces. "No, that was Shelton Banks, the rich businessman Mona is watching."

"Right, Shelton Banks," she says. "The same man Vicky saw a minute ago when she drank the tree sap."

I stare at her. "How do you know they're the same when they have different names?"

Exasperated, she throws her hands in the air. "What are you talking about? It's the same name!"

Maël gently places a hand on Kessley's arm. "I think the alcohol is getting to your head again, Kessley. We are talking about two different men. Shelton Banks, who is responsible for the death of Taylar's brother, and Shelton Banks, who may have murdered Vicky's grandmother."

Kessly presses her hands against her temples. "Aaargh!"

I exchange a quick look with Maël and rise to my feet. "Are you okay?"

She looks up when I walk over and sit down in the empty chair next to her. "You're serious, aren't you? You really don't know you're saying the same name twice."

"But we're not," I say with a comforting smile. "You're the only one who thinks that."

"I—"

"It's okay," I tell her. "I don't blame you for being confused. You're so tired from everything that happened since I summoned you that your mind starts to play tricks on you." I gesture at her head. "And then there's this drunk thing you're dealing with. I think you just need some rest."

Her gaze shifts from me to Vicky, and then to the other side of the table, where Taylar, Charlie and Gisella are watching with concerned frowns. "You're not pulling my leg, are you? It's not some kind of initiation prank?"

We all shake our heads, and she leans back in her chair with a sigh. "In that case, you're right, it must be the booze. I'm sorry for interrupting you. Please continue."

I stand up. "Are you sure you don't want to go and rest?"

"I'd rather stay here. There's so much I still don't know about what you've all been through."

"That's true." Grateful for her dedication to our mission, I walk back to my own chair at the head of the table and slide back onto it. "So, where were we?"

"We were trying to remember everything we know about the man that killed Vicky's grandmother," Charlie says, pushing the last of the toast into his mouth.

"Right. So, we know what Mrs. Delaney told us. She was a friend of Vicky's grandmother. She said Banks was creepy."

"And he has a big library," Vicky adds.

"And Quinn!" I suddenly remember. "He had a relationship with your grandmother, didn't he, Vicky?"

"I still can't believe that," Charlie says. "I mean... I know magic can be crazy, you know, but that story is wild."

"Why?" Kessley asks. "Angels can get very old, right? And they have feelings too, I guess."

"They do," Vicky answers, "but Quinn wasn't an angel then. He was an old, white man."

Kessley's mouth forms a perfect *O*. "I see."

"We could ask him what he knows about Shelton Banks." I lift my eyes to the ceiling, as if that makes any difference, and call out. "Quinn? Do you have a moment for us?"

No answer.

"Quinn?" I repeat.

Still nothing. No whoosh to announce his arrival, no bright light, no glimpse of his friendly face.

Charlie's fingers tap the table restlessly. "Something's wrong. We haven't heard from him or seen him in ages."

I swallow the fear that rises in my throat. "They're probably still working on restoring the balance in Heaven."

"No." Charlie shakes his head. "We fixed that when we sent the souls back to Purgatory, remember? Something else must be wrong. You haven't received the new set of Cards of Death either. They normally arrive soon after we save a soul."

"You think the two have something to do with each other?" I let that idea bounce around my head for a second. *Is it possible that the cards are sent from Heaven?*

Charlie gets up and rummages through the cupboards. "I need more food to think."

Taylar rests his head in his hands. "I wish Mona was here to make us something."

"Hey!" Kessley calls out. "What was wrong with the breakfast *I* made?"

"Nothing!" he says hastily, and a blush creeps from his neck to his cheeks. "Nothing at all."

Gisella collects the plates. "I think Mona puts some of her magic in her food and drinks. She uses her sparks to take away some of our worries and fears."

She hasn't even uttered the last word when tiny yellow lights whirl between Charlie and the kitchen table.

"Did I hear my name?" Mona asks, appearing in a shower of sparks.

I shoot her a big smile. "Yes, we were talking about how much we miss you."

"More like your cooking," Charlie mumbles with a whole cookie in his mouth.

"You maybe," I scold him, "but I actually miss having Mona here." *And Mom and D'Maeo and Jeep. They're all family now, and I feel incomplete without them.*

Taylar turns to face her. "Did the police pick up Shelton Banks?"

Her face lights up. "They did!"

I jump from my chair immediately. "Then we'd better get going. It might take us a while to find more evidence in his house, and I have a feeling his staff won't be too happy to see us."

"I agree," Mona says solemnly. "He's got a household full of pixies and trolls, and they've been instructed to kill all trespassers."

"No problem." I grab the two notebooks from behind my waistband and sit down again. "So we need a spell to capture them."

"You mean to kill them," Taylar says, an angry glint in his eye.

"Well…" I hesitate. I'm not crazy about the idea of killing creatures when it's not absolutely necessary. "Capturing should be enough, shouldn't it? Shelton Banks could have cursed them or something. We'd be killing innocent beings."

Mona clears her throat. "Although I am against murder of any kind, I think the risk of leaving these creatures alive is too great." Her shoulders sag a little as she continues. "Pixies and trolls are evil by nature. They will come after you if you don't kill them."

"I have no problem killing them," Taylar says.

Mona places a hand on his shoulder. "I understand that, but please keep in mind that no good will ever come from torturing in the name of revenge."

"How about torturing for fun?" he replies without a hint of sarcasm.

Mona lowers her head. "Please trust me on this, Taylar. The pixie and Mr. Banks will pay. There is no need to torture them. Do not lower yourself to a place you can never return from."

A couple of sparks jump from her hand onto his arm and make their way to his head.

He jumps up and tries to wipe them away. "Don't try to influence me like that!"

Mona bites her lip. "I'm sorry, Taylar. I shouldn't have done that. But I'm worried about you. There's so much hate in your heart. Try to turn that into relief. You'll feel much better, and it's far less dangerous."

I hold out my hand to touch him but change my mind.

I consider telling him that his brother wouldn't want him to be consumed by hatred. But that's such a cliché. He knows this and saying it out loud will only make him angrier.

"I cannot imagine what it must feel like to finally face your brother's killer," I say instead, diverting his attention from Mona to me. "And to be honest, I think I would react the same way you do."

His lips curl up a bit, but his smile freezes when I continue.

"But… we have a rule here. We do not torture people or monsters."

Mona sends me a hopeful look over Taylar's head. Guilt flows through me. She won't like what I'm going to say next.

"I will stick by that rule," I continue, "and I could order you not to torture that pixie, if we find it. But that is not the way I work. I refuse to order you guys around, because I don't think I'm wiser than you are. The choice is yours. I only hope that your choice will not interfere with our plans to make the Shield stronger."

I can tell my words are getting through to Taylar. His eyes reflect the battle raging inside him.

I lean closer to him. "I know you don't believe it, but you are just as important to me as the rest of my Shield. I want you all to be in the best shape possible. No, I *need* that."

He nods, and I smile at him. "When the time comes, please make a decision based on your heart, not on the hatred raging inside it. Can you promise me that?"

He raises his hand like a scout making his pledge. "I promise I will think before I act."

"Good." When I lean back in my chair, I glance at Mona. It amazes me that instead of disapproval, I read a mixture of admiration and wonder in her expression.

After a short silence, she claps her hands together. Her bright smile returns. "Right. Who wants some hot chocolate?"

With an eager "Me!" Charlie breaks the last of the tension.

CHAPTER 24

It feels good to have Mona back with us again. We drink hot chocolate and she tells us about the things she saw at Shelton Banks' house. We're all concentrated but relaxed, until Mona suddenly stops talking and looks up at the ceiling.

"What is it?" I ask. "Did you hear something?"

*Is someone in the mansion? No, that's impossible. It's well protected.*

A worried frown takes over Mona's perfectly smooth forehead. "Something's wrong."

Taylar follows her gaze and pulls his head in. "With what?"

Without a word, Mona reaches up and pulls something out of thin air. The sight of it makes us all recoil.

The glass box we locked D'Maeo and the Black Void in shudders in Mona's hands. She places it

222

gently on the table. We all move back our chairs, except for Maël.

"Is it escaping?" Charlie asks, downing his hot chocolate in one go.

"I'm not sure." Mona holds the box down with one hand and peers into it. The brown and green spots block most of what goes on inside. Vaguely, I can see the darkness swirling. I can't make out any shapes. Which is probably a good thing, because I don't want to see parts of D'Maeo tumbling by.

Vicky's fingers wrap around the edge of the table. "Is it killing him?"

Mona bites her lip. She doesn't answer.

A tear falls from Vicky's eye when I grab her left hand. "I'm sure he'll be alright. D'Maeo is strong."

She shakes her head and pulls her hand free. "No, Dante. Look at that box."

When I keep my eyes on her, she stands up and points at the box. "Look at it!"

I gulp and do what she says. The glass seems to wriggle under Mona's hand.

"What does that look like to you? Does that look like D'Maeo is winning?"

Mona holds up her free hand. "Don't panic, Vicky. This is as terrifying to me as it is to you, but there's no way to know what it means."

Vicky opens her mouth, changes her mind, wipes her eyes angrily and sits down again.

"It does look bad to me too," Charlie says after a short silence. "So, what else do you think it could mean, Mona?"

The fairy godmother is staring into the glass box again. Sparks crawl all over it, and the box seems to bounce a little less.

"I think it means that they are fighting," she says slowly, "but there's no way of telling who has the upper hand."

"Sure there is," Vicky says in a low voice. "We know how strong that chaos residue is, we know it was taking over D'Maeo from the inside, bit by bit, and we know it took a lot of power to lock it in that box." Her voice rises again. "Now that it's in there, you think D'Maeo will be able to beat it by himself?"

I stare into her eyes, pleading for understanding. *This choice was really hard for me. She sees that, doesn't she? She can read my emotions. She must see that I'm also torn by this.* I try not to think about it, to focus on other things, to solve as many problems as we can. But the search for a way to free D'Maeo is always in the back of my mind, as are the cases of Mom and Jeep.

I try to send my feelings and thoughts to her through my eyes and silently beg her to understand. I simply can't risk the safety of the whole world for the afterlife of one man.

Guilt washes over me. *Who am I kidding? D'Maeo is important. He's part of my Shield. We need him. Of course he's worth the risk. Vicky is right, I made the wrong choice. But there's still time to fix....* My thoughts come to a halt. *Wait a minute...*

With my teeth clenched, I tear my gaze away from

Vicky's. The guilt lessens immediately.

I push my chair back, stand up and slam my fist onto the table. "How dare you use your power on me!"

"How dare you keep D'Maeo trapped like this?" she counters.

A rumbling goes through the room, and I search for the source.

It's the glass box. It's shaking violently now, even though Maël tries to hold it down.

"Stop arguing," the ghost queen says. "Your anger is feeding the chaos residue."

Vicky jumps to her feet. "I'll go somewhere else for a while."

"Wait! Vick..." I hold out my hand to her, but she's already gone.

I sink back onto my chair and rub my face. *I can't believe she influenced my emotions. I know she cares about D'Maeo, but still...*

"Don't be too hard on her," Mona says.

When I look up, the box has settled down. Sparks still crawl over it, but more lazily now.

Gisella clears her throat. "I think Vicky is feeling guilty because we spent a lot of time trying to get rid of her curses. Time we could've spent figuring out how to free D'Maeo."

I shift in my seat. "You think that's it?"

Gisella holds up her hands. "Yes, but I'm not the one that can read emotions. If you want to know for sure, ask her."

"I will." I push myself up again but pause when my eye falls on Mona's sad face.

I walk around Vicky's empty chair and hug Mona from behind. "Are you okay?"

She pats my hand. "These are hard times for all of us, Dante. But I have faith in D'Maeo. In his will and his strength." Her voice breaks, and she swallows half a sob. "But I do miss him. So much."

I kiss her temple and hug her tighter. "I know. We'll come up with a solution soon."

She squeezes my hands. "Thank you, Dante."

"If you think of something, let me know."

She nods.

I gesture at the box. "Or if you think he's in trouble."

"Will do."

I give her one last kiss, turn and make my way out of the kitchen and up the stairs.

I find Vicky in her own bedroom, where she's hardly spent any time lately. She's lying on her back on the bed, staring at the ceiling.

I knock on the open door. "Can I come in?"

"You can do whatever you want. You're the master."

With a sigh, I lower myself on the foot of the bed. "That's true, but I would never use my powers on you or the others unless I really needed to. We are on the same team. If we disagree on something, we can talk about it."

"Sure," she sulks, "but in the end, you make the

decisions."

I can't argue with that, so I say nothing.

After a long silence and hundreds of thoughts crawling around in my head, I put the right words in the right order and say what my heart tells me to. "You know, babe, I *am* the one who makes the final decisions, and honestly, I wish I wasn't. I'm the youngest here, with the fewest knowledge of the magical world. I would gladly transfer the responsibility to someone else. But I can't."

I find the courage to look at Vicky again. To my surprise, she's watching me intently, but with no trace of anger anymore.

"Also…" I hesitate. "I think I shouldn't leave it to someone else. We all have a role to play in this world, and this is mine. Although I don't like it, I take it very seriously. Lucifer isn't only threatening the existence of me and the ones I care about, he will kill most of humanity if I screw this up. Which means I need to make impossible decisions sometimes. Leaving Mom in Trevor's care is one of them. So is leaving D'Maeo and Jeep to fend for themselves while we try to find a way to get them all back." My throat tightens, and I swallow. "It's difficult to get our priorities sorted here, and I pray I'm not putting them in the wrong order. I try not to think about what could happen if I choose wrong."

Tears well up in my eyes as the full force of our situation hits me again. I can almost feel the weight of the whole world on my shoulders. Long, wet lines tickle my cheeks, but I don't move. I don't want to break eye contact.

Finally, Vicky sits up, takes my hands and pulls me to her. She presses my face against her cold, silent chest. "I'm sorry. It wasn't you I was angry at. This is not your fault."

"I love you, Vicky. I don't want to see you hurt."

"I know." She kisses my neck, follows the trail of tears to my eyes and then drops down to my mouth.

She tastes sweet and salty at the same time. Soon, I get lost in her kiss. I sink into it gratefully.

"I love you, Dante," she whispers, and my sorrow is pushed to the back of my mind for a moment.


Back in the kitchen, I concentrate on the spell to use on Shelton Banks' servants while the others discuss strategies and blink upstairs to check out the arsenal in the storage room.

As soon as everyone is provided with tea or coffee, Mona vanishes to get snacks, since Charlie ate our whole supply. We don't mention the box anymore. I think we all know we need a decent plan before we throw ourselves at that problem.

When Mona gets back, Charlie hands her some cash and throws me a couple of bills too. "Here, I don't want you guys to pay for everything."

"That's sweet of you, Charles," Mona says. "But how will you pay for all of this if you don't have a job?"

He shrugs. "I saved some money. It's fine."

Mona and I shove the cash back at the same time, laughing when our hands touch.

"Keep it," I say. "I'm glad to pay for food in return for you fighting at our side."

"Oh please." He snorts. "I'd still fight with you if I had to bring my own food."

"Sure, but you wouldn't be of much use. You'd run out of food in an hour."

Vicky giggles from the chair on my right. "More like half an hour."

Mona throws several packets of cookies and about twenty chocolate bars across the table. "For your endless pocket."

Charlie gapes at it, then shakes his head and grabs the bills in front of him again. "Take the money, Mona. I'm serious."

Mona quickly walks around the table to her seat next to Kessley. "I don't want it. You'll need it more than I do when Lucifer is beaten."

Charlie looks down at the bills with a frown. "I will?"

"Yes, I'm paid well for my services as a fairy godmother."

My eyebrows move up even further than Charlie's. I should concentrate on the spell I'm writing, but this fascinates me. "Mom pays you? I thought she didn't know what you were until recently?" And I thought being a fairy godmother was sort of a charity job. It never occurred to me that she needs money to stay alive.

Mona moves her fingers, and her sparks scatter around the table to pick up the dirty cups and take them to the sink. "We are paid by the magical government."

My mouth falls open, and so does Charlie's. "There's a magical government? Why haven't I heard of them until now?"

Mona smiles brightly. All eyes are on her, even Maël's. I thought she knew almost everything about the magical world, but this must be new to her too.

"Our government only interferes when needed," Mona explains. "Contrary to non-magical governments, ours knows that most things will solve themselves. And if they don't, they don't."

"So it's like a 'do whatever you want, we don't care' policy?" I ask.

She chuckles. "Not entirely and I wouldn't put it like that. The magical government, MG for short, makes sure that people with magical jobs, like me, get paid, so we can buy houses, clothes and food, and blend in with the non-magicals."

I scrunch up my nose. "So we need to pay magical taxes too?"

"Not at all. There are some that can create money. They work for the government."

"All of them?" Charlie asks. "What if they don't want to? I mean, it's not as if they need to work when they can create money out of thin air, you know."

Mona shakes her head. "It's one of the few forbidden things. To keep the magical community running and under the radar, there are certain rules."

A chill suddenly runs up my spine. "What about murder? Can we be arrested for killing all those demons? Or for opening a portal into the Shadow World?"

Kessley bounces up and down excitedly in her chair. "What about Trevor and his demons killing and kidnapping people, can they be arrested for that?"

Mona ignores the bouncing next to her. "No, there are no laws for such things. The MG believes in the natural balance, which basically means that good will defeat evil if the balance tips and the other way around. This is also why they won't offer us help in dealing with the Devil."

"Wow, really?" Kessley scratches her head. "Isn't that a little bit crazy?" Her voice goes up at the end of the sentence. She stumbles over her next words as they roll from her lips at rollercoaster speed. "There shouldn't be too much bad in the world, right? We don't want to trip over demons every time we step outside, or be afraid to go to the supermarket because monsters roam the aisles?"

"We don't need to go to the supermarket anymore," Taylar points out. "Or to any shop."

"I know that!" Kessley carries on. "I mean people in general. People who are still breathing. But sure, also ghosts. If there's as much evil in the world as good, there'd be no safe place left!"

"Kessley?"

The sixth ghost whirls around to face Maël. "Yes?"

"Please stay calm."

"I'm trying." Kess waves her hands in the air, as if to get rid of all the worries and frustrations inside. "It's the booze again. I can't stop talking!"

"It's fine," Mona replies with a twinkle in her eye. She sends some sparks to take a teacup from the cupboard and fill it with tea. "Drink some of this, you'll feel better."

Kessley picks the full cup up when the sparks set it down in front of her and breathes in the smell. "Yes, much better."

"And you…" Mona points at me with a semi-reprimanding look. "You should be writing a spell. We don't know how long it will take for the police to question Mr. Banks. And I expect them to get a search warrant too. You don't want to run into a police search team while sneaking around his house."

"You're right." I close the notebooks and stand up.

I walk to the adjacent room, the annex. To my surprise, I find an armchair and wooden side table there. Last time I walked through this room, it was empty. We've been decorating in between fights and solving curses and such, and I wanted all the old furniture gone, so the ghosts threw them out. It's probably all piled up somewhere at the back of the garden, out of sight. Remnants of Dad's secret life, memories of battles I was never a part of. Thinking about it still stings my heart, even though I know Dad was only trying to protect me and Mom.

Since I don't recognize the chair or table, I conclude that Mona must have put them here. It's a nice chair, comfy too, but the rest of the room is still chilly and dusty. *I think I'll let Mona and Mom decide how to decorate it once our mission is completed. It'll be nice to have a cozy room to get together in instead of always sitting at the kitchen table. We could relax, watch movies together, play games, eat snacks and drink beer. Listen to some music.* The thought makes me happy.

Until I remember that the "we" in those sentences will consist of only six people. After all, the Shield will move on when we defeat Lucifer. *It will be Mom, Mona, Quinn, Charlie and Gisella sitting here with me. I'll be alone. Mona will be alone.*

My heart sinks at the thought. Then I shake my head feverously. *No, I can't let that happen. There has to be a way to keep us together.*

But even while I'm thinking it, I know my fantasy of this big happy family can never come true. 'Most of us want to move on. We want peace, we want to see our families again.' Didn't Jeep say something like that? He wants to see his wife again, Taylar misses his brother and Maël longs to be reunited with her tribe. And Vicky…

I rub my face hard to drive out the sad thoughts. I can think about this later.

*Focus on getting everyone together now. On keeping the Devil in Hell. Take it one step at a time.*

I throw my feet over the side of the chair and close my eyes.

233

Soon, the words for the spell roll through my mind.

I write them in my Book of Spells and leaf through Dad's notebook to find ingredients that will amplify the power of my words. I choose black candles. Those will stand for banishment.

As soon as I've scribbled it all down, I return to the kitchen. I find it empty, but a peek through the back door window locates my friends. To my surprise, they're training in the protective circle. In my concentration, I hadn't even noticed the noise.

Happy with their efforts to get better, I leave them to it and go through the cupboards until I find most of the herbs I need. I also set aside some salt and a bowl.

From the doorway, I call out to Vicky, "I need some herbs. Can you check your endless pocket?"

She breaks off her fight with Maël and Gisella and blinks to my side. "Of course, what do you need?"

"Do you have any agrimony seeds?"

"To banish negative spirits? Sure. Good choice."

I smile when she hands me a bottle filled with dried green leaves.

"How about some fern leaves? To prevent getting jinxed, and to ward off evil spirits."

Her hand disappears into her pocket again. "Got those too. I stocked up with everything I could think of recently."

"Black candles?"

"Yep."

She sets it all down on the table. "Anything else?"

"Let's see." I scan my list again and check off the ingredients. "I've already got rosemary, saltpeter and regular salt."

Vicky peers at my list. "You've got a lot of herbs that banish or ward off evil."

"Yes, because Shelton Banks is powerful, and there are a lot of pixies and trolls in his house. We've got a lot of evil to defeat there."

"Oh yes, it's a great idea. But what about…" she reaches into her pocket again, "some aloes powder, to silence the lips of those who speak evil."

I gape at her. "Really?"

With a chuckle, she sets the bottle on the table. "Yes, really."

I rub my chin. "I thought it kept your skin smooth."

She throws her head back and laughs. "That too. It all depends on the words you use them with."

"Anything else I should put in?"

She wraps her arms around my neck. "No, I think this is a pretty strong combination." She kisses me on the nose. "Need any help mixing it all?"

"That would be great. If you do that, I'll heat up the calamus oil."

"Used to control a situation or dominate a person," Vicky says.

"Or both," I add. I smile down at her. "You know all of them by heart?"

With a shrug, she pulls away. "Not all of them,

only the most common ones."

I grab the bottle of oil from the kitchen counter and pour the liquid into a saucepan. "Now you're just being modest."

"Not really," she answers, shaking herb after herb into the bowl. "There are thousands of plants that can be used in spells. It's impossible to remember them all, unless you're a Mnemonist."

I snort. "A what?"

"A Mnemonist is someone who can remember lots of things. They can memorize whole lists of data. The term is even used in the non-magical world, but of course no one there knows it's actually a magical power."

I turn up the heat under the pan. "Sounds awesome."

Vicky appears next to me and kisses my neck. "Not as awesome as being able to control the weather and throw balls of lightning."

With one hand, I pull her against me tightly. "You're so hot when you're flattering me."

A loud "Wow!" from Kessley and a sudden veil of darkness makes us turn to the back garden. We hurry over to the back door simultaneously and freeze there.

A giant cloud hovers above the garden. Gisella is standing under it with her hands raised. The others are either watching her or the cloud in awe.

Vicky and I exchange a worried look before hurrying over to our friends.

"What happened? Are you guys okay? What is that thing? Is it a new demon?"

Kessley wakes from her shocked frozen state and starts hopping up and down. "No! It's not a demon, it's a cloud made of shadows. Isn't this brilliant?"

My gaze shifts to Gisella. "No way. Are you doing this?" *I knew she could move shadows now, but to create something steady like this, and of this size…*

"You made this?" I ask again.

Instead of answering, Gisella moves her arms down to her side and then up again like a ballerina.

The cloud separates into hundreds of small pieces.

The werecat-witch holds one hand still and twirls the index finger of the other hand. Half of the clouds turn into small vortexes. With a quick downward move of her hand, Gisella makes them soar down. When she pulls her arm back, they change direction. Dozens of whirlwinds shoot straight at us.

I force myself to stay put. I have nothing to fear from Gisella. Still, my stomach swarms with restless bees.

Leaves and small rocks are pulled in as the vortexes make their way over to us. From the corner of my eye, I see the others stepping back. Kessley stopped hopping, and Charlie calls out a warning.

Three feet until they reach us. Two feet… My clothes are blown in all directions, as if five people are pulling them at once. One foot… I prepare to duck, but a fraction before one of them hits my nose, Gisella holds up her hand in a stop motion. Abruptly, all of the whirlwinds come to a halt and stop turning.

"Holy crap, Gisella!" I call out, releasing my anxiety and admiration all at once.

I shake the trembles from my hands. "How did you manage this in such a short time?"

She shrugs and moves her hands to the sides. All the shadows in the vortexes and clouds pull free and return to their natural places.

"It started as a reflex. I was collecting shadows, but way too slow. So I braced for impact when Charlie threw a giant grease ball at me. That accidentally led to the huge cloud you saw."

Still stunned, I stare at her without moving. "You are amazing."

Kessley comes hopping back. She slaps Gisella on the back several times. "She's brilliant, isn't she? We are so gonna kick Satan's ass." She dances around us and back to the others, where she grabs Taylar by the hand. Together, they perform a manic dance around the protective circle.

Vicky comes to pat Gisella on the back too, and then whispers in my ear. "Interesting couple they make."

When I frown, she nods at Kess and Taylar. My eyes grow wide as I realize what I've overlooked.

"You think…?"

Gisella bends forward. "Don't tell me you hadn't noticed their little moments yet."

I turn away when I feel a blush rising to my cheeks. "Of course I have." I walk back to the mansion. "Gather in the kitchen everyone!" I call over my shoulder. "The spell is almost ready. We're leaving for Shelton Banks' house soon."

# CHAPTER 25

Shelton Banks' estate lies between Blackford and Mulling, to the north-east of our town. We passed it without knowing when we saved the priest.

A high iron gate blocks our way, just like Vicky said. I bring Phoenix to a halt and pull Dad's notebook from my waistband to find a spell to open it when Gisella gets out of the car.

"What is she doing?" I ask Charlie, who's sitting next to me.

He shrugs, but we don't have to wait long for the answer.

With a couple of swift wrist movements, Gisella gathers a handful of shadows from the nearby trees and sends them into the lock in the gate, where they wriggle around for a while. With a soft creak, the gate swings open.

Gisella sends the shadows back and hops into the

car.

"Wait," Charlie says when I put my foot on the gas.

"Why?" Phoenix gives an impatient roar when I press the brakes.

"Aren't we walking up to the house? We're not going for a grand entrance, are we?"

"Why not?" I ask. "We've got everything we need to take them out. A spell, weapons, cages."

He pulls his blond hair back and ties it together slowly. "True, but Mona said there are a lot of servants. Do we really want them all to see us before you get a chance to cast the spell to kill them? And what if the spell doesn't work as expected? Or if there's another creature in there that Mona didn't know about. One that's more powerful than we expect. It could knock you down, or even unconscious, before you get a chance to finish the spell."

I watch him intently until he starts to shift uncomfortably in his seat.

"What?" he says eventually.

"I was just thinking, you're a lot smarter than you look, Charlie."

He punches my arm hard. "Twerp."

Kessley giggles from the back seat, where she's merged fully with Taylar, because of the lack of space.

I chuckle and punch him back. This goes on until Gisella leans forward. "Excuse me, children. Weren't we in a hurry or something?"

We straighten up instantly. Kessley giggles even louder.

I put Phoenix in reverse and park her between two trees.

"If you park three feet back, the car will be hidden," Gisella remarks.

I recoil. "You're not serious, are you?"

She gives me a blank look in the rearview mirror, and I turn to face her. "You think I'm going to drive Phoenix into those bushes? She'll get scratches all over her!"

Her mouth forms a silent *O,* and she turns her head to look out the window. To hide the fact that she's rolling her eyes, most likely.

I'm about to explain that Phoenix isn't like a regular car, that she was Dad's and...

Before I can even form a solid sentence in my head, Gisella has stepped out.

Without a word, she walks into the forest and comes back with her arms full of red osier dogwood, which she places in front of the car.

Kessley disappears too and flickers back into view next to Gisella.

"Wow! Did you see that!" she calls out. "I apparated!"

"Well done," I compliment her, taking the plants from her. "But try to keep your voice down, in case Shelton's servants are nearby."

She slams a hand against her mouth. "Oops, sorry."

Gisella is off to get another batch of bushes, and Kessley follows her at a run.

Vicky watches her with a grin. "That girl is amazing."

She helps me place the dogwood on the hood, and when Gisella and Kess deliver another supply, Phoenix is fully hidden behind strings of green.

We collect our weapons and the herb mixture from the trunk, and I read my spell one more time.

"Everybody ready?" I ask, taking in all the determined and expectant faces around me.

They raise the weapons they found in the storage room. Small cages to lock the pixies in and maces and shields to hit the trolls or pixies with, since swords and blades won't do us much good against them. Trolls have thick skin, and pixies are agile and small. So what's better than a couple of sticks with spiked balls to swing at them?

"Maël, can you take the lead, please?" I ask. "Vicky will close ranks to make sure no one sneaks up on us from behind."

I could put the strongest fighters on each end, but Maël and Vicky can both use their senses to detect living beings, so this makes the most sense. They'll warn us if someone approaches, and we can all get ready to fight.

Slowly and as quiet as possible, we make our way through the forest to the mansion. A whiff of chlorine hits my nose, and in my mind, an imagine pops up of a sparkling pool surrounded by sunbeds under parasols. Waiters walk around with trays full of cocktails and disappear into a dark mansion about the size of Darkwood Manor. Mold creeps up the walls and covers most of the windows. Cries of dismay bounce around inside. I almost shiver at the thought.

But when I finally catch sight of the house between the leaves and branches, my mouth falls open. It's nothing like I imagined.

Hidden behind a small hedge lies a shell-shaped pool in front of something that I'd call a castle rather than a mansion. Or simply a three-story mass of balconies and glass.

At one end, there's a tower, dwarfed by a strangely placed chimney, whilst the other end has the look of a converted garage slapped onto the main building. Between the two are layers upon layers of balconies, flanked on both sides by elegant round stairways leading from what I'm guessing are the living areas down to the pool. In the center of the mansion, there's a massive stack of windows that reflects the sunlight, crowned with an arch that takes up half of the main roof.

It's massive, it's excessive and it screams "I have money!". But it's also light and inviting, nothing like I was expecting. It looks as if the architect couldn't decide what kind of tower he liked best, had a love for chimneys in strange spots and didn't know when to stop adding new parts. And although I hate to admit it, I kind of like it.

We all watch it silently for a minute.

"Are we sure he lives here alone?" Taylar asks, voicing my thoughts exactly.

Maël nods. "Yes, we did some research on the Pentaweb, and Mona said she never saw anyone other than Shelton and his servants here at night. There is no woman, there are no kids, and the friends he has never stay overnight, as far as she knows."

"Then what does he need such a large house for?" Taylar says. I can tell by his tone of voice and the angry frown in his forehead that he's getting more annoyed by the second.

"Who cares?" I answer. "Let's do what we came here for. Kill his servants, collect all the evidence we can find about his involvement in your brother's death, and get out of here."

He wraps his hand firmer around his mace and presses his shield against his chest. "Gladly."

I turn to face Vicky, who's scanning the tree line behind us. "Do you sense anyone?"

She shakes her head.

"Good. What about you, Maël?"

She forms the okay sign with her fingers.

"Then we're moving in. Remember the plan."

Without hesitation, they form a circle around me. It feels weird. As if I'm a king or something, more important than the others. I'm not. I'm the one casting the spell, and they will try to keep me out of the fight, if it comes to one.

Maël counts from three back to one, and we move in formation. One step at a time, to a silent rhythm in our heads. We practiced this only once back at Darkwood Manor, but now, it's as if we do this every day. We leave the protection of the trees and move steadily past the pool to the middle of the building.

As soon as Maël, still in front, comes to a halt next to the large window, we all do. From here, I should be able to reach the most inhabitants with my spell. Not all, since it's a big house, but most will do.

Vicky puts the four black candles from her pocket down on all sides of me while the others close ranks to protect us. I sprinkle salt around myself in the shape of a circle.

"What are you doing here?" an unnatural high voice says.

I set my curiosity aside and keep concentrating on the spell.

"We would like to speak to Mr. Banks," Maël says calmly.

I block out their voices and light the black candles one by one without a word.

A strong smell spreads when I open the wooden box with the cooked mixture I prepared at home.

Something lets out an alarmed shriek and comes soaring toward me. Someone lifts a mace and smacks the creature in the head.

"Hurry up, Dante," Vicky says from behind me. "We've been noticed, and they are going for the cold welcome."

I take a handful of herb mush and get down on my knees to draw a circle inside the line of salt.

As soon as it's complete, I call out my words over the noise of approaching trouble.

*"Forces of nature, hear my call.*
*Let all evil creatures fall.*
*Take away their strength and sound.*
*Make them move as if they're bound."*

Quickly, I collect the herb mixture again, in reversed direction, and disperse it over the salt line.

*"Forces of nature, hear me now.*
*Let to us all evil bow.*
*Grant us entrance to this home.*
*Make sure we can safely roam."*

As the pixies and trolls filing out of the mansion drop down one by one, I press a finger full of herb mush against each of my friends' foreheads to make sure they are included in the spell. I finish by putting a dot on my own forehead.

*"Forces of nature, hear my plea.*
*Show us what we're meant to see.*
*Keep us safe and make us find*
*the secrets of the owner's mind.*

*Forces of nature, hear my cry.*
*Give us all a keener eye.*
*Leave no traces of our stay.*

*Wipe all evidence away."*

All candles are blows out at once. The smoke that rises slithers around us. The wisps touch our foreheads, and the herb dots evaporate. The smell of rosemary lingers in the air when silence settles upon us.

Taylar and Charlie collect the pixies lying motionless on the cold tiles and put them in the cages we brought. Then they put all the unconscious trolls in a heap and form a barrier around them.

"Ready?" Vicky asks me.

I nod solemnly. I know killing them is the safest solution, and the world will be a better place without them, but slaughtering monsters when they're not able to defend themselves feels unnatural.

"They'll kill us all if we don't kill them first," Gisella says over her shoulder.

When I don't respond, she steps out from the circle. "I can do it for you."

"No, don't. Give me a second." With all the evil powers inside the werecat-witch, I can't let her use an incantation. It would almost be like inviting the Devil in.

With an impatient nod, she steps back into the circle.

With a couple of deep breaths, I get ready for the second spell.

I place the black candles around my friends. The incense stick from my pocket shakes in my hand when I light it. I never thought I would find myself in a situation like this, ending the lives of creatures that lie helpless at my feet. My whole body resists my efforts, but I have no choice. If we let these creatures go, we will be in big trouble later.

So I lift the two cages, that look like bird cages filled with pixies that remind me too much of Tinkerbell, and hand them to Vicky, who places them on top of the troll pile. She puts the burning incense stick on top.

With another matchstick, I light the black candles again and walk around my friends a second and third time.

*"Burn these creatures without pain.*
*Let their struggles be in vain.*
*Make sure none of them survives.*
*Send them to their afterlives."*

The incense stick shoots sparks down, and soon, a small fire spreads through the pile of bodies.

I avert my eyes and continue.

*"Leave no trace to us behind.*
*Let the search for us go blind."*

A horrible mixture of blood, herbs and burned hair and bones rises, accompanied by black smoke.

I swallow several times. The candle flames sway restlessly, as if they don't want to be a part of this either.

But I've come this far. Now I should finish it.

*"Let these bodies disappear.*
*Let their souls no longer fear.*
*The wind will pick up all the dust,*
*and they will end up where they must."*

My voice doesn't sound as confident as it usually does, but it works, nevertheless. The burned body parts, clothes and even the cages are turned into dust and taken away by the wind.

"Very smart," Vicky comments when the candle flames die. "You made sure they won't end up somewhere they shouldn't."

I shoot her a faint smile. "I learned from my mistakes."

Vicky puts everything back into her endless pocket, and I join Taylar, who's hovering by the glass doors that lead to a giant kitchen and dining room.

I'm surprised at how calm he has been.

"How are you feeling?" I ask him. "Was she among them, the pixie that killed Lleyton?"

He rubs his temple. "I'm not sure. I don't think so."

"Maybe she isn't here anymore. She could work for someone else now."

His eyes narrow. "Maybe."

"Or maybe she died."

Now he shakes his head and clenches his fists.

"No, she's alive."

"What do you think then?" The anger that starts to emanate from him is making me nervous.

"She's probably running errands or trying to get Shelton Banks out of prison."

"He's not in prison yet, Taylar," I say, lifting my arm to put it around him but thinking better of it. "That's why we're here, to collect the evidence that *will* put him there and keep him there for a very long time."

Taylar doesn't move. "But he's not the only one who should be punished. He's not the one who actually killed Lleyton."

I feel the others shifting uncomfortably behind us. We can't stay for long. If someone catches us…

"I know," I say. "And if we find her, we will take care of her. But please try to keep a clear head. Don't get carried away by hate, Taylar."

He breathes out slowly and unclenches his fists. "I'll try."

A look over my shoulder tells me everyone is eager to go in. "Remember, don't wander off alone, in case of surprises, and holler if you find anything useful."

They all nod solemnly, and Taylar and I step forward as one.

Only to hit our heads against an invisible wall.

## CHAPTER 26

I squeeze my eyes shut until the flashes of lightning stop piercing my brain. Vicky's hands touch my back, preventing me from tumbling backwards. I hear Taylar moaning beside me.

"Why did Mona not tell us about this security wall?" Maël ponders aloud.

Slowly, I regain my balance. The pain in my head subsides, but dots of bright light still dance through my vision.

"They probably put it up when Shelton was taken in for questioning," Gisella says. "I might have an idea on how to trick it."

I hold up my hand. "Don't use an incantation."

She pushes me out of the way gently. "Don't worry. All I need are some shadows."

I pull a flashing Taylar toward me, and we watch quietly as the werecat-witch gathers shadows from all corners of the house.

"I'll try this on myself first," she says. She makes a twirling motion with her index finger, and a handful of shadows wrap her up from head to toe. Her hand, now covered fully by shadows, is dropped to her side, making her look like a dark statue. Until she suddenly vanishes.

"Fingers crossed!" her voice says close to me.

I peer through my eyelashes and tilt my head, but I still can't see her.

A couple of seconds later, the dark figure appears again, inside the house.

"You did it!" I call out. "That's amazing!"

"Brilliant!" Kessley agrees.

The shadows unwrap themselves, and Gisella smiles at us. "Okay, stay still everyone, and don't panic. This might itch a little."

As she moves her hands, the shadows that still linger near the doorway shoot left and right and wrap around each of us. It feels a bit claustrophobic, especially when a shadow folds around my head, making it impossible for me to see anything. The wriggling of the shadows feels more like a tickle than an itch, and that comforts me a bit. Although Gisella uses her dark powers to control them, the shadows themselves aren't evil.

I breathe in and out slowly until I can see again.

"Okay," Gisella says. "To prevent collisions, I'll call you in one by one. Step through the barrier slowly and stand next to me."

She calls my name first, and I step inside without trouble.

"Okay, I made it," I say when I reach Gisella.

The shadows release me at her command, and she calls in Taylar, who was standing next to me.

One by one, we make it inside safely. I laugh at the sight of Kess dancing through the dining room as if she just got into an amusement park.

I turn to Gisella to thank her. "That was a great idea. How did you know this would work?"

She sends the shadows to the corners of the room. "Remember the invisibility spell? That uses shadows too."

"You're right! I hadn't thought of that."

"I wasn't completely sure it would work," she confesses.

Charlie walks up to her and kisses her on the cheek. "It did, and I'm so proud of you."

"Thanks, Lee."

I clap my hands to get everyone's attention. "Okay, now that we're inside, we'll split into twos, as agreed, and—" I fall silent. "Where's Taylar?"

Everyone turns around in search of our youngest ghost. There's no sign of him anymore.

A worried frown takes over Gisella's face, and I follow her gaze.

A shadow slithers along the floor and around the corner. We hurry after it at the same time, the others following close behind.

We find Taylar at the foot of the stairs leading to

the next floor. Several shadows have wrapped themselves around him again. *Are they obeying him now?* His complexion is unnaturally gray. His jaw is set and his mace held tightly while he looks up at a pixie, hovering halfway up the stairs.

"I've come for justice," he says, his voice dripping with hate. The last word comes out as a venomous hiss.

The pixie raises her tiny chin. Her wings flutter rapidly to keep her in the air. "What I did was justice. You both should've died that day."

Taylar climbs the first step with a violent roar. "We deserve to die because we stole food to stay alive?"

She crosses her small arms. "Stealing is a sin. You can work for food and shelter. That is no excuse to steal or to live in someone else's house." Her voice is so shrill and vicious that it hurts my ears.

While the two bicker on and Taylar moves closer to the pixie one step at a time, I discretely point at Vicky's back pocket. She takes the hint and pulls out the remains of the herbs. She hands them to me behind my back.

In my mind, I practice the words again to make sure they come out fluently.

Vicky reaches for the black candles when everything spins out of control.

We're swept off our feet with force and bang into each other near the ceiling. The box of herbs slips from my hand and hits the floor.

Maël is hovering near me. She holds her staff firmly in both hands, and her lips are moving.

"Oh come on!" the pixie screams, and the next moment, we all tumble up and down again. I hit the ceiling hard and see Maël's wand sailing down and landing in the herbs that decorate the floor.

The flying creature flutters toward the ghost queen and produces a shrill laugh. "You didn't really think you were stronger than me, did you?" She taps Maël's cheeks mockingly.

She passes by each of us while we hang glued to the ceiling. "You think you can come in here and kill all of my friends?" Her tiny face turns a bright red.

"We did kill all of your friends," Gisella responds, moving her hands to call the shadows to her.

The pixie is next to her in the blink of an eye. "No, you didn't. You think I was alone here? Think again, bitch." Her whole body shakes with another burst of laughter.

From behind her, the shadows draw nearer. Gisella is seconds away from wrapping her in them.

But then, the pixie dashes out of the way, and the shadows hit Gisella in the face. She splutters and moves her hands frantically to get them off. She directs them back to the pixie, but without even moving, the creature turns us all sideways. Gisella loses focus, and before she can recover, a rope folds itself around her wrists.

Once again, the room spins around us. Without guidance, the shadows retreat to their corners.

I try a lightning bolt, but before there's even a spark in sight, my hands are bound too.

Then, there's another roar. *Taylar.*

He's still surrounded by shadows, and they tilt him back onto his feet. He's turned solid, but his skin is still a sickly shade of gray. Red veins pulse wildly as the shadows propel him forward. The pixie flees out of reach again, but the shadows are faster. They lunge, grab her ankle and pull her into Taylar's waiting arms. He catches her and presses her tightly against his chest. She shrieks in pain, but the sound is soon muffled by the darkness that squeezes against her.

I want to tell Taylar to stop. That we can take care of her in a better way. A less cruel way. But when I open my mouth, my stomach turns upside down again. The floor gets closer at frightening speed, and I collide with the floor. Maël, Kessley and Vicky manage to slide through it. They get to their feet unharmed. Me, Charlie and Gisella are not so lucky. We stay down, moaning and grumbling in pain.

Maël hurries over to Taylar, whose face is contorted with hatred as he squeezes and squeezes.

"I will handle it from here," the ghost queen tells him.

He looks up at her with dark eyes. "No, she's mine."

"Please, Taylar," she begs. "Do not let these dark emotions control you. Hatred is what killed your brother. She will pay, but this is not the way to do it."

I manage to sit up. My ribs hurt so much I can

barely suck in air.

Taylar's expression sends chills down my back. *I should've watched him more closely. I should've known that taking him here was a bad idea.* The fact that the shadows obey him can only mean that part of him has been pushed to the dark side by his anger. Maybe even all of him. The thought makes me sick. *What if we can't get him back?*

Maël gently reaches out to him. "Hand her over, please."

Finally, Taylar relaxes. The shadows move to his waist and neck, and he holds out his arms.

There lies the pixie, motionless, all the color drained from her face. Her mouth and eyes are wide open in panic. Her chest no longer moves.

"Oh, Taylar," Maël whispers.

The darkness slithers around the young ghost like a bunch of snakes.

"She deserved it," he says without blinking.

I can't argue with that, but I sense the same thing Maël does. Taylar crossed a line. He didn't just kill the pixie, he made sure she suffered. And he controlled the shadows, which is an evil power.

All we can do now is hope that he can step back over the line. Back to the light.

Maël forces a smile onto her lips. "Can I have her, please?"

After a short hesitation, he drops the pixie into her outstretched hands.

Immediately, a weight seems to be lifted from his

shoulders. With a strong shake of his arms, he chases the shadows away. His see-through skin turns back from gray to its normal shade of pale. His eyes get lighter every time he blinks.

He rubs his face, and I gesture to Maël to get rid of the pixie. She blinks out of sight with a worried look on her face.

Carefully, I step closer to Taylar. "How are you feeling?" I'm afraid to touch him, but I do it anyway.

I expect to be thrown back or to get a shock. Instead, Taylar lowers his hands and shoots me a guilty look.

"I'm sorry."

My hand wraps firmer around his shoulder, as if that will send more comfort through him.

Maybe it does, because a weak smile turns the corners of his mouth up. "Thanks for caring, Dante."

"Of course," I say, and I hear the surprise in my own voice. *Why wouldn't I care?*

"I'm fine now," he adds. "I feel much better."

My hand still rests on his shoulder. I'm afraid to let go. Afraid to lose him.

Guilt flashes across Taylar's face again. "I'm sorry I scared you. I just had to do this."

I swallow. "I understand, but not like this."

Maël aparates back in with empty hands. Her jaw is set tight as she nods at me to step aside. She places both hands on Taylar's chest and closes her eyes.

The white-haired ghost waits patiently for the verdict.

Finally, the African queen pulls back. "He seems okay."

"How is that possible?" I ask. "Even I sensed the evil inside him."

Taylar doesn't even flinch at my words. *What is going through his head?*

Vicky appears on my left. "Let me look at him."

He turns to her and meets her eyes without fear while my heart goes in overdrive. I have a lot of faith in Maël's abilities to sense evil, since she's shown them before, during our search for the fairy for instance, but Vicky's power of empathy goes deeper. There's no tricking her.

My hands are clammy by the time Vicky finally tears her gaze away. But instead of stepping back and telling us Taylar is okay, she flings her arms around him and presses him against her chest. "Don't ever scare me like that again."

"I'm sorry," he repeats, and he hugs her back.

I let out a sigh of relief and finally look around. "This place is crazy."

Several shrill outbursts of laughter answer me, breaking the tension in the large room.

Gisella walks to the space behind the second set of double glass doors. "Look at this kitchen." Her hand glides over the shiny counter that takes up at least thirteen feet on the far wall and about ten feet on the other side of the kitchen island. There are two large ovens under an enormous ventilation hood. The whole room is decorated with marble and big white ornaments that are supposed to make it look like something from the Roman empire. Large ionic columns support the upper floors. They look small in the giant space until you step under them. As soon as the sun hits the white and sparkly interior, we're all blinded. I see everyone raise a hand to shield their eyes.

Then, I'm knocked over, and the room fills with heavy footsteps and a loud fluttering of wings. Only now do I remember the words of the pixie. "You think I was alone here?"

"Gisella!" I call out. "Use the shadows!"

When I peer through my eyelashes, I see that the blinding light doesn't come from the sun at all.

The troll that climbs on top of me is carrying some sort of lantern, which flashes on and off, giving me a headache. I can barely keep my eyes open, but if I don't, I'll never get this heavy creature off me. Its face full of lumps and rotten teeth hovers over me. The giant nose moves as it sniffs my face. "This one smells important."

Immediately, two more trolls saunter over to me, and a pixie also joins the party.

I stay still while I concentrate on conjuring a whirlwind to pick them all up and slam them against the ceiling like the pixie did.

"Can I have a bite?" one of the trolls asks, only to shove his friends aside without waiting for an answer.

His foul-smelling mouth comes closer and opens wide. The pixie above my head claps and cheers.

"Yeah! Kill him, crush him, show him who's boss!"

I push all the anger I have to my hands and throw them up. Between them, a twister forms, and I hurl it away from me.

The trolls and the pixie are sucked into it. The lantern falls onto the floor and extinguishes. There are more lights in the corners of my vision, but I'm able to ignore those.

With my eyes fully open again, I can send the twister wherever I want it to go. So I sit upright and steer it toward Vicky, who's wrestling with another troll. *How many of these creatures were in here anyway? We already killed so many before we came in. It's like a village in here.*

The wind knocks the troll out of the way, and I make sure it slams into the wall, hard.

I prepare to send it to where Charlie is trying to avoid the ivy stalks created by two nature pixies, but something pushes me in the back. I tumble over and manage to pull myself upright on a column. Without looking, I throw a lightning bolt over my shoulder.

There's a pained grumble and a thump, and I turn to face another troll. Near the ceiling, several shadows chase another pixie. She raises a hand, and my feet leave the ground. I try to hit her with lightning, but a ball of grease slams into her face before I can even move. Once again, the floor comes closer, but this time, the landing is softer. A well-aimed blow to the head knocks out the troll I landed on.

A loud battle cry drowns out all other noises, and

all trolls and pixies come to a sudden halt.

When I scramble back to my feet, I see Maël standing in the doorway, her staff held firmly in front of her. The agate stone inside it burns bright, and Maël's face is contorted with concentration.

"Hurry," she says in between the words of her time spell.

I stare at the frozen creatures scattered through the kitchen and dining room. "Eh… we can't hurt them when they're frozen in time."

Vicky starts to pull herbs and candles from her endless pocket. "No, but you could cast a spell to overrule that."

All of the Kessleys between us are sucked back into the original ghost. "Brilliant idea!"

Vicky must sense my hesitation, because she slides all kinds of herbs to me across the floor. "Don't overthink it. Use these ingredients to make sure we can hurt them even though they're stuck in time, then repeat the spell you cast outside, to make them disappear."

I follow her advice, and about three minutes later, everything is ready.

I position myself in the middle of the room. "Cross your fingers!"

## CHAPTER 27

My spell works like a charm. One by one, the trolls and pixies release their last breath and go up in smoke. Maël nearly collapses on the floor. Charlie and Gisella rush to her side to support her.

"I am fine," she says, but I can tell freezing time this long took a lot of energy.

"Why don't you stay here and rest for a little while," I suggest. "I don't think there are more servants in here. Kessley can stay with you."

Maël lowers herself onto a kitchen chair and waves my words away. "I will be fine on my own. I will join you in a couple of minutes."

"No." I shake my head firmly. "I don't want anyone to be alone while we're in here. Who knows what other surprises Shelton Banks has left behind for us."

Kessley sits down next to the ghost queen. "I don't mind staying with you for a while, Mäel. We can get to know each other a bit better while you rest."

"Wait," I interrupt as a sudden realization hits me. "Shelton Banks…"

Gasps fill the room, and we all look at each other in shock.

"Shelton Banks is the same guy that killed Vicky's grandmother?" Charlie says incredulously.

"He is!" Vicky calls out.

Kessley crosses her arms. "I told you."

"You did," I confess. "But we heard two different names." I shoot the others a questioning look. "Didn't we?"

They all nod.

Maël taps her staff against the floor in thought. "It must have been a spell cast by Shelton Banks. Entering his house must have undone it."

I shake my head. "No, that doesn't make sense. We've been inside for a while already." I pace from the living room to the kitchen and back with my hands in my trouser pockets. My fingers touch something grainy, and I come to a halt. "What's this?" I grab the grains and pull them out. They're in both pockets.

"Look at this." I hold both hands up to inspect the sandy material. The grains seem even smaller than sand, and they glow.

Vicky puts her hand in her pockets and pulls out the same stuff.

One by one, the others do the same, except for Kessley, who doesn't have pockets.

"Pixie dust," Taylar says.

Gisella lets the grains from her pockets slide through her fingers. "The glow is fading. It must have stopped working because we killed the pixie it came from."

"So, it was... what? Some sort of hallucination pixie?"

"An illusion pixie actually," Maël says. "They can also make themselves invisible, which explains how she managed to dust us without us noticing. She must have done it ages ago."

Charlie empties his pockets on the floor with a look of disgust. "I put on clean clothes yesterday, so how come I didn't know Shelton Banks was... well, Shelton Banks before?"

"The dust travels with you, even if you change your outfit. It can even cling to you if you do not have any pockets." The African queen demonstrates that last fact by patting her dress. Two piles of sand form beside her.

With a frown, I turn to Kessley. "Then why doesn't Kess have any pixie dust?"

The sixth ghost answers before Maël can. "Because I joined your Shield after the pixie dusted you."

The full meaning of it finally sinks in. "Which is why you knew they were one and the same all along."

"Exactly. The man that killed Taylar's brother is the same guy that killed Vicky's grandmother."

"And the same guy that put the curse on me,"

Vicky adds. She wipes her hands on her black pants. "Which means he wants me dead too." She tilts her head in thought. "And the pixie, one of his servants, got close enough to dust us. Why didn't she kill me? Or all of us, for that matter."

There's a short silence.

"Maybe something got in her way," I say eventually. "It's definitely something to think about. Why does Shelton Banks want to kill you, and why did he put that curse on you? He's powerful. He could've just ended you or sent you to some other world. What is he waiting for?"

"For his master to say the word?" Gisella offers.

"His master?"

"Satan? Lucifer? The king of Hell?"

I scratch my head. "You think he works for the Devil?"

She shrugs. "Wild guess."

"If that's the case, we should be able to find proof in here somewhere."

"I'll check upstairs," Taylar says, already on his way back to the hallway.

"Yes," I agree. "Let's get to work. We need answers." I nod at Charlie and Gisella to follow him, and Vicky and I decide to start on this floor. *We've got a lot to explore. I hope we're able to find something useful in this giant mansion, preferably before Shelton Banks returns. I hope the spell shows us where to look and what to inspect.*

Vicky opens a door that reveals stairs leading down. "He's got a basement too?"

I shrug. I can't say I'm surprised. By the looks of the house and the kitchen, Shelton Banks isn't the kind of man that stops at "rich". Too much for us is not nearly enough for him. Why settle for a three-floor mansion if you can also have a basement?

Vicky gestures at the stairs. "After you."

"I can't wait to find out what he's done with it," I say sarcastically.

Vicky leans over and whispers in my ear. "It's probably a dungeon."

Chuckling to ourselves, we descend. We're about halfway down when someone calls to us from above. "Wait!"

I squint against the light from the doorway. "Maël? Is something wrong?"

Her head goes up and down. "I heard something from below."

I frown. "More servants?"

She joins us on the stairs and holds out her hands. "Not servants. Something darker."

"I'll get the others," Vicky says, and she blinks out of sight.

We wait for her to come back with Taylar, Charlie and Gisella. Meanwhile, I prick up my ears to find out what we're dealing with, but all I can hear is a soft scraping.

Kessley steps closer and clears her throat. "I can disguise myself as a troll and take a look, if you want?"

"That's a great—"

Maël cuts off my sentence. "No, it is too dangerous. A horrible thing happened down there."

She shivers, and it's as if her chills jump over to me. "What kind of thing?"

"I cannot sense that."

Hurried footsteps approach from above.

"We're here," Vicky says.

"Okay. Be careful, everyone."

I start walking further down. At the bottom of the stairs, there's a narrow hallway. My hands search for a light switch, but can't find one, so I conjure a lightning ball in my palm and send it to the low ceiling. A couple of feet away, I spot a closed door. I walk over to it, closely followed by my friends. With a wave of my hand, I extinguish the lightning and count back from three softly. Then I open the door.

Bright golden shapes move along the far wall like giant ants. The light emanating from them, and from the puddles of gold on the floor, almost blind me.

The creatures come to a sudden halt when the door creaks. They turn and look at us with giant, bulging eyes, three of them on each round head. Steam rises from the gold on their bodies as it drips down. Their long, pointed noses turn up, sniffing the air as if to determine how dangerous we are.

"What the heck are they?" Kessley whispers.

Vicky slowly brings her mace forward. "The demons from the fourth circle of Hell. The punishment there is smelting gold."

My whole body grows cold. "What are they doing

here? Were they expecting us?"

"If that's the case, why are they leaving?" Kessley points at a dark vortex appearing in the wall behind the monsters. "Wouldn't they stay to fight us?"

I stare at the demons, backing up and jumping into the portal one by one, and suddenly it hits me. I know it even before I see the limp body in the claws of one of the monsters. "They've got the sixth soul!"

It came out a lot louder than I intended, and my friends interpret it as a starting shot. They move forward as one, and I have no other choice but to join the attack. I adjust quickly, pulling out my Morningstar and aiming it at the golden demon that carries the child we were supposed to save. The spiked ball hits the middle eye, and the monster goes down. The body it carries slides from its grip and comes to a halt about two feet from the portal. Another demon reaches for it with its abnormally long arms, but a big slab of grease knocks it over.

Maël comes to a halt in the middle of the basement and slams her staff down on the floor, ready to slow the demons down in time. Vicky apparates to where the victim is lying and reaches out to pick it up.

"Watch out!" I yell as two demons tear a handful of hot gold from their skin and hurl it at my girl.

Vicky ducks, and the limb body is snatched from under her fingers.

I haul in my weapon and throw it again, but this demon evades the incoming ball easily.

Taylar jumps in between the demon and the portal, his shield held high to protect his solid body, his mace swinging wildly.

I lose track of everything that happens. Steaming gold flies in all directions, maces hit bulging eyes, and there are shrieks and angry cries everywhere. The demon carrying the one we need to save moves in slow motion, but that doesn't help Vicky. While she kicks several demons in their protruding noses, the small body is thrown into the air. It soars over Vicky's head and past Taylar's swinging weapon.

"Dante!"

My head swings left at the sound of Kessley's voice. *What is she doing on the other side of the basement?*

She bends over and picks something up. When she turns back to me, I gasp. A copy of the victim lies motionless in her arms. Now I see that it's not a child at all. It's a troll.

"There's another one," Kess says.

I shake my head in horror. *That's not another one. That's the same troll. Its soul has already left the body. If the demons manage to take it with them through the portal, Satan can open another circle of Hell.*

"Leave it there," I tell Kess. "We need to save the other one."

She places it back hastily, and a whole stack of coins rolls from its pockets with a loud clang. The evidence of its sin, greed. *It must have dug into Shelton Banks' money supply.*

*No time to ponder that now.* I turn back to the fight

and find myself face to face with a steaming demon. It wraps its long arms around me and squeezes. I yell in pain as the gold burns through my clothes and skin.

*Ice, turn to ice!*

Frost collects on its nose, and it shakes its head. But it doesn't let go.

I picture a large block of ice coming down from the ceiling and landing on the three-eyed head. A second later, the demon is flattened. It goes up in black smoke.

I pick up the chips of ice that came off on impact and press them onto my arms and chest. They relieve the pain only a little, but it'll have to do for now. I'm about to dive into the fight when Kessley calls out from behind me, "Move out of the way!"

I step aside, and a giant version of the golden demons stomps by. It has the same round body and head, but it's almost three times bigger. It pulls itself forward using its long, twiggy arms. Melted gold flies in all directions as it launches itself at the demons closest to the portal.

"Watch out!" it calls out with Kessley's voice.

The other ghosts apparate out of her path while Charlie and Gisella roll away.

The Kessley monster knocks several demons aside as if they're bowling pins and slams into the wall with a loud crash. Pieces of plaster fall down and disappear into the puddles of gold. Kessley sinks her sharp teeth into several demons' necks, and black smoke fills the air around her.

I use the momentary confusion of the monsters to hit them with small blocks of ice. I hit a couple of them, but they only screech and keep fighting. Taylar has turned to follow the demon carrying the troll's soul. Charlie is getting to his feet, a ball of gel in his hand.

They're both too late.

I yell as the troll is carried through the portal. The remaining demons flee after it before Kessley gets the chance to knock them over and tear them apart. She comes to a halt inches from the portal and wipes some gold and grease from her bald head. Panting hard, she turns back into herself and shoots a smile at me. "Did we win?"

I lower my hands. "No, they took the soul with them."

Without hesitation, she turns back to the portal. "Then we go after them!"

She steps forward. Taylar pulls her back just in time. "No!"

She almost tumbles backwards, but he catches her.

"Why not?" she asks, straightening her dress.

Maël waves her staff in their direction. "That portal leads to the fourth circle of Hell. It is too dangerous for us there."

"But the soul—"

"There's nothing we can do about that anymore," I interrupt her. "If we'd known the soul was here, we would've come down sooner. But we didn't."

Vicky pats my shoulder. "We still only lost two souls and saved four."

"We should've had six wins," I say. Then I take in the solemn faces around me. "But Vicky is right. We're still ahead of Lucifer. They had another win, and that sucks. But he's still stuck in Hell, and we're going to make sure he stays there. Forever."

"Hear, hear!" Taylar calls out, and Vicky, Gisella and Charlie join in.

Maël and Kessley are distracted by something on the floor that's blown our way by a mysterious wind.

Kess points at it. "What's that?"

I follow her gaze and frown. It's not hard to recognize the objects. "The Cards of Death."

"How did they get here?" Vicky wonders aloud.

I squat down. "I have no clue."

When I pick them up, they crumble to dust immediately. A confirmation of the bad news: we lost another soul.

"I found something else," Charlie calls out. I hadn't even noticed him walking to the other side of the basement.

"Look at this," he says over his shoulder. "I think it's some kind of secret room."

He presses his hand against the wall next to the door through which we entered. A panel slides open to reveal a storage room filled with wooden boxes. They've been knocked over, and coins of all sizes and colors are spread over the floor.

"That must have been the work of the troll. It got

greedy and robbed its own boss."

"The sin of the sixth circle," Vicky whispers.

Charlie doesn't say anything. He stands there in the doorway frozen, as if someone put a spell on him. Then he sucks in his breath with a choking sound.

"What's wrong?" I ask, hurrying to cross the distance between us.

I place a hand on his shoulder and try to look him in the eye. "Charlie? Talk to me. What happened? Are you in pain?"

Gisella runs to his other side, with an equally worried look on her face. When Charlie doesn't respond, her gaze moves through the hidden room. She freezes too. Her eyes grow wide. "Eh… Dante?"

My heart beats unnaturally loud and fast when I turn my head. All strength floods from my limbs, and I collapse onto the floor. I can hear my own breathing, unsteady and wheezing. I want to look away, but I can't. Behind the fallen crates, the shape of two giant wings are burned into the wall. And although I've never seen anything like this before, I instantly know what it means.

An angel was killed here.

# CHAPTER 28

"Quinn." His name comes out choked, and I swallow.

"You don't know that," Charlie says, but he doesn't sound convinced. "Do you have any idea how many angels there are?"

"No," I answer.

He lowers his head. "Me neither."

Gisella squints at the burn marks on the wall. "Call him."

I bite my lip. *Quinn hasn't answered my calls for a while. He said he was busy restoring the balance in Heaven. What if he needed us? What if he died because we didn't help him?*

"Quinn?" Charlie calls out so loud I jump.

I wipe my hands on my pants and look up at the ceiling.

There's no answer.

"Please no, please no," I whisper.

Vicky grabs my hand and kisses it. I ball the other

one into a fist.

"Quinn?" Charlie repeats. "Please answer us." His voice almost breaks. Tears form in my eyes.

A long silence follows, and I think of all the great times I had with Quinn. Playing basketball, poker, singing karaoke... it all feels like another time, another life. Another world even. And it is. I lived in the non-magical world then with no idea of what was hidden right under my nose. Another world, a magical one, that gave me power, friends and a wonderful girl. But also a world that took away both of my parents and showed me so many ugly things. And now, it took—

"Dante?"

My head snaps back up to the ceiling. "Quinn?"

Charlie breathes in sharply. "Do you hear him?"

I nod. "Yes, but he sounds far away."

"Dante, can you hear me?"

"Yes, I can hear you!" I call back. "Are you okay?"

"I'm fine, but I cannot enter the house you're in."

"What is... where... why didn't you answer us sooner?" I stutter.

"I'm sorry, it has been crazy in Heaven lately. Before you restored the balance of the universe, something broke into Heaven. It took us some time to track it."

"But you found it?"

"Yes, it was a demon. We killed it."

My eyes grow wide, and the others send me questioning looks.

"What?" Charlie asks. "What is he saying?"

I give them a recap, and they all gasp.

"What kind of demon was it?" I ask Quinn.

"A golden one."

I bite my lip. "He was sent by Trevor. I'm sure of it."

"We don't know that," Vicky says.

"Well, we saw Trevor leading the wolf demons of the sixth circle. They were all killed, so it makes sense that he'd be in charge of the demons of the fourth circle now. And Shelton Banks is probably helping him." I rub my face hard. "I think the Devil has broadened his plans for domination."

"You think Lucifer will also try to take over Heaven?" Quinn sounds stunned. "That's a bit ambitious."

"Is it?" I retort. "I mean, how many demons have you seen in Heaven in your time as an angel?"

"Only this one."

"Exactly."

"Anyway," Quinn says. "I need to get going. I'd better report this, and we've got a missing angel to find. I hope that has nothing to do with this."

I clear my throat. "Eh… Quinn? I'm afraid I've got some bad news."

"More bad news?"

I glance at Charlie. *Is this the way to tell Quinn?* He shakes his head.

"Can we meet outside in the garden?" I signal to Charlie to take a picture of the burn marks, and he takes out his phone.

"I really don't have much time, Dante. Just tell me."

I hesitate. Vicky squeezes my hand. "Trust your heart, it knows best."

Another look at the shape of the wings on the wall tells me enough. "We're going outside. I want to tell Quinn in person."

We walk back to the stairs in a silent, solemn procession. Quinn is waiting for us on the other side of the pool in his human form. He looks tired and worried. I walk up to him with Charlie while the others keep a respectful distance.

We bump fists as if we're in the schoolyard waiting for the first day of school. *If only things were still as simple as they were in those days.*

"I'm so glad you're okay," Charlie says. "You scared us, you know."

Quinn slaps his shoulder. "I'm sorry, I didn't mean to." He turns to me. "What's the bad news?"

Charlie grabs his phone, but I stop him. "Not yet."

Quinn's dark eyes flick from Charlie to me. "What is it? Tell me already."

The air around us gets colder when Quinn reads our thoughts. "An angel was killed."

"Yes, in the basement of this house. By demons."

"How do you know?" Quinn asks softly.

Without a word, I gesture at Charlie, who hands Quinn his phone.

Our friend gasps and stumbles.

I place a hand against his shoulder to steady him. "I'm sorry."

"Did you know him? Was he a friend?" Charlie asks.

Quinn closes his eyes for a second and hands the phone back. "I am God's right hand. I know all the angels." He doesn't answer the second question, but the look on his face tells us enough.

I'm not sure what to do, so I follow Vicky's advice and listen to my heart. It tells me to hug him.

Quinn lets me. I feel his chest contracting as he holds back his tears.

"Is there anything we can do?" I ask when we let go.

Determination takes over his face. "Do what you were born to do. Finish your mission. It will save us all."

He vanishes before I can respond.

Charlie lets out a deep sigh. "I've never seen him like that."

"He never lost a friend like this before, and I think he never witnessed an attack on Heaven before either."

My best friend looks up at the sky, as if he can find a trace of Quinn there. "This wasn't an attack yet, you know. This was a scout. The attack is yet to come."

I turn to look at the mansion. "Then we'd better start turning this place upside down. There's a reason the angel was killed in there."

We split up in twos and threes again and each take a floor to search.

Me and Vicky start in the basement, where we search for any more hidden rooms. It's hard not to look at the wing marks.

"I think that angel was supposed to take the Cards of Death to us," I say when I turn over the last crate of coins and find nothing interesting in it.

Vicky stares at me through the doorway. "You think Heaven has been helping us in secret?"

I nod. "They've seen my grandfather and my father lose. I guess they figured I could use a little help."

"Well, they were right. But now the Devil knows about it. Maybe that's why he wants to attack Heaven too."

I kick an empty crate and head for the door. "Come on, there's nothing else to find down here."

The kitchen and dining room don't hold any surprises for us either. We turn all the cupboards upside down, take everything out of the china cabinet and inspect loose tiles on the floor. There's nothing there. We move on to the bottom floor of the tower.

"Now it gets interesting." I throw Vicky a smile over my shoulder as we walk into a giant library. It spans all three floors, and it's filled to the rim with old books.

Vicky presses her hands against her temples. "How are we going to find anything in here? This will take weeks to go through."

Charlie and Gisella appear in the doorway above us.

"I agree," Charlie says. "There are so many books here, and we don't even have an idea of what we're looking for, you know."

Silently, I take in the rows and rows of books.

"I'll cast another spell."

Charlie pushes a stray lock of blond hair from his eye. "How? You don't know what we're looking for."

"No, but magic will. I already put something about it in the spell I cast outside, but it probably wasn't strong enough. There must be some extra protection on these books, because we did find the secret room in the basement. Another spell on top of it might do the trick, though." I turn to Vicky. "Right?"

She puts the book in her hand back on the shelf. "Maybe. It can't hurt to try."

I take out my Book of Spells and sit down in the armchair next to the winding stairs in the middle of the tower.

"We'll check for hidden doorways and such while you write a spell," Vicky says.

With words already spilling into my brain, I only nod. I pull out a pen and start writing.

Once the spell is done, I flip through my notebook and Dad's to choose the ingredients.

I beckon Vicky and prepare everything with her before calling out to the others. "Get ready to grab whatever the spell reaches out to."

They nod, and I step inside the circle of salt I drew

on the floor.

"Need candles?" Vicky asks from my left, holding out different colors.

"Of course, I almost forgot." I grab the one in her right hand. "Orange for attraction please. Four of them."

While I place the candle on the east, Vicky takes three more from her pocket and puts them in the right spots.

"Thank you, babe."

She blows me a kiss and steps aside. "The stage is yours."

I pick up the incense stick and light it. Once the smoke reaches the next floor, I start turning.

*"Let the smoke spread high and wide.*
*And cover every inch inside.*
*Let it show me what I need.*
*Give me what I need to read."*

After the third turn, I light another match and ignite the four candles. Then, I drop the incense stick into the herbs I mixed together.

As soon as the stick hits the herbs, the candles burn brighter. The smoke in the room thickens. I can no longer see anything, not even my own hands or the flames of the candles. That is, until the flames grow higher and higher. Sparks fly everywhere and connect with the smoke. It whirls around the books, searching. Now and then, there's a bright flash, and the smoke halts at a book, but then it moves on.

After several minutes, I'm starting to worry. "I don't think it's working. I'm not strong enough to compete with Shelton Banks' powers."

Vicky's voice comes from my left. "Patience. There's a lot of books here."

Another flash, bigger and brighter than the previous ones, lights up the whole tower. The smoke starts to gather in three different places. One cloud hovers next to the highest shelf on the top floor, one close to where Gisella is standing and one to my right. Vicky walks over to it but keeps a safe distance. I stay inside the circle, afraid to disrupt the spell.

All three smoke clouds dive between the shelves and pull out a book. Three books tumble down while the smoke disperses. Charlie, Gisella and Vicky each catch one of them. The last of the smoke tumbles down like ash and dissolves on the floor. The candles are blown out by a gust of wind.

I walk over to Vicky, who has opened the book in her hands.

"Look at this," she says, pointing at a page in the middle.

Quickly, I read a couple of lines. "Is this the book your grandmother read before she was killed?"

She shivers. "I think so."

"Then the spell definitely worked." I look around for a bag but can't find one. "Do you have a bag in your pocket? Or three? Those books look heavy."

"Sure." She digs up three sturdy bags and hands

two of them to Charlie and Gisella, who have come down the stairs.

"You want to take the books with us?" Gisella asks with a frown.

"Of course. There's no time to read them now."

She shakes her head. "If we take them, Shelton Banks will come and find us."

"He won't know it was us," I counter.

She snorts. "Sure he will. He's a powerful Mage. He has ways of getting information, just like we do."

I start pacing the room. "So, what do you suggest?"

She holds the book out to me. "Use that spell again. The one we used on my aunt. Make it look like no books were taken."

Charlie nods enthusiastically. "Great idea. And then we make it look like something chased us away before we had a chance to check out this tower. We block all the doors from the outside, or something, you know. Make him think we never entered his library."

"Sounds like a good plan," I say. I gather the three books and turn to Vicky once again. "Do you remember what I need?"

She smiles. "Of course."

CHAPTER 29

Several minutes later, I've got three fake books in my hands. I put them next to the real ones and squint to find something that doesn't match.

"They're perfect," Vicky says. "He won't notice until he grabs one of them."

I sigh. "I hope so."

Vicky apparates from one floor to another to put the three fake books in place. Then she helps me clean everything up.

Gisella and Charlie go back to the upper floor to see if the others found anything, and we follow them, after putting another spell on the library to make it look like we left without entering it.

My feet are itching to check out the rest of the house, but we've been here for far too long already. *If Shelton Banks comes back and finds us here, we'll lose a lot more than the three books we confiscated.*

Taylar, Maël and Kessley are leaving a ballroom-sized bedroom when we reach the top floor. I'm relieved to see that Taylar still looks like his normal, transparent, pale self. No dark eyes or gray skin.

"Did you find anything?" I ask when I take in his content expression.

"A note with me and Lleyton's name on it." He holds it up. It's a list of names. Some have been crossed out with red ink.

"Good," I say. "We can hand that over to the police. Anything else?"

He puts the hit list in his trouser pocket. "Not yet, but we've got one more room to go."

When we reach it, Charlie and Gisella are already collecting all kinds of dark stuff from a room that looks like a shrine to the Devil.

"Holy crap!" I call out. "Was this room unlocked and in plain sight?"

Charlie looks up with a grin. "Nope. Gisella removed the shadows that hid the door and used them to open it."

"Nice job." I enter the room and look around. "Can someone take pictures of this room? The police might be able to use them."

Charlie holds up his phone. "Already did. They'll think he's insane."

I hold up my thumb.

Vicky passes me and looks around. "We should take all of this. There might be something valuable here, and even if there isn't, it will slow down his plans."

"I agree, but how do we hide the fact that we took his stuff?"

"Maybe we shouldn't," Taylar comments.

I raise my eyebrows at him. "You want to leave an open invitation for an attack?"

He picks up a black cup, decorated with inverted crosses and eyes. "I think he'll find out it was us anyway. Covering our tracks sends him the message that we're scared of him."

I throw my hands in the air. "I *am* scared of him!"

Maël steps between us. "Taylar makes a good point. Whether we are afraid of this man or not does not matter. Eventually we will come face to face with him. It is best if we make a good impression, now and later. Show him we are strong and confident, even if we are not."

Taylar smirks at me over her shoulder.

I sigh. "I suppose you're right."

"So, we take it all?" Taylar asks eagerly.

"Yes. See if you can find any boxes to put it in."

"This will never fit into your car," Vicky says. "It's too small."

"*She* is fine the way she is," I retort. "And *you* can all blink home carrying three boxes each."

She chuckles. "Of course, master. And I can put the small stuff in my endless pocket."

I grab her hand before she gets the chance to drop some knives in it. "Don't. All of this emanates evil. I don't want you carrying so much of it close to your body."

She kisses me on the lips. "You're so sweet."

A loud rumbling makes us both look up.

There's a hiss followed by the moaning of an animal.

Charlie stumbles back and bumps into me. "I opened the door to another secret room."

*A hidden room within a hidden room? This can't be good.*

We all back up, and I grab Vicky's hand again. In the other, I conjure a lightning bolt.

Charlie creates two gel balls, and Gisella turns her hands into blades. Maël raises her staff while Taylar picks up the shield he put on the floor. Kessley multiplies several times, each copy holding a mace out threateningly.

The wall has slid almost completely open now, showing us a shimmering portal to a dark world.

We all prepare for an attack. What hits us instead, when I send my lightning bolt closer, is shock and relief.

"Jeep?" we call out as one.

\* \* \*

Dante Banner returns in **The Seventh Crow** – Will he be able to take Jeep home safely or is he too late to help his friend?

An unexpected enemy blocks his way to the next soul, and this one cannot be taken out easily… Will

Dante and his friends find a way around this enemy in time, or will they lose another soul to the Devil?

Turn the page for a sneak peek! Or pre-order the book online NOW!

# Make a difference

Reviews are very important to authors. Even a short or negative review can be of tremendous value to me as a writer. Therefore I would be very grateful if you could leave a review at your place of purchase. And don't forget to tell your friends about this book!

Thank you very much in advance.

# Newsletter, social media and website

Want to receive exclusive first looks at covers and upcoming book releases, get a heads-up on pre-order and release dates and special offers, receive book recommendations and an exclusive 'look into my (writing) life'? Then please sign up now for my monthly newsletter through my website: www.tamarageraeds.com.

You can also follow me on Facebook, Instagram and Twitter for updates and more fun stuff!

Have a great day!   Tamara Geraeds

# Found a mistake?

*The Sixth Ghost* has gone through several rounds of beta reading and editing. If you found a typographical, grammatical, or other error which impacted your enjoyment of the book, we offer our apologies and ask that you let us know, so we can fix it for future readers.

You can email your feedback to: info@tamarageraeds.com.

# Preview

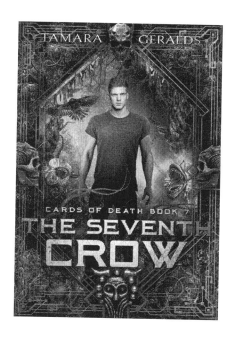

Cards of Death book 7
# The Seventh Crow

# CHAPTER 1

A couple of weeks ago I would've considered what I'm seeing now impossible.

I'm in a secret room, looking into another secret room with a portal in it. That's weird enough to begin with, but it gets crazier. I'm surrounded by several ghosts, who are all part of my Shield, which means they protect me, because I'm the chosen one, the only one capable of keeping the Devil in Hell. Every time I think about this, I question my sanity. Maybe I fell asleep and got caught up in a really long, crazy dream? Did I get into an accident and end up in a coma? That could explain the weird turn my life suddenly took. I mean, an angel as a friend? Two friends who turned out to work for the Devil himself? Making love to a ghost? Traveling to other worlds, meeting the ferryman of the Underworld, Saint Peter and the Four Horsemen? All in my head, right? I made all of this up in my dream, to escape from Mom's horrible fits, Dad's disappearance and… a car accident? The weird things started happening after we all drove home from school in Quinn's car, so why not?

Sure, Mom's fits were also weird. And weird is an understatement here. At least once a week she acted like she was possessed by a demon. Of course, demons don't exist, so we searched for some other cause. Brain damage? Severe epilepsy with something else on the side? It was none of that.

My mind short-circuited and came up with this explanation. The world is filled with magical beings. Humans with powers, monsters of all kinds, demons, and to make the horror complete: Lucifer. Maybe Mom's lunacy was hereditary. That makes much more sense.

I shake my head to get rid of the images from the past that roll by before my eyes. I see Jeep, the necromancer of my Shield. He's trapped behind the portal in the secret room. Can a dream feel so real? Can you love the people you meet there? Because my heart breaks at the sight of Jeep suffering like this. Just after he died, his wife was attacked by a bunch of ghosts. He was able to fight them off and save his wife, but the only way to beat the ghosts was to trap them in his tattoos. He's been fighting to keep them there ever since, and now they're escaping. Being trapped in the empty world behind this portal must have consumed the last of his energy.

The tattooed ghost doesn't look up when we call

out his name. He doesn't even seem to hear us, although that's hard to tell with only a faint, small light shining down on him in an otherwise completely dark world.

Vicky is the first to break the stunned silence. She dives forward before I can stop her. Then, with her nose inches from the portal, she comes to an abrupt halt. "No! Jeep!"

The ghost is on his knees with gritted teeth and closed eyes. He trembles violently. Stretched-out bodies rise from his tattoos. Bony, transparent hands push bodies from the pictures that have been their prison for so long.

"Do something!" Taylar yells behind me.

My foot moves forward on its own. It bumps against an invisible wall. My heart stops beating when I hold out my hands to find the same obstacle.

"No…" I breathe. *Why is this happening? We finally found Jeep. The thing we've been fearing for a while has come true, and there's nothing we can do about it. There's no way of reaching him.*

I put my arm around Vicky and pull her close. All we can do now is watch in horror as our friend gets surrounded by the evil souls he trapped under his skin. Souls that have been yearning for revenge for decades.

Vicky's hand clutches mine as we watch helplessly, an invisible wall between us and our friend.

I close my eyes and will myself to wake up. *Enough of this. I want my life back. I'm going to wake up now, in a hospital bed. I will find Mom sitting next to my bed, with an exhausted, but relieved look on her face.*

"Dante?" Vicky's voice makes me open my eyes.

I realize I'm swaying on my feet.

"Stay with us, Dante. We need you. We need to figure out a way to get to Jeep, and help him."

She sounds desperate. There's a mixture of emotions in her eyes I can't fully read.

Mom's voice comes to me from the corner of my mind. A Christmas memory. Me and Mom sitting at the dining table. Me with my sketchbook, Mom with her sewing machine. *Winter Wonderland* playing in the background. Mom is staring at me and I put down my pencil. 'What is it?'

She smiles. Pride and love shine through her eyes. 'You are so talented.'

I look down at my drawing. It's a portrait of a snow owl, surrounded by trees covered in white bliss. I shrug. 'It's okay.'

'It's more than okay, Dante. Can't you see that?'

'Not really.'

'You should apply for art school. If you want to make a living with this.'

It's probably the tenth time she brings this up. 'I don't know. I'm not *that* good.'

'Yes, you are.'

'I'm good at one thing, Mom. Drawing animals. Nature.'

She stands up and walks around the table. With her arms wrapped around my neck she studies my work again. 'You could draw something else. Practice with other materials, see what else suits you.'

'That's just it, Mom. I'm not really interested in anything else.'

She lets out a sigh. 'Try a fictional animal then, to start with. Do it for me.'

Of course I agreed to try it, but it didn't work out. Not enough imagination, like Dad would say.

With a jerk I jump back to the present. *Not enough imagination.* Dad wasn't only talking about when I am awake. Even my dreams are much more realistic than those of other people. Even in my sleep I lack imagination. Which means I could never come up with all these powers and this whole crazy plot about the Devil wanting to escape the nine circles of Hell by myself. Which means… this is all very real.

I blink and see Jeep hunched over on the floor, alone and unable to defend himself against the angry souls that pull themselves from his tattoos.

"This isn't right," I say, and I take a step back, pulling Vicky along. I turn my head to face my other friends. Charlie, Gisella, Taylar, Maël and several Kessleys. That last ghost is certainly something I could never have imagined myself. Someone with the ability to shapeshift *and* multiply? No way. "Everyone, hit the barrier with everything you've got, in three… two… one…"

It rains lightning, gel balls and weapons around me. But they all bounce off against the invisible wall. Gisella slashes away with her blade hands, but although sparks fly everywhere, they don't penetrate the barrier.

"Again!" I yell.

We hit it even harder, Maël with her staff and Vicky with powerful kicks.

Nothing.

We seize our attempts, panting hard.

"Vicky, try going invisible," I say.

She vanishes instantly and the wall lights up.

"Yes!" I cry out. But my excitement is premature. Vicky appears again, on our side of the portal.

We have some success though. Jeep looks up from his place on the floor. The souls still swirl around him, most of them attached to a tattoo with only a small sliver now.

"Jeep!" Vicky and I call out at the same time.

I move closer to the portal. "Can you hear us?"

"Guys?" Jeep's voice is hoarse.

"Yes, it's us!" Vicky shouts.

"We can't break through," I explain, although I'm not sure he can hear us. "Try to damage the wall from your side."

A glint of hope flickers in Jeep's eyes. He swats the souls away that try to wrap around his face. Two other ones grab his wrists, but his newfound hope makes him stronger. He pulls his arms free and reaches for his bowler hat, which is lying two feet away.

"Hit the wall once more with everything you've got when Jeep's hat connects with it," I order the others.

They all prepare, their faces contracted in concentration.

Jeep's hand is an inch from the rim of his hat when one of the souls finally manages to pull free. The tail of the dark wisp frees itself from the tattooed skull and shoots up high into the emptiness of the world Jeep is in.

"Watch out!" I yell as it drops back down.

But Jeep is too late to avoid it, because the other souls hold him down. The sliver of black mist slams into him and he screams in pain.

I pound my fists against the wall. "No! Leave him alone!"

Vicky joins me. "Keep fighting, Jeep!" Tears stream down her cheeks while she moves her fists forward with all her might.

But Jeep stays down. One by one the souls pull free from his tattoos and slam down on him like bricks. They wrap around his wrists and ankles and pull.

Jeep moans and screams.

"Make yourself invisible!" I tell him.

He flickers like a bulb that's about to die. It's no use, the souls keep him in a death grip. They will literally tear him apart and we can only watch as they do it.

Vicky stops pounding and rests her forehead against the invisible wall. "If you can hear me, Jeep, I want to tell you something." Her voice is fragile and full of sorrow. "You mean the world to me. You watched out for me from the moment I was added to the Shield. You supported me, taught me how to fight and had faith in me. You never failed me."

Jeep stops struggling and looks up at her. He wants to answer, but as soon as he opens his mouth a dark sliver covers it.

"I want to thank you for the great time we had together, Jeep," Vicky continues. "I never thought it would end like this, and I'll miss you terribly." She wipes her nose and looks Jeep in the eye. "I love you, Jeep."

For a second Jeep's mouth is uncovered and his lips form into a sad smile. "I love you too."

The ground rumbles and a thin golden line trickles from Jeep's forehead. Vicky grabs her head as the same happens to her. Slowly the two lines stretch toward each other. Vicky's travels through the wall unharmed. The moment the two lines touch, the rumbling gets louder. I jump back as invisible bricks hit me in the chest.

Vicky reaches forward and steps over the shattered wall and into the empty world. I follow her, afraid of the wall mending itself. The ground still shakes and the souls loosen their grip on Jeep. Vicky has reached him and pulls him up with both hands.

I bend over to pick up his hat before hitting the fleeing souls with lightning.

Balls of gel zoom past my head. Something tugs at my leg, but I kick it with my other foot and it lets go.

Four Kessleys take their place behind us and fight off the souls that are trying to reach Jeep again.

One by one Vicky and I pull the rest of the slivers away from him. Mouths appear at the end of one and snap at me. Others have blinking eyes and I even see an arm.

"They are transforming back into their human forms," Maël says, smacking a half-formed head with her staff.

"What happens after that?" I ask, throwing Jeep's arm over my neck.

"I do not know."

"I'd rather not find out," Gisella says, while she cuts souls in half with her blades.

Taylar holds his shield up above Jeep's head as two souls dive down. "Can we lock them back inside this room?"

Maël and I answer at the same time. "I hope so."

Slowly but surely we get closer to the portal. I try to ignore the feeling of oxygen getting sucked out of my lungs with every step I take. There's something off about the air in here. It's unnaturally dry.

The Kessleys, Taylar, Charlie, Vicky and Gisella try to block the souls' way back to Jeep.

Maël moves faster than me, unaware of the lack of oxygen flowing to my brain.

"Hurry, Dante," she says, and I urge my feet to keep going. But the longer I am in here, the foggier my mind becomes. All strength floods from my limbs and suddenly I'm on the ground. In the corner of my eye I see Jeep tumbling to the ground as Maël loses her grip.

I gesture at her to pick him up. "You go… on. I'll… follow."

"No!" Jeep's voice is suddenly strong. He lifts his head and meets my eye. "You… safe…"

Maël hauls him back to his feet and he leans on her heavily. "I'll take him out and come back for you."

I nod and rest my head on the ground for a moment.

"Babe!" I feel Vicky's cold touch on my cheek. "Don't give up. It's only three more steps."

"I can't," I whisper without moving. All energy has left my body, as has the will to even try to get up.

"Vicky! Hurry up!" I hear Charlie yelling.

Then Taylar's answer, "We'll never be able to trap them in here. Can you use the shadows, Gisella?"

Someone tugs at my arm. "Come on!"

My eyes have closed and no matter how hard I try, my eyelids refuse to open.

Then something wraps around my ankles and drags me along. Hurried footsteps follow me.

I force my eyes open and see shadows hovering in the air, diving left and right whenever a soul tries to pass. Fresh air flows back into my lungs and I push myself into a sitting position.

Vicky is still on the other side of the portal, with Taylar and Gisella. When I turn my head, I find Charlie next to me on the ground, gasping for air.

I pat him gently on the back. "Take it easy. You're okay."

He takes another gulp of air and wipes the sweat from his forehead. "I couldn't... breathe... you know."

Maël helps us both up. "It was the climate in that world. Hardly any oxygen in the air."

I point at Gisella, who's directing the shadows with some simple hand movements. "Why isn't she gasping for air?"

Charlie frowns. "Good question."

## WANT TO READ ON?

Buy the next book now, on Amazon!

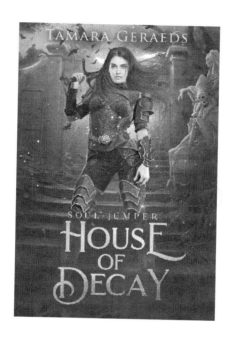

SOUL JUMPER
HOUSE OF DECAY

Welcome to Vex Monster Tours.
Please press PLAY to watch this video.

PLAY

Loading....

Loading....

Loading....

"Hi there, and welcome to Vex Monster Tours. If you're looking for an adrenaline-filled adventure, you've come to the right place. My name is Vex and...

You're laughing, aren't you? I don't blame you. I would too if I were you. But it's not my fault that I'm called Vex. My parents had a great sense of humor, or so they thought. They were both Soul Jumpers, of course, like me, and thought it was ironically funny to name me Vex, since they trained me to be a nuisance to any kind of monster.

Anyway, in case you don't know what a Soul Jumper is, I'll explain it to you briefly.

A Soul Jumper is a human with special powers, born and trained to kill monsters. We are stronger and faster than regular humans and have more endurance and agility and some other extras. When we touch the last victim a creature killed, a connection is made with the next target of that monster. When that target is attacked and about to lose the battle with the monster, our soul jumps into the target's body. From that moment on, our natural strengths are doubled, as are our senses. This gives us the power to defeat the monster before it kills another person. While we're inside the victim's body, they have no control over their moves but can still feel everything and talk to us. If they die, we jump back into our own body, which is protected by a flock of birds. Hawks, in my case. We have special Soul Jumper battle outfits, like I'm wearing now, connected to our souls to make them jump with us. They have some neat gadgets as extra back-up.

So, where was I?
Oh yes, Vex Monster Tours offers you the chance to see and fight any evil creature up close. To increase your chances of winning without my help, you get a day of training. That doesn't sound like a lot, but I'll give you a cupcake that contains a special mixture. It will give you the ability to pick up everything you learn a lot faster, and it builds up muscle at triple speed.

A blood vow is made between me and the monster of your request in which we agree not to attack before the arranged time. I will protect you the best I can while letting you fight the monster for as long as possible. Sounds cool, right?

But why, do you ask, would a monster agree to fight two people? Well, for one, most monsters are cocky, and two, these days, there are so many hunters roaming the streets that they have a hard time finding a quiet place to attack. They think they have a better chance for a meal when they're just fighting you and I… but we'll prove them wrong.

Have any questions? Feel free to email or call me!"

# CHAPTER 1

I sense something off even before I see it. My muscles tense at the feeling that I'm not alone, like I should be.

Custos lands quietly on my shoulder while I peer left and right. Everything seems normal. There are no odd sounds, no footprints on the path or in the earth around the trees.

Then I notice it. The door to the training barn is ajar. It's just a crack, and there isn't enough wind to make it move, but I know something is wrong.

Custos cocks his head when he notices it a second later. He nudges my neck with his beak, as if to say, 'Go check it out!'

Slowly moving closer, my mind whirls around the possibilities. *Did I fail to properly close the portal after the last training session, making it possible for the monster to escape?*

I shake that thought off. Even if I didn't close it completely, the portal only lets monsters cross halfway. It's not really a passage; they can't get through to this world.

With narrowed eyes, I watch the creak in the door. My ears try to pick up a sound, any sound, that could give me an indication of what to expect. When they finally do, just as my hand moves to the doorknob, I freeze.

Custos lets out a disrupted croak as the pained whimper drifts toward us.

"That sounded human, right?" I ask him quietly.

He nods, and I wrap my fingers around the doorknob. "Good. That rules out the worst."

Before I get the chance to pull the door open, the leader of my protective kettle pulls my hair.

"Ouch," I whisper. "What was that for?"

The hawk swoops down to the ground and pulls at my pant leg.

A smile creeps upon my face. "Oh yes, good thinking, Custos."

I pull out the short blade hidden in my boot and wait for Custos to settle back on my shoulder.

"Ready?" I ask, and his talons dig into my shirt.

With one fast movement, I pull the door open. It takes me a millisecond to realize I won't need my weapon. No one is jumping out at me. The whimpering has stopped, but there's no doubt where it came from. Several of the traps that line the walls have been set off. Whomever broke into my barn managed to avoid the first trap, judging by the three arrows lodged into the wall on my right. Dodging them slowed him down enough to get doused with flammable liquid and set on fire.

I scan the floorboard in front of me. Yep, burn marks. The trail of black spots leaves no room for doubt about the intruder's next move. He dove for the bucket of water on my left, that has tipped over and is still dripping.

"And there it is," I say manner-of-factly.

Three small steps take me to the edge of what is normally a pretty solid wooden floor with no more than slits showing the dark void below. Now, the boards have moved aside and down, creating a large hole with a view of the endless blackness. Inches from the tips of my shoes, bloodied fingers are straining to hang onto what remains of the floor.

I lean forward so I can see my unwanted guest. "Hello there. How can I help you today?"

The man attached to the fingers is about nineteen years old. He has black hair covered in grease and green eyes that look up at me with a mixture of relief and despair. Scorch marks decorate his arms and face, and there are burn holes all over his shirt.

I study him shamelessly while he searches for an answer.

Custos scurries over and softly pecks at one of the fingers.

With a squeal, the man pulls back his hand, swinging dangerously by the other before wrapping it back around the floorboard five inches further to the right.

"Help me, please," he finally manages.

"Sure!" The fake smile on my lips almost hurts.

I squat down in front of him. "But first, I'd like to know what you're doing here."

One finger slips, and he groans. "I'll tell you everything. Please help me up."

"I will," I answer, examining my fingernails, "after you tell me."

"Fine." His voice goes up a couple of octaves. "I was hiking in the forest when a bear attacked me." My gaze drops down to his green shirt, which is streaked with red between the holes. There's a gash in the side that could've been made by a bear's claw, but it could also be the result of climbing the fence around my premises.

I frown. "Where's your backpack then? Did you drop it?"

"I did." He nods. His dark eyebrows are pulled together when he sends me a pleading look. "It fell into the pit. Please don't let me fall too. Please."

He sounds convincing, yet something about his story is off.

"Tell me exactly what happened with the bear."

He groans. "Please pull me up first. I can't hold on for much longer."

I stand up and take a step back. "I'm sorry, but I don't trust you. Your story doesn't make sense."

"Why not?" he exclaims. "I encountered a bear; I swear! I've never seen one so big in my life."

"What kind of bear?"

"A black bear, of course; it's the only one that lives here."

"Hmm." Anyone could know that.

And then it hits me. The thing that doesn't add up in his story.

"Bears never come close to my home. They sense

the monsters that visit frequently."

The muscles in his arms are starting to shake from the effort of holding on. "Please… I don't know what it was doing here. I'm telling you, it attacked me, and I figured climbing over your fence was my best shot."

I tap my lips with my finger. He is so full of bull that it's almost funny. Even if a bear would come close, climbing over the fence would trigger my alarm. *What are the odds of a bear approaching and my alarm failing on the same day?* And I'm not even counting the tripwires set up everywhere.

I cock my head. "You don't seem surprised to hear that monsters visit me on a regular basis."

He focuses on his fingers, trying to get a better grip. His breathing is fast, and sweat trickles down his temples and over the stubble on his cheeks. "Monsters are everywhere, why would that be a surprise?"

"No…" Slowly I shake my head. "You know who I am, what I am. You know what I do."

He clenches his teeth. "I swear-"

He yells in panic as his other hand slips from the edge. I drop back down quickly and grab it.

"Didn't your mother teach you not to swear?" I say. My voice is low with repressed anger. My patience has vanished. "Now, tell me the truth, or I'm throwing you in."

"All right, all right!" He swallows and licks his lips. His weight pulls at my arm, and I grunt.

"You better hurry."

"I know who you are. You're Vex Connor, a Soul Jumper, *the* Soul Jumper." He gives me a sheepish grin. "Everyone admires you. I just wanted to see how you did it all, you know. What kind of tools you use, how you live…" His voice trails off, and he breaks eye contact.

After a short silence, I shrug. "Well, that still sounds crazy but much more plausible than your other story." I grab his arm with both hands and haul him up.

He collapses on what remains of the floor and clutches his hands to his chest.

Custos shrieks, and I nod at him. "Yes, turn off the traps for a minute, please."

The hawk flies to the other end of the barn, close to the ceiling to avoid the booby traps that are higher up on the walls. I block the intruder's view as Custos picks up a rope, drops the loop at the end around the handle of the device I built and pulls.

With a sound like a collapsing bookcase, the floor boards pop back up until the black void below can only be seen through the cracks.

I stick out my hand. "Let's go. I'll give you a cup of coffee before you leave. You can wash up while the water boils."

\* \* \*

Want to read on? Order this story on Amazon now!

## IMPORTANT NOTICE

All *Soul Jumper* stories can be read in random order. You can start with the story that appeals to you most. It is, however, recommended to start with Force of the Kraken.

I hope you enjoy them!

# ABOUT THE AUTHOR

Tamara Geraeds was born in 1981. When she was 6 years old, she wrote her first poem, which basically translates as:

*A hug for you and a hug for me*
*and that's how life should be*

She started writing books at the age of 15 and her first book was published in 2012. After 6 books in Dutch she decided to write a young adult fantasy series in English: *Cards of Death*.

Tamara's bibliography consists of books for children, young adults and adults, and can be placed under fantasy and thrillers.

Besides writing she runs her own business, in which she teaches English, Dutch and writing, (re)writes texts and edits books.

She's been playing badminton for over 20 years and met the love of her life Frans on the court. She loves going out for dinner, watching movies, and of course reading, writing and hugging her husband. She's crazy about sushi and Indian curries, and her favorite color is pink.

Printed in Great Britain
by Amazon